BYE BYE BABY BOY, BIG BOY BLUES

Denis Hayes

PARTRIDGE

A Penguin Random House Company

To order additional copies of this book, contact
Toll Free 800 101 2657 (Singapore)
Toll Free 1 800 81 7340 (Malaysia)
orders.singapore@partridgepublishing.com

www.partridgepublishing.com/singapore

Author's Note

All the characters portrayed in this book actually lived and all the events really happened. Any views and opinions expressed are those of the author's.

Names have been changed where necessary to protect the privacy of innocent and guilty alike.

For convenience some events have been combined, several different experiences have been grouped together, not necessarily in strict chronological order and on occasions various characters have been made into one.

The lives portrayed in this book should not be judged on the basis of our so called enlightened 21st century attitudes.

The period 1940-1960 was one of great political awareness but not of political correctness. It was a time of contradictions. It was a time of hardship and recovery. The mainstream of British Society was quite conservative and prudish.

We were born mature but never grew up.

The British Army, along with the general public simply had little tolerance of homosexuality, racial or female equality partly because of prejudice but mainly because of ignorance. Such things had to be fought for, accepted and understood in the future. Tolerance had to be learned Enlightenment is not part of this story.

Other books by the same author

Children's Books: Silly Animal Stories for Kids
                    Silly Fishy Stories for Kids
                    Silly Ghost Stories for Kids

Teenage Books: Silly Alien Space Stories for Bigger Kids
               Silly Alien Space War Stories for Bigger Kids
               Silly Alien Time Travel Stories for even Bigger Kids
               Out of this World Stories

Adult Books: The Misadventures of Wunderwear Woman
               The Misadventures of Wunderwear Woman in
               America
               Hard Travellin' Man Blues

Bye, Bye Baby Boy, Big Boy Blues

(words and music by Denis Hayes. Slow standard 12 bar blues in E major.)

e   e7   slide chord to a7
I was born in the Great Depression, raised in World War Two,

a7   a∂7 ⇒ **a7**⇒   slide chord to b7
I was born in the Great Depression, raised in World War Two,

b7   slide chord to a7   e
Bye, bye baby, got those baby boy, big boy blues.

Yeah that Great 'ole Depression would greatly depress you,
Survive that Great Depression would surely depress you,
Get a chance to die in World War number Two.

Hell fire and lightning thundered in the sky,
Hell fire and lightning thundered from the sky,
Down on God's earth so many surely die.

Kids in my school played at fighting war,
The poor kids in my school played at fighting war,
Then one morning my friends they came no more.

War was over, freedom came that's true
The war got over, freedom came that's true,
So why was I so big boy, baby boy blue.

Cos I was gone for a soldier, fighting God know's who,
Gone for a soldier, fighting against God knows who,
Bye, bye baby, lost those baby boy, big boy blues.

I have never needed to agree with someone to in order to appreciate their
greatness.

Churchill is an example. Politically I would have clashed with him nearly everyday but the man truly wanted in his way the best for everyone, set an exemplary example, and fought for it regardless. I just disagreed with how it should be achieved and what the result should be.

I first heard his name when I was young at the beginning of the Second World War.

It was a tough introduction.

BOOK ONE

"Baby Boy Blue"

"Us kids in my school joked about the war,
Those kids in my school joked about the war,
Then one day those kids they came no more."

A Bad Night in the London Blitz

I was going as fast as my short legs could carry me but it was not nearly quick enough for my mum. She was striding out in a nervous, breathless hurry, dragging me along beside her, glancing up at the clear blue summer sky every few seconds.

This was London in the middle of 1941, the blitz was at its height, and the air raid warning had sounded sometime before. It was not a good idea to be caught in the open.

We lived high up on a hill at the top of Maxey Road in Plumstead. We were close to both Plumstead and Woolwich Common which meant we were also close to the anti-aircraft guns and balloons.

That was the good news. We were also next to the borough of Woolwich, in South-East London. That was the bad news.

Woolwich possessed the historic Royal Dockyard, the Royal Arsenal, Army barracks, the HQ of the Royal Artillery, the old Military Academy and miles of Dockland spreading up and down and across the River Thames. Add dozens of factories to this and you can see why the area was a prime target for the German bombers.

It wasn't a place that felt safe even in an air raid shelter.

Although it was re-assuring to hear the sound of your own guns firing at the enemy and to see your own fighters attacking them you also had to be aware that all that exploding ordnance had to land somewhere. The lucky ones fashioned ashtrays, coasters and flower vases out of the shrapnel and cases. The unlucky ones landed in hospital or the mortuary.

That was before even one bomb had dropped!

We were on our way to my gran's house. My gran's house on the Irish side of the family. My dad's mum.

My mum had been taking it in turns looking after an older sister dying from cancer who lived in the shadow of a large army training depot. We had left her in the hands of another family member and had popped home first, then set out for grans'.

Even though the bombers were coming in continual streams day and night, life had to go on and the wonderful Londoners carried on cursing, moaning, laughing, helping and working through it all.

This was fine but we were only just coming up to Woolwich Arsenal Station wanting to cross General Gordon Square to go down Powis Street, the main shopping area. That would take us within sight of the Arsenal's main gate across Beresford Square. If we managed to traverse half of the length of the Arsenal, go past the Woolwich Ferry, we would then come to the Dockyard and factories and we would still have a way to go. No wonder mum was worried.

"What do you think you're doing? Where are you going? Get in a public shelter now!" bellowed a huge voice.

It was an air raid warden on his rounds making sure people were as safe as possible. Mum ran into a doorway.

"Don't be daft, it's not bloody raining, it's an air raid. You can't put an umbrella up and dodge this bloody lot. You're not Churchill!"

That was the first time I remember hearing his name.

Mum spluttered a bit as the warden told us to go to the underground shelter beneath the square ahead. He pointed it out and watched us as we made our way there.

Before we got there he disappeared around a corner so mum said quietly and quickly, "come on, run, get round this corner."

We did.

As we were going down Powis Street we heard that well known throb, throb, throb of the German bombers following the river.

The river Thames, day or night was like a guiding beacon. They flew across from France or Holland, found the estuary, and followed it straight to the heart of the capital.

The balloons had already gone up, this kept the bombers flying higher but didn't stop them dropping their load. Then our guns opened fire.

For those who have never experienced war it is impossible to imagine the sound of dozens of heavy and light artillery anti-aircraft guns firing rapidly nearby. The ground shakes, the body shakes and the ears nearly concuss.

We had a worm's eye view. We could see the bombers. So many that they looked like a swarm of bees. We saw a few fighters engage and a few bombers hit. Normally we cheered but not today.

We sheltered in the doorway of the large Co-op department store near the end of the street.

We were lucky. Woolwich was not the target this time. They were going further up the river.

Mum said, "Some other poor sods are in for it this afternoon. Come on."

We shot past the Granada and Odeon Cinemas and the old smugglers pub opposite the present site of the Woolwich Free Ferry. During redevelopment years later a number of secret smuggler passages were discovered leading from the pub to the river.

The next door church yard held the grave of the old World Champion barefist fighter Tom Cribb.

We made it to grans' just as the all clear sounded.

The family thought mum was a looney but pleased she made it.

They made a big fuss of me. Well I was only a young whippersnapper.

Gran said that they had made some tinned salmon and cress sandwiches in brown bread with the crusts cut off just as I liked them. Good ole' Gran, these were real luxuries. Food was short.

I had never seen a banana, orange, lemon, ice cream or grapes. Meat, cheese, butter, and other necessities were rationed and clothing was issued on coupons.

We lived our lives in the ground, in Anderson shelters, curved corrugated iron plates linked together to cover dirt holes dug in the ground. These were then covered with turf, stones and sandbags.

The deeper the shelter and the more covering that had been applied then the safer it was. It was a do it yourself job.

However Gran was old so the council had put hers in, strictly according to regulations—no short cuts. Short steps went down to a hinged wooden door.

Consequently when the warning went Gran was joined by a number of neighbors who felt safer in Gran's shelter than their own.

I was used to shelters. We all were. Mum put me down at night to sleep on one of the hessian and wood bunk beds pushed against one of the sides.

On the other side were another camp bed and a couple of chairs. My cousin had fitted up a few compact shelves and on two of these there were small spirit lamps. They were lit when I went down and my cousin would come and choose a story from my Boy's Big Book of Adventure Stories. I would read the story, turn out the light and go to sleep.

Mum slept in the flat, only coming down when the warning went, which was several times a night. I slept through it all.

In the morning you went to school and were used to friends not coming again, ever. The names were no longer called out at morning prayers. There were now so many it was considered bad for morale. They were not forgotten though.

The damage was there to see every day but to us kids it was one more play area. The half houses with collapsed walls, floors and stairs hanging precariously, wallpaper in shreds and rafters exposed were paradise. We played war. We all wanted to be the good guys, no one wanted to be a German so only those who we didn't like were the Germans and of course they always lost.

We learnt the rules of survival. Don't pick up unexploded ordnance of any kind, don't kick tins or pick up pens or pencils in the street. They could be anti-personnel mines. Keep mouths tight shut in case spies were around and report anything suspicious. We all studied the shadow outlines issued by the government showing the shapes of the German aircraft, ships and tanks. Every kid kept a sharp lookout seeing the possibility of enemy everywhere. We all took this very seriously believing we greatly contributed to the war effort.

The government ensured that all school children got a spoonful of concentrated orange juice, a spoonful of cod liver oil and malt and a third of a pint of milk twice a day. We were all served from the same jars and the same spoons which we licked clean and then passed on to the next kid in line. The job of milk monitor was highly prized. Nobody missed the nit comb. This was a stout stainless steel comb that was dipped in disinfectant. It was passed through all the children's hair, each one carefully inspected for fleas, lice or nits. If you were okay then you went back to class while the district nurse swished the comb in the bowl of disinfectant for the next kid in line. It was a terrible embarrassment and disgrace for anyone pulled out for further investigation. We would all run around the infected one pretending disgust and reluctance to stand close, real friendly and supportive like!

Shortly after Gran made tea the warning went. This time Woolwich was the target. Before we made it to the shelter guns were firing and bombs were dropping.

We all made it in.

We were packed a bit tightly.

The usual crowd was there, jovial and friendly and were putting on a brave face.

It was the common belief that if you heard the bombs whistling down then they were not for you. The one that hit you, you didn't hear.

We heard plenty of whistling, the jokes stopped, and faces looked anxious as the ground shook. "This is a bad one," some one said, shaking his head. Then!!!???

No more shelter, no more people. I was looking up at the stars with flames around my feet.

I was having trouble hearing and speaking and had to keep wiping dirt away from my eyes. Close to me were two bodies, or what remained of them. I couldn't recognise them. I looked towards the house which was badly damaged. Doors were blown off, windows were gaping holes with curtains torn to shreds flapping in a heat haze caused by dozens of small fires and there were huge holes blasted in the walls. I saw my mother picking herself up from the garden path.

Like all mums her first concern was for me. She was crying, covered in blood, and bent down and lifted me out of the hole. There was nothing left of the shelter and I was the last survivor out.

Mum and I must have been unconscious for some time as Gran and some others were already on the way to the hospital. We picked our way through what was left of the house into the nightmare in the street outside. There were police, fire brigade and ambulances all rushing with a sense of urgency trying to get to trapped people. Flames were shooting up in the sky as a gas main had been hit which lit up the area.

Hoses were spread like dozens of snakes across the road and water controlled and uncontrolled was pouring out. A bomber had dropped his whole load of bombs in a line and that line had been our street. One entire side of the road had been destroyed. Casualties were very heavy and the soot grimed faces of the rescue workers were grim.

They had seen a lot but were still shaken. Unfortunately they would see far worse before this war would be over and so would we.

We were ushered into an ambulance and taken to the War Memorial Hospital on top of Shooters Hill.

My mum showed me first to the nurses as I was covered in blood. I was dealt with as priority. It took them nearly two hours to clean the imbedded dirt and debris off me, only to find that miraculously I was totally unhurt. The blood had come from mum. Luckily she had been treated quickly and her wounds discovered and dressed.

We were discharged about four o'clock in the morning and my poor old mum, damaged and confused went to wait at the bus stop.

We could see across half of London and it was a spectacular but disastrous sight.

We had survived one of the biggest bombing raids of the war and London was smashed and burning. Hundreds had lost their lives. The bombers had gone and left havoc behind.

A small car came up the hill, over the top and stopped beside us. The driver, an elderly man got out, looked at mum and said, "What are you doing here, my dear? There won't be any buses for hours and the service may not be any good anyway. Can I help, take you anywhere?"

Yes he could.

He was a part time policeman going off duty. He was stationed outside London and so had missed the raid. He lived a little way down Shooters Hill which had also missed the bombing.

Mum explained everything, how she was looking after her sister and was worried. We went there first. No need. The area was flattened. The bombs had missed the barracks but hit the houses. There were very few survivors. None were family.

The kind man took us home to Maxey Road. He had a battery portable radio in the car and tuned in on the way. I was fascinated, a mobile radio, wow. Having a car was luxury enough but a radio!!?? Was he a secret agent?

He searched and found that Lord Haw Haw was broadcasting.

He was the traitor William Joyce, who broadcast from Germany telling the British that resistance was futile and we should give up. His call sign was, "Charmany colling, Charmany colling." Tonight he was cock a hoop. "Crawl out from your rat holes you Londoners and look at your city in flames. This is what will happen over and over until you are destroyed or surrender. The might of Charmony is against you. You stand no chance. Give up."

Every one in Britain who could do so used to tune in to Lord Haw Haw. He boosted British morale no end and the Germans never caught on.

He was captured and executed after the war.

Our man dropped us off at the end of our road.

His closing remark just about summed it all up. "I'm so sorry, this has been a bad night."

Mum had one more big worry. My dad. He was in the London Fire Brigade and had been in the middle of everything since the blitz on London had begun. Was he okay?

We couldn't afford cars, motor bikes or telephones in those days so we just had to wait. Some one would get us a message and some one did. Dad was all right.

Mum and I were evacuated to Yorkshire to recuperate while family sorted things out for us. Dad got his first leave, got to Yorkshire and nine months later back in London I got a baby brother! Mum called him her Ilkley Moor baby because, although he was born in the British Home for Mothers and Babies evacuated to Kent, he was conceived in Yorkshire.

We were hit so many times during the war that the family thought that Hitler had a personal grudge against us.

They never worked out that whenever we were bombed we found a new house or flat in the same area. It never occurred to them to move out into the countryside. Good lord, we were Londoners, East and South Londoners no less, salt of the earth. Let Jerry do whatever he liked he would never beat the cockney. I truthfully believe I was privileged to grow up with such people. We will never see such quality and resourcefulness in adversity again. In an age when common sense now is in such short supply they had it in abundance.

Perhaps because they had so little else.

The ladies young and old had outgoing personalities and were full of fun. Kid's my age never saw their fathers. They were all away in the armed forces.

We had lovely parties with a few cakes and buns and played silly games such as grunt piggy grunt, charades and pass the parcel. We all made our own music, sang and danced to the cockney music hall songs and invited allied soldiers who attended local churches to come and join us.

These men showed us their family photos, talked of their lives and dreams and died soon afterwards. We received many letters from widows, mothers and sisters thanking us for our kindness, saying that the visit to us was the last good thing that had happened to their soldier relative before he was killed. We shed many tears for them.

Mum said many times that when this awful war was over she would never worry again. But she did, all the time, bless her heart, until the day she died at ninety one years of age. She had a lot of time to worry.

My dad died two years earlier, also ninety one. They couldn't bear to be separated. They had a lifelong love affair.

Little did I know then that it was not the war to end all wars. Oh governments and decent people tried but politics, religions and ideologies were never going to give way to common sense and common interest. Too many people with differing opinions and self interest thinking that only they were right. I was to fight in several countries, including Malaya, only to find that what we left behind were pyrrhic victories.

Thirty five years later in a much different world I was a senior executive with a large retail group and along with a few colleagues I was attending the Frankfurt Fair in Germany. This was a huge affair and covered every service and industry. A must visit sort of place.

We took a taxi and noticed that the taxi driver was listening intently to our conversation. We paused, looked at each other and then looked at him.

"Yeees?"

"Wovon kommen sie?" he asked, "sind sie Englander?" (Where do you come from, are you English.)

"Ja, wir sind Englander, von London," I said. "(yes, we are English, from London.)"

"Ach, Ich kenne London, ich habe London gern," He offered. "(Oh, I know London well, I like London.)"

"Prima, wo bleiben sie als sie nach London fahren? Machen sie eine Reise?" I asked. "(Great, where do you stay when you go to London, do you tour?"

"Ach, was? Ich bin nicht nach London gegangen." He said. "(Eh, what? I've never been to London.)"

"Aber sie haben gesagt das sie—" I started to say "(but you said that you—)"

"Nien, nein, im kreig habe ich es jedenes nacht gebombt!!" he exploded. "(no, no, in the war I bombed it every night!!)"

"Stimmt das? Wirklich?" "(Is it true? Really.)"

"Naturlich stimmt das. So ist das Leben" "(Of course it's true. Such is life.)"

I translated all this for my friends who were gobsmacked—silence.

Then I burst out laughing. "Dummkopf, aber meine Schule nicht, warum?" Sie haben meine Schule verpassen.

(Idiot, but not my school, why? You missed my school.)

One of my friends came in with, "of course he missed, that's why he's just a bloody foreign taxi driver. If it had been a London cabbie he would have been right on the mark!"

We arrived and got out before I could translate.

We do indeed live in a different world. Pity it's not a better one.

Buzz Bomb Alley

We were winning the war. At last.

However Herr Hitler just couldn't stop killing. He knew he was beaten but was not prepared to give anyone a break.

The same applied to the Japanese.

Stupid people who couldn't face surrender but were facing defeat.

Of course the Allied attitude didn't help. They demanded unconditional surrender although in point of fact it couldn't sensibly be anything else after all the horrors perpetrated by the Axis.

The days of coming to terms with, excusing and accommodating mass murderers was still in the future.

We had survived the blitz and could survey the ruins of many of our English cities in relative peace except for London.

We were in range first of the V1 pilotless jet aircraft (the Buzz Bomb) and second the V2 rocket. The first was noisy, the second silent. Both packed tons of explosives and were far in advance of anything the Allies had.

The invading Allied Armies had landed in Normandy, broken out in France and were advancing through Italy but had not yet reached the launch sites in mainland Europe. The Russians were mopping up the men and miles in the east.

We woke up to the smell of cordite. Over the five years of war we had come to know it well.

We were in our Anderson shelter in the middle of our garden which had been our bedroom for years. As a young boy I hadn't known much else other than sleeping in a hole in the ground covered by corrugated iron and dirt.

It was daylight, seemed sunny outside, and dust was floating about in the air. We also felt the aftermath of concussion so we knew that something had gone off somewhere while we were sleeping.

We pulled open the wooden door and were confronted with a dirt wall almost up to the top of the shelter. The steps cut into the ground had disappeared.

My older cousin's face was framed in the gap and he took our hands and pulled us out. Everything was intact but our shelter had been pushed down about three feet into the ground.

Buildings were intact but doors and windows had been blown out.

We walked through into the street and joined the crowd of neighbours looking down the hill.

"It was a buzz bomb. It hit Taylor's yard," said my Aunt Violet, who was called Voil to match boil!! "they lost everything, all gone to blazes."

"Couldn't be much, it was all junk," laughed my Uncle Sid, "it was a scrap yard. They didn't even keep the horse and cart there."

"Don't be wicked Sid," said my Aunt, "go and check on Ada, she's not that far away from it."

However my Aunt Ada was coming to us.

"Bloody hell Rene," she said to my mum, "a right mess down there. Family's all right though, no one hurt thank god. The junk flew all over the place. The pub on the corner looks more like the 'Hole in the Wall'. Kid's are having a field day nicking the packets of crisps."

"Oi! Where you two going," Uncle Sid called after me and my brother just as we were sloping away.

"Nowhere," we said innocently, "just wandering around."

"Well you'd better wander a bit quicker if you fancy some crisps. Don't blame me if you get caught. Get out of it."

"Oh Sid, is it all right? You are a bugger you know encouraging 'em," said my Mum.

"Bloody hell Rene, let 'em go and 'ave some. The poor little sods 'aven't 'ad much 'ave they?"

We were already halfway there.

We came back later with arms full of packets of crisps and a few nuts and raisins. We handed them over to anyone who wanted them, we were stuffed full and couldn't face another mouthful.

People started to get choosy. There were no varying flavours in those days and all were supplied with a small blue packet of salt but even so the packets were examined for any minute advantage.

Slowly people started to look up and over behind us. We lived on the side of a hill overlooking the River Thames, the Docks, the Arsenal and the Dockyard as well as miles of army barracks and factories. Behind us Shooter's Hill rose even higher. This had led to a false sense of security in the belief that any buzz bomb or rocket that could clear the hill would go flying on down to the river or even over it.

The German's put enough fuel in to reach London, where the engine would cut out, the weapon would crash and the bomb would explode.

Sometimes their calculations were wrong and they either put in too much or too little. In the main they were right on.

Sometimes we would watch the Spitfire and Hurricane pilots fly up and tip the wings of the buzz bomb to divert it away from the city and into the countryside. This was a delicate maneouvre and needed skill and courage. Everyone always cheered and waved like mad. If the pilot succeeded he would fly low along the side of the hill waving back and sometimes would do a victory roll.

As we looked a buzz bomb came over the hill with the sound of it's peculiar spluttering motor clearly reaching us. We all kept watching. As long as the engine was running so would the plane. If the engine cut out then it could either glide on for a fair way or drop down like a stone. We all moved closer to our shelters to be on the safe side.

Sure enough the engine cut out just after passing overhead.

"Blimey," exclaimed Aunt Ada, "not another one on Taylor's yard."

"Nah," said Uncle Sid, with more conviction than he felt, "this one's going over."

And it did. We watched it as it slowly dropped into Silvertown on the other side of the river. We saw the clouds of smoke go up and then the muffled sound of the explosion reached us.

"Poor sods," said Aunt Ada, "let's hope it dropped onto a bombsite."

Aunt Ada lived in a house opposite buildings that had been obliterated and laid waste by a landmine.

London had been hit so often that the same place was frequently hit two or three times making more ruins of the ruins.

Water dams had been built on a lot of them to aid the Fire Brigade to have much quicker access to water to fight the incendiaries. We sailed makeshift boats on them.

We had many playgrounds like that. Bombed houses and buildings, tops of concrete tank traps to leap across, abandoned pill boxes and shelters to hide in, huge craters made by land mines to roll in and of course the water dams.

In winter we broke the ice on them and in the summer they were full of naked boys and girls cooling down until some interfering old busybody chased everyone off.

We made do. Ropes were tied to lampposts to make merry go rounds and also to trees to make swings. Everything else had gone to support the war effort.

We were winning but the costs were phenomenal for all those countries directly in the field of fire.

As this was the third time our family had suffered my brother and I were evacuated to a family in Castleford, Yorkshire, near Leeds. The house faced onto farmland just over the road from the rows of houses.

The man of the house worked in the mines as a maintenance engineer. A good job and a vital one which was why he wasn't in the armed forces.

He had a large coloured map of Europe on the wall.

The map was full of pins with flags showing the Stars and Stripes of the USA, the Union Jack of Britain and the Hammer and Sickle of Russia.

A piece of wool was stretched around the pins showing where the Allied forces were in Europe. Everyday the man listened attentively to the radio and moved the pins in accordance with the news.

All over Europe those who could were doing the same, risking their lives listening to the BBC and living in hope. For so many liberty would come too late.

I was fascinated.

My brother and I were also in school.

Northern adults were inclined to be kind to Londoners. They knew and understood what we had been through. The Northern kids did not.

We were like foreigners. They were more or less able to make out Oxford English due to the BBC but had never heard anyone speak as we did. We also looked a bit pale and dirty. They were inclined to take the piss or try to bully us which was not a good thing to try on backstreet slum city kids. We were always in trouble and of course it was always our fault. We saw more of the teachers in detention than we did the kids in our class.

We looked forward to the summer holidays when we thought we would get some relief.

Wrong.

We went pea picking to earn a few bob on the local farm. We worked so hard for so little that we felt the need to do a bit of private enterprise. My little brother and I set up a box beside the road and offered a handful of peas for a penny. We lasted about ten minutes before our peas were confiscated, our box chucked away and were marched off home in disgrace.

We were told not to come back.

That did it. The paperwork was done, labels stuck on us, train tickets purchased, telegrams despatched to parents and we were sent back to London with a few others.

The Northerners said that they would rather take a chance on the Germans.

Mum welcomed us home and we told her that we were sent back because we cried every night and were homesick. The family said, "ah, the poor little loves," when they should really have said, "what right little horrors."

We played it for all it was worth and only told Mum the truth years later when we were too old to beat up.

Anyway we firmly believed that you could die from too much fresh air which was just as well if you lived in London.

The river Thames often raised a mist that was trapped in the Thames Valley and was changed into choking fog by pollution. Autumn was the worst time.

Early in the war it hadn't mattered too much if you couldn't see because there was a general blackout imposed at night. If the Germans had invaded then they would have been as confused as we were. Later on when shaded lighting was allowed buses, cabs and cars operated on low level dipped lights and people carried low powered torches. This was a slight improvement on before but no use at all in a smog. They were frequently thick pea soupers where any light, no matter how strong just reflected back and made the situation worse. The air, what there was of it, was filthy.

If you blew your nose then your handkerchief was full of large black spots.

On the buses the conductor had to climb down, walk to the front, and bang on the mudguard of the bus to keep the bus close to the curb and going in the right direction. The bus driver couldn't see and frequently lost the conductor. In that case passengers had to get off the bus, form a chain, and direct the conductor back to the bus and everyone would set off again. Nobody regarded this as strange.

After the war orange sodium street lighting was introduced which penetrated far deeper than other types but the problem was never cleared up until smokeless fuels and central heating became normal.

Within a few years the infamous London Smogs were no more and the pop song 'A Foggy Day in London Town' so beloved of American crooners was consigned to history.

Shortly after our return two rockets fell in South London both bad enough but one was truly awful. It was a Saturday afternoon and the German armies were being rolled up everywhere which had led to a lot of life returning more or less to normal. Or at least as normal as could be under the circumstances.

A false sense of security prevailed.

Woolworths store, close to New Cross Gate Southern Railway Station was packed with shoppers eager to get at whatever was on sale. Out of the blue a V2 rocket hurtled in and obliterated the store and most of the shoppers.

The carnage was terrible. Bodies and mutilated remains were still being recovered days later. Woolworths raised a new store on the site with a commemoration plaque to remember the dead and swore to maintain a store there for ever. Unfortunately Woolworths didn't survive for ever and neither did the new store.

The other explosion was from a V1 Buzz Bomb landing at the very bottom of our street opposite the Matchless and AJS motorcycle factory. The factory wasn't damaged and wasn't making motor bikes at the time either. What they were making was classified.

The bomb made a direct hit on a huge pub cum hotel and tore a gaping hole in a warehouse at the back. Word went round amongst all the kids. Get down there and see what you can grab. We hardly knew what toys were as everything went towards the war effort but we understood there were great playthings to be had.

It was dreamland.

The warehouse was a store for theatrical props.

The surrounding streets were soon chock full of Greek and Roman soldiers fighting Zulus and Roundheads. Saxons were fighting Normans which made a welcome change from us acting as Spitfire pilots shooting down German Messerschmidts which immediately became old hat.

This went on for a few days until the authorities, with co-operation from unpopular parents, recovered most of the stuff. We were upset but we did have a ball. For a very short time Buzz Bombs enjoyed a period of popularity.

Around the same time a rocket dropped into Woolwich Arsenal during a working day. The explosion was ten times larger than normal as it hit a red zone area. The government tried to cover it up, never announced the number of casualties, and tightened security. They thought that as the war was being won then the death toll would be bad for moral. They were probably right.

The extra security didn't help one threesome however. The Woolwich Arsenal and Woolwich Dockyard cops were the only armed police in the country at that time directly in contact with the public. They manned the gates and patrolled the exterior as well as the interior. Public transport, workers and shoppers in Beresford Square Market were right up against them at the main gate.

One gate guard spied his wife out with her lover shopping hand in hand in the market, who had mistakenly thought her husband was on a different shift.

He ran over to them, shot them dead and then shot himself in front of dozens of witnesses. That couldn't be kept quiet.

They tried to review the rules but what could they do. Give enough people guns and sometime and somewhere at least one of them is going to go off with a bad result.

It was a credit to the people that they could still be upset by such a tragedy after nearly six years of brutalising war.

An adults idea of a chat with children is always different to that of the children.

Things are never straightforward. Children go sideways. Nana Hayes decided to have a little chat with me.

"Denis, I hear you are a good reader. That's good. What books do you like? What is your favourite?" she asked gently and encouragingly.

"Dunno really nan, I like a lot," I said. I was worried and panicking because I was frantically trying to remember names. To my mind I read stories, not books.

"But you must have a favourite, one you love to read over and over again. I know I did when I was a little girl," nana said.

My mind boggled. Nana was a little girl once? She had always been old ever since I was born. Of course I read the same story many times. There was a war on, there weren't that many books around anyway. You hung on to what you had.

My mind went blank. "Come on," I thought, "don't disappoint Nan. She's lovely."

I grasped at a slip of memory and blurted out, "The Three Mustardeers." This was a comic cartoon strip produced by Coleman's Mustard as a bye line to their newspaper advertising campaign.

As soon as I said it I regretted it. Even to my young mind it didn't seem suitable.

However luckily for me Nan misheard.

"Wonderful" she said, "come with me."

I followed her as she opened a cupboard in the forbidden front room.

"Here," she exclaimed triumphantly, "here, this is yours, just for you."

In her hands, held out to me was a beautifully bound copy of Alexandre Dumas 'The Three Musketeers'.

I took it from her totally bewildered. I wanted to tell her she had got it wrong but couldn't manage to get one single word out.

Nan, bless her, thought I was speechless with gratitude.

"It's a wonderful story. It's a favourite of mine too," she said kindly. "I hope you enjoy it and treasure it for years."

I managed to mumble, "thanks Nan," and started to skim through it with Nan looking on benignly. If only she knew. Perhaps she did and was trying to guide me.

I will never know. I never read the book until years later. The copy Nan gave me was destroyed by bombs. But I have to agree. It is a wonderful romantic adventure story.

Grandad was Irish through and through. He was a hard working, hard fighting, hard drinking, hard swearing man. He had worked all over the world but had little to show for it except decay. He was a devout Catholic and so would go and confess his sins on a Sunday morning. He was gone a long while!

In later years he would go down the Irish Catholic working man's club on a Saturday night, sing and drink the remainder of his life away and then get into a fight with the Northern Irish who he regarded as traitors and the police who he regarded as ignorant defenders of the British Empire. Nan often had to burn policeman's helmets and truncheons in the boiler when doing the Sunday wash. He didn't at all like seeing his battle trophies used in that way but as it was a Sunday he tried to behave himself.

He was such a wonderful role model that all his fifteen surviving children became protestant, didn't drink and didn't swear much. They figured that if they did the opposite to their dad they would be better people. They were. They only had one or two children.

Much to my Mum's horror he would sit me on his knee, sing patriotic Irish songs and tell me the powerful stories of the heroes who fought for Irish freedom. I still treasure the illustrated book I have called "The Fight for the Irish Republic."

Legend has it that his grandparents spoke no English and never left Ireland. Grandad apparently fought in the Cork County Irregulars, hated the British Auxillaries and Black and Tans even though he had earlier fought in the British Army against Germany in the first World War. He was later one of the earliest members of the newly formed Air Force, his discharge papers showed he was a fitter.

He left Ireland during the civil war when he found out that the Irish Free State was not free for Republicans. Grandad was a Republican through and through and although he would fight the British for Independence he would not fight Irishmen.

So he did what thousands of Irish have done ever since. He took the ferry to Britain.

He saw nothing contradictory in sitting spellbound in tears listening to the King's Christmas speech. He never missed it. His children laughed and called him a hypocrite but he didn't care less. It was a beautiful thing and if only the Irish appreciated it then so be it.

He called me his "little Dinney" which horrified my Mum. She called him a terrible excuse for a man and he called her "Angel Face." In Grandad's eyes she was wonderful. She was. My Dad, although one of the younger sons, was the first to stand up to him and protect Nan from the violence. Dad never forgave the older sons for not doing the same.

He died suddenly of pneumonia. The doctors said he had had so many tropical illnesses and injections that nothing worked any more. His immune system didn't function. The priest winced at his deathbed confession but absolved him all the same.

I still have this old photo of a big stern man sitting on a chair in Africa with his "boy" standing dutifully next to him. The story goes that this servant paddled Grandad down the Congo to hospital when he was riddled with malaria and slept under his bed until he recovered. Grandad never said what happened to the servant. Probably didn't care. Typical white colonial who being Irish should have known better.

Nan died from cancer in her bed at home. She told everyone that she didn't want people to be unhappy. She had wonderful children, lived to see the Nazis defeated and was going to live with Jesus who she had loved all her life.

So many women like her through the ages have been the unsung heroes. Not so sure about today's lot though?

Finally the news came through. The last of the unmanned bomb sites in Europe had been over run.

We celebrated but not for long. At almost the same time pictures appeared on newsreels of concentration camps being liberated with the horrifying revelations that in fact most of them had been death camps. Belson, Dachau, Auschwitz, Sobidor and too many others became household names. The victims were not casualties of war they were victims of planned genocide. Most were guilty only of being Jews but others suffered too.

The free world recoiled in horror especially as a few months later Japan surrendered when the torture they had inflicted on innocent people became general knowledge also.

Very few at the time had any guilt about the two atom bombs being dropped on Japan. The casualties there were in the thousands whereas the world was still recoiling from the horrors of millions of dead and dying.

The feeling was, 'if you start it, don't complain when it comes home to you and you lose.'

Peculiarly it became fashionable to extol compassion to the inhabitants of Dresden, Nagasaki and Hiroshima and skate over the atrocities propagated by Germany and Japan. The suffering and deaths they had inflicted had not only been larger and unjustified but thousands of times greater.

Ask the survivors of Nangking, where the Japanese slaughtered many more innocents who didn't want war, if they felt sorry for any Japanese killed in Hiroshima in a district which supported the war. No contest.

How anyone could view people being killed by a bomb as deserving more sympathy than those men, women and children dying in agony after being bayoneted in cold blood dozens of times by Japanese soldiers beats me. Common sense seems to fly out of the window when pretended outrage takes over. Usually the protesters are those who have never experienced true bloody hardship. To them going to hell and back is usually knowing someone spending time in rehab, or experiencing a little upset from time to time. Poor dears.

Everyone was prepared to end the war under any circumstances— the world was war weary. The Japanese were probably secretly relieved they had been given a good reason to surrender although that was never apparent. They broadcast the propaganda that they were willing to fight until the last man, woman and child. Surrender was unthinkable. Many still couldn't accept it years later.

Any Allied Premier who had the means to end the war but didn't do so would have been justifiably vilified. God only knows what would have happened had the Axis got hold of it. To vilify the leaders of the free world for doing so is quite ridiculous and can only be construed that there are always those who wish to make mischief rather than use common sense.

We all celebrated the end of the war with street parties. Unfortunately it was yet again not a war to end all wars.

It was not an end but only a beginning.

Communist Russia and Communist China were about to kill more of their own people in peacetime than their enemies did in war and Governments committed to freedom went on devising weapons that were capable of not only exterminating whole cities but the entire population of the world.

Unbelievable but true! Somehow we lived through it all.

Cynicsm

Our generation had had an early overdose of reality. World War Two was over and the clearly defined enemies were soundly beaten. Ourselves and our allies were heroes.

Except they weren't.

Our allies Russia and China who had suffered so much from our enemies were no longer our friends. In Churchill's words, "an iron curtain had descended over Europe."

Mao Tse Tung was chasing Chiang Kai Chek onto the island of Formosa, later to be renamed Taiwan.

At the same time our previous enemies almost overnight had become friends.

This should have been confusing but it wasn't. We took it all in our stride.

We understood that the enemies of our enemies were our friends until they became our enemies. Nothing difficult in that.

Many of us went to Malaya where we were fighting communist guerrillas who had been trained and decorated by our side for heroically fighting the Japanese. Then we went for R&R in Hong Kong where we patrolled the border with China supporting the communist troops on the other side.

The guerrillas claimed to be fighting colonialism but carried on the killing after independence.

In East Africa we fought rebels with primitive rituals who were obviously nowhere near ready for democratic independence but had to negotiate and deal with their murderous leaders for years.

We were fighting battles against regimes that pretended they were fighting for high ideals when they were just trying to grab and hold onto power for themselves while at the same time we were supporting others who were just the same.

Countries supported Independence groups in neighbouring states, not with the aim of setting them free but with the objective of taking them over.

A different form of Imperialism and Colonialism was arising expertly practised by Communist China and Soviet Russia.

The naive approach of the Americans added to the confusion. In order to obtain millions of dollars in aid and military support it was only necessary to claim to be anti left wing. In fact the Yanks even fell for the blackmail whereby certain rulers said they would go left if they didn't get the arms and money. They got it.

We accommodated all of it, not comfortably, but we seemed to have had a much more pragmatic approach to everything than people years later.

The USA didn't help. They put some out of control nutter called McCarthy in charge of investigating supposed non-American activities together with holier than thou J Edgar Hoover and the world lost the balance it had fought so hard to protect.

Unfortunately although it hadn't become clear then it was actually the start of a decline that continued until now.

America looked as though it was roaring ahead when it actual fact it was being slowly undermined from within. And it was from the Right not the Left. As the old folk song said, "they say America first but they put America last."

Then, as now, everyone was spying on everyone else. Even the spies were spying on spies whose job it was to spy on spies who were spying. Huge blunders of security were made with surprise defectors on both sides who at times were not defectors but only pretended to be.

Spying had always been part of the silly season but this was chaos making a silly season almost seem normal.

Spies used every device available to them and we all thought why not.

Sun Tsu had done so centuries before, in fact he made a living writing books about it. Or maybe it was not him??!! If he was alive today he would have amassed a fortune in royalties.

Nobody thought it particularly shocking or surprising. Only those who were caught doing it.

Nothing much has changed except that undermining from within seems to have become the norm and perversely even viewed as admirable by some.

What a sad world when cynicism becomes unacceptable.

The Operation

I t was nearly the end of my first year at Askes School. I had just had my twelfth birthday.

I woke up to get ready for school and doubled over with a pain that took my breath away. Before I could reach the toilet I was hit again and again.

After a few minutes I realised it was not a toilet pain.

I staggered down stairs to the kitchen.

"Not good mum," I groaned, "got a pain in me gut."

"Good one slacker," shouted my little brother, "original, original, original! Can I have one like that too mum? No school ha ha."

I could see the doubt in my mum's face but before I could swipe my brother I started to vomit and didn't stop for some minutes. Even then I was still heaving.

"Want this then do you," I managed to moan, "come on then, take this on."

He had gone green at the sight of the mess and he did almost join me. He ran for it.

Mum looked concerned, "get yourself to bed, I'll bring up a hot water bottle. Wrap it up and put in on your stomach while I just call the doctor."

Actually the doctor's surgery was nearer than the public telephone box so she ran all the way.

She came back breathless.

"Doctor will come straight after surgery," she said, "will you be all right?"

"'Course mum, not good though. Pain down here is real bad. Hurts a lot," I said quietly."

"Were you sick while I was gone?"

"Yeah a bit, on an' off. Kept it in the bucket though."

When the doctor came I was doubled over. He told me to lie still, took my temperature and prodded and pushed around my stomach locating the pain.

"Right," he said, "hospital for this fellow. I'll go back to the surgery and phone for an ambulance. Pack a few things as I am recommending admittance."

Mum went pale. "Is it serious doctor, what's wrong, why hospital?" she asked urgently, obviously worried.

"Appendix," he said curtly, "acute, needs attention now."

"Wow oh wow. An ambulance. Now that's living," I thought, "please, oh please carry me out on a stretcher, don't just make my day but make my whole life."

Then a more sobering thought hit me. The only ambulances seen in our street since the end of the war were to take old people away who never came back. Maybe I'd tell the doc I could walk.

No chance. When the ambulance came I got the full works. Wrapped in red blankets, strapped in a stretcher and carried out by two ambulance men.

Oh I did feel good. All the old girls in the street were out in their pinnies, turbans and curlers, looking serious and gossiping like mad.

I wanted to wave but couldn't because of the straps so I tried to look long suffering and brave instead.

I failed.

I was hit by a wave of pain which made me wince and totally ruined my image.

I had to go alone with the doctor as mum had to get my brother to school first and wait for my dad to arrive home from nightshift.

They would come later after they had made arrangements with my aunts to pick up my brother from school and look after him.

I was on the way to St. Nicks. Saint Nicholas hospital in Plumstead was typical of all the wonderful local do it all medical centres. About the only thing they couldn't cope with was brain surgery.

I was rushed into emergency. They asked me how I felt.

"Very brassed off," I uttered moodily.

"Oh dear," exclaimed a worried looking nurse, "we'll soon get you right though. That's why we're all here," she finished on what she obviously thought was a cheerful note.

"You can't," I said defiantly, "upset 'enn I? The ambulance driver didn't ring his bleedin' bells did 'e?"

They were all a bit taken back until a medical orderly pushing my trolley to the wards began shouting, "ding, ding, ding, dong, ding-a-ling."

Everyone laughed, including me.

I was admitted to the surgery ward and within minutes my bed was screened off and a hospital doctor appeared along with my doctor and several nurses.

I had to undress. No problem. I had been through the war where delays because of modesty could get you killed. I played rugby, football, did cross country and cricket and washed in communal baths full of mud, blood and piss in all seasons of the year.

I was examined thoroughly and then told to turn over facedown.

The white coated doctor pulled on a pair of rubber gloves, covered them in vaseline and stuck his fingers up my arse.

Whoops, made my eyes water.

He probed around. Pulled out, took off the gloves and said, "very swollen appendix, close to seepage, slight touch of peritonitus, operate 6am tomorrow."

They all left. Screens were removed and I looked around at my fellow inmates.

They did not look in good condition, especially the old guy next to me who was being shaved by a younger guy I guessed to be his son. The old man's face was so cavernous I couldn't believe he wasn't cut by the razor.

The shaver, looked across, smiled at me, nodded and went on with his work.

I was the only kid in the whole place of about thirty patients.

I was examined again several times before my parents arrived at visiting time in the evening.

Rules were strict and unbreakable. There were two hours visiting twice a day. If you missed them then it was too bad, come the next day and be on time.

If you wanted to die in the arms of your relatives then you had to arrange it in visiting times. Outside of that they could see you in the morgue.

All patients had to be in bed at visiting time, even if walking, tucked up tight in disciplined hospital sheets. Sister's word was law and matron's word came directly from god.

Doctors were there to help you get well, nurses were there to make sure you did. They were, and still are, fantastic dedicated people.

I didn't have a clue what was going on, nor did I understand what was wrong with me nor what they were going to do to put it right.

So I was calm and blase.

Everyone thought I was so brave but I was actually totally ignorant.

I did notice that mum and dad were unusually grave and concerned. Mostly they believed that my brother and I either faked illnesses or exaggerated them so as to hop off school and of course they were usually right.

Their serious attitude should have tipped me off but I was too busy lapping up the total attention.

I wanted to know where the chocolate and fruit was as we had done hospital visits before but I was told I couldn't have them just then. Perhaps the next day.

I still didn't cotton on.

During the night I was disturbed as the old man next to me was carried out dead. He had been dead a while as he was stiffening up and there was a fuss around the trolley trying to fit him on. If they got him on one side his arm on the other side was sticking out, pointing at me. I wasn't one of those auto-suggestive silly kids so I saw no significance in his gesture. War made you understand that the dead were just dead.

I told one of the concerned orderlies that it seemed as though he wanted to pick a bogey out of my nose and grinned. He didn't think it was funny.

Ah well. My mates would have laughed.

There was no point in sleeping anyway as it was close to six o'clock.

Right on time screens were wrapped round my bed.

Sister appeared and asked, "have you had your pre-med yet?"

"What's that?"

She turned aside, snapped at one of the nurses, "well, has he? Right then do it now."

I was given some medicine which they said was to relax me and then had the cheek to give me an enema which meant shoving a tube up my bum to inject my bowels full of soapy water. I was stuck on a bed pan just in time to catch me unloading everything stored up inside me in about three seconds flat.

I was congratulated on co-operating so wonderfully.

Bloody hell I had no choice and no idea what was going on.

Next my pyjamas were removed and I put on a white flowing gown that looped over my head and fastened at the back with tabs.

I laid on the bed and nurses lifted my gown up around my waist.

Whey, hey.

One of them had a mug of warm water, a shaving brush and a cutthroat razor.

Not so whey hey!

She shaved what little pubic hair I had at the time. Actually the shaving brush had more.

Then washed and dried me.

So far so good.

Then another nurse smothered all my nether regions with yellowish brown iodine, stuck a label on my toe, and a small disc near my right groin.

Not so good.

By then I was becoming very dreamy.

By the time they took me to the theatre I wasn't really interested although they talked to me sweetly.

I was placed under bright lights, examined closely and then told to bite on a metal plate put between my teeth. I did so.

A full face mask was placed over my moosh and that terrible claustrophobic feeling you got from the anaesthetic in those days took over. Everything heaved up and down, in and out until weird dreams took over and you knew no more.

I slowly came round, floating in and out of consciousness, vaguely aware that I was being sick in front of my parents sitting beside my bed.

Eventually I made it back to the land of the conscious and the living.

My parents were so relieved but not as relieved as I was.

Dad signalled to a nurse that I was awake.

Sister and a nurse came up, gushing about how brave I had been and an orderly said he was sure I hadn't been making a fuss so as to avoid an operation. If only.

Mum was just a little bit weepy but held onto it well. You didn't display your hurt in those days, nor discussed it. You always soldiered on regardless.

Laughter and happiness could be shared but sorrow never. Everyone had suffered so much over twenty or thirty years that there was no patience for those who used hardship as an excuse or wallowed in self pity.

I was only allowed liquids for a couple of days and then graduated to soups, custards and jellies. Heavy foods were out.

I had to lay down and move as little as possible. I drank out of a little pot like mug, covered with a spout on the side.

The doctor came and told me I had been very lucky. In layman's terms my appendix had burst, peritonitis was setting in and it was all just short of being very serious. I was going to have to have a tube stuck in the cut and be drained three times a day. This would delay my recovery but I was in no danger.

My goodness I was treated like royalty. The nurses told me that the grown men should take me as an example. They were all moans, groans and complaints and apparently in total agony most of the time. I was just a quiet kid who lay down, read a book and told adventure stories to old men who were capable of listening.

Slowly I was allowed to sit up, then try to stand up and then taught myself to walk again by pushing the tea trolley round for the tea ladies.

The pain hung on though. I was told it was not because of the appendix, that had gone, but it was wind trapped trying to force it's way out.

It slowly subsided.

Then the tube came out.

The doctors pronounced themselves satisfied and that I could go home after two days and attend outpatients afterwards.

They were critical of the scar. It was not as tidy as they would have liked due to the complications but as far as I was concerned it was immaterial.

Ironically whether it was neat enough or not didn't matter because seven years later my guts were ripped apart by hand grenade fragments in almost the same place leaving a scar alongside that was really ugly.

Thank goodness we don't know what the future holds!

During my convalescence I visited my class at school who stood up and applauded me as I came in. I was so embarrassed that I didn't handle it well.

When the new term came I turned up at my usual class but was turned away by the form master. I had been relegated.

I wasn't having any of that. I walked out of the class I had been sent down to and went back to my old class. I told the master, with a few tears in my eyes, that I had suffered enough with the illness so I didn't deserve to be punished at school. I didn't belong with the relegated, I belonged there.

He was superb, called it great spunk, and took me to the headmaster.

He was a formidable figure, straight and perceptive. He peered at me through strong glasses and said, "give the boy a chance."

That was it, I was back in. I didn't know it then but I had attracted the notice of the school authorities in a positive way and in spite of a number of stupid growing up pranks I would be given a number of opportunities of leadership that I would never shirk and always embrace.

At the end of my second year I finished in the top ten out of thirty in the class.

The form master when he signed off the end of the year said quietly, "and this is the lad they wanted to send down. You never know do you?"

That was all I needed.

I would have to go backwards several times in my life but I would never go down.

The Gunpowder Plot

"Quick, come over the fields and don't act suspicious," whispered one of my mates Johnny conspiratorially.

So we did and although we thought we were quick and not acting at all suspicious we actually looked like a coven of foreign spies about to blow up an Archduke.

He huddled over and looked around him furtively and we all followed suit.

He reached inside his jacket and pulled out an air pistol.

Our eyes went bigger than our heads.

We were speechless for a while then managed to gasp, "it's beautiful. Where did you get it? Can we touch it? Have you got any pellets?"

"It's my brother's and I've got pellets but you can't touch," he said triumphantly.

"Bet you can't shoot it. Bet you don't know how." we said.

"I do, watch," and he put a slug in the end of the barrel, pressed in the spring against a tree, aimed at a flower, pulled the trigger and missed.

Nobody cared.

This was living and living dangerously.

Not from the gun but from his brother. If Johnny got caught then either his Dad or his brother would kill him.

This was the high spot of our day.

I rushed home and shouted, "Dad, dad, can I have an air pistol, Johnny's brother's got one and he let's Johnny use it."

"Then he's got more money than sense. I'll have a word with his father tomorrow."

Oh, oh, I realised I had just made a big mistake in letting my mouth run away with itself.

"Can I have one though Dad?" I carried on hoping to smooth over it.

"You can have a smack round the ear if you carry on, you are too young," he said, "anyway what on earth would you use it for?"

"Rabbits, squirrels, rats and that. You know, over the fields," I explained earnestly.

"When did you last see any of them round here? The foxes got them ages ago."

"Well I'll shoot the foxes then or Mrs. Grainger's cat. The one that moans all night cos you said he's so randy," I managed to shout as I ran flat out through the back door just dodging the blows coming my way.

My mum's voice followed me down the path, "language!! Wash your mouth out. Don't be late for tea."

The pursuit of air pistols became our prime aim.

We couldn't buy them but big brothers could. So they were pursued continuously.

I didn't have a big brother—I was a big brother. I had a little brother which only re-enforced all of our opinions that little brothers were a waste of space.

We lived on a council estate which wasn't quite finished so there was still a mixture of mature settlement, open spaces and construction. Plenty of ways to make ourselves a nuisance but air pistols were something else.

We needed them.

Some of my mates were successful. By playing one off against another, they got a few brothers to fork out and soon there were even two air rifles to examine.

We practised over the fields and managed after a short while to mainly hit what we were aiming at.

This got boring.

We needed fresh challenges but needed to be careful. If we got caught then our game was over.

However, when did common sense and foresight ever feature in a kid's brain?

We came onto the streets looking like old time gangsters which did not draw much attention. Our gang was usually acting stupid so no one paid very much attention to our latest mood.

We popped off a few pellets at Mr. Davison's homing pigeons, thankfully missed the glass coverings of a number of street lamps and focused on the toilet windows set on the side of some of the houses.

It was summer and most of the windows were latched open.

We sat down to wait. Hardly innocently but again no one took any notice.

Very frustrating when you are young as you always want to be noticed.

The art of anonymity only comes with maturity.

We didn't have to wait for long.

It was early evening when the light in the toilet went on. Evidently the occupant was intending a long sit in reading the paper before using it to wipe his backside.

Two of us lined up the opening in the window in our sights.

One, two, three, fire.

Bullseye.

The two slugs zinged through the window and ricocheted around the little room.

As soon as we heard the first yell we were on the move, down the road and around the corner. We took it in turns to do a few more before it was time to go home.

The next day there was a lot of neighbourly consultations going on.

At teatime Dad repeated the latest scandal to Mum who was horrified.

"What's up Dad?" I asked not very hopefully. Most times we were told to be quiet and not to listen to adult conversations as they weren't for young ears.

This time I got a surprise.

"There's been some irresponsible shooting around the estate. Old Mr. Foster, you know, the one with the gammy leg, hurt himself falling off the toilet dodging air gun pellets. It took Mrs. Foster a long while to clean up the mess. Thank god we didn't let you have one. You lot had nothing to do with this did you?"

"Come on Dad, be fair, you were going to give me a smack round the ear just for asking. Blimey dad, we are done if we did it and done if we didn't. Grown ups are not fair."

"All right, don't over do it but the police have been called so watch yourselves."

We met over the fields for a council of war.

Johnny and Tony were missing. They had the air pistol and the air rifle.

We were worried, would our friends crack and drop us all in it.

No worry. They appeared two days later in top form. Minus weapons.

We were disappointed in them.

Apparently no one had associated us with the events. Only the brothers who had a damn good idea what was up.

They had been warned and lectured by the police who believed their alibis but were unhappy with the lackadaisical security. The guns were locked up.

The older brothers had warned our pals that they would get their own backs later.

We were at a loss.

We tried bows and arrows, catapults, slings and spears but nothing came close to matching up to the air guns.

Then Johnny appeared excited again.

His brother had told him that he needed to make a real weapon and had told him how.

So at woodwork lesson, during the metal work period, Johnny had secured a metal tube to a handle, sealed off one end and made a hole into the tube from the top of the body.

He nicked a few chemicals from Chemistry and bought a bit more from the chemists and made gunpowder. He wouldn't tell us the exact formula, that was to be his secret.

He rammed a wad of paper soaked in oil down the barrel, put in powder, wadding, and then ball bearings and then packed in more paper and wadding. He rammed it all down tightly.

He stuck a match in the hole, lit it with another match, watched it flare up and work it's way down into the barrel.

We all stood back.

After what seemed an age there was a flash, a muffled bang and the ball bearings shot out and dropped about 10 feet away.

Wow! He was a hero.

He was also ambitious.

We all made one, hid them under leaves near our camp in the woods and learned how to make a more balanced mix so that we had more controlled power.

It was a wonder that no one died.

Johnny told us he was up to something that would make our eyes boggle.

One day he came out from his backyard pulling a dog's lead.

Yeah, what? He'd bought a dog? Big deal.

No, it was a small cannon, roughly made, but certainly recognisable as a lethal weapon. Lethal to whom was the question which was shortly to be answered. Johnny was in test mode.

We proudly marched off to the fields.

Anyone would have thought that we were making a kid's version of "The Gun."

We all eagerly assisted in making it up and getting it set and then we just as eagerly backed away.

Johnny lit the fuse.

It fizzled out.

It fizzled out three times more.

We had all backed further away each time it was lit.

We were now standing well away.

Johnny blamed the malfunction on our cowardice.

The wind was too strong. The flame was blowing out before it had time to catch on.

We needed to huddle round, pack closely together and it would work.

As we would be huddled down we couldn't keep watch so a volunteer was needed to go up on the road as lookout.

I was there before anyone else moved.

I looked down on the scene.

There in the field below was a group of boys packed closely together apparently in the middle of receiving a team motivation session.

Suddenly there was a puff of smoke and then a flame that shot straight up in the air from the middle of the group.

All the heads flew backwards at the same time as another puff of smoke blew out from between their legs and a muffled explosion reached me.

A cardboard box set up as a target 10 yards away leaped into the air and was later found to be peppered with holes.

I rushed down to congratulate my mates.

I hardly recognised them.

They had black and grey faces, no eyebrows and singed hair.

They were also partly deaf for a few hours.

It was decided, without any further consultation, that cannons were out and handguns were safer.

One sensible decision and one mistake.

We carried on for a while until one idiot threatened a girl, peppered her legs with shot needing her to see the doctor.

He delivered an ultimatum with the agreement of her parents.

If all the guns were chucked in his dustbin by the next morning no further action would be taken.

We did it and that was the end of that.

Scrumpin'

We were out. Walking along but early teen style walking. In other words not normal. It was running ahead a bit, turning, and rugby style zig zagging menacingly back with an imaginary ball. It was shoving and shouting nonsensical impressions from the radio, especially the Goons. It was hurtling towards walls, running up them and turning a backwards roll. It was indulging in mock boxing matches or wrestling for fun until one got upset and started a real fight with the rest of us pretending to try to stop it at the same time as egging them on. Sometimes a blow went wild which brought others into the fight until a passing adult waded in whacking us with hands or newspapers eventually calming us down. Only then did the losers tell the winners that they were lucky the fight was stopped when it was, a little longer and they would have been real sorry. That would cause a flare up all over again.

The more adventurous would try to smoke the odd dog end they'd picked up in the street still alight if possible. We couldn't afford even a single whole cigarette let alone a packet. They would hold it backwards in the palm of their hands or have it hanging sneeringly out of the corner of their mouths gangster style. You had to be careful. If adults saw you they would knock it out of your mouth or hand and scuff it under the heel of their shoe.

Those were the days. Everyone took responsibility.

We were hungry. Of course we were always hungry at that age.

We were on the lookout.

Allotments and easy to reach gardens were a favourite as were fruit trees hanging over a garden wall.

We loved to raid for carrots and potatoes. We would shoot in, rip up what we needed and shoot out. We would scrub the dirt off the raw carrots by scraping them on the wall and munch away like rabbits. The potatoes we would take to building site night-watchmen who would bake them on their braziers.

We tried raw onions but some were so strong they nearly blew our heads off. Tomatoes were delicious but had to be carefully cleaned on our shirts as they tended to grow biggest and tastiest in manure.

Everything was very seasonal so we had a limited few months to enjoy.

We picked blackberries, raspberries and strawberries wild, usually along hedgerows but apples, pears and cherries were more difficult. Crab apples grew wild but just a few would cause days of the shits. Good for an occasional clear out.

We learned to avoid the farm orchards. They were a livelihood for the farmer, not a garden summer bonus, so the fruit was well protected. The farmer had a shotgun and would use it. One had cleared some gypsies off his fields a few weeks earlier. He hadn't shot to kill but he had shot in warning and if that was good enough for the gypsies it was good enough for us.

That left the front and back gardens of householders who had carefully pruned and nurtured fruit trees for years in a difficult climate. They looked forward and valued their fruit year after year.

So did we.

We were exploring a side alley, playing hide and seek with a military theme, when we spotted the tops of apple and pear trees showing on the other side of a high wall.

High walls were no problem. We were on top in seconds.

Wow, bingo. A large garden was before us full of fruit trees including plums.

The trees largely concealed us from the back of the house.

Utopia.

We needed to check if anyone was alert or in the house.

We sent a lone scout up to the back window.

He reported back. No one in the kitchen, just an older couple in the back room asleep in armchairs by the fireside. No fire—it was summer.

We needed a threefold operation. Three teams taking it in turns. One team outside the wall pushing up team number two who would haul up team number three who would go into the garden and nick the fruit then be hauled back up and dropped outside. We would take it in turns.

I was in team three and first in the garden.

We sampled the fruit, eating some, while stuffing the rest into our shirts which were soon bulging. We had a large sample of apples, pears and plums stashed away. We had taken our time being selective so were abused by our mates when we got back outside on the ground.

We had a bit of a row and were resentful of their attitude.

We shoved them up to the team on the wall and they took their turn in the garden.

We looked at each other and said, "yeah."

We wandered away nonchalantly, trying to look as innocent as possible. A few of us stayed in view of the wall watchers. I and a couple of friends walked up to the front door munching away on juicy pears.

We rang the bell and the door was opened by a bewildered looking middle aged lady, dressed like a headmistress, obviously just woken up from a nap.

Very innocently we informed her, with serious faces, that it was our civic duty to tell her that some rough boys from a bad neighbourhood were in her garden stealing her apples. We didn't think it right as she was a nice person and such behaviour was disgraceful.

She looked at the half eaten pears, scrutinised our stuffed shirts and hesitated. She made up her mind.

She shouted, "clear off," slammed the door and called for her husband.

We went round to the side entrance.

Within seconds the wall was full of our mates, scrambling like mad to get out.

They joined us on the run, some with fruit, some without.

We stopped a few streets away.

"What went wrong?" we asked innocently throwing away the remains of the pears and starting on ripe apples.

"Dunno?" they said, "one minute it was all quiet, the next all hell broke loose. They came flying out the house swinging brooms with a couple of bloody great dogs."

"Should have been more careful," we said, "probably made too much noise. Did you get anything?"

"Yeah, a bit but not a lot. You going to share or what?"

"No, if we share you won't learn. Better next time eh?"

We wandered home.

I went in through the back door. Mum was cooking in the kitchen so I said triumphantly, "look what I got mum, keep us going for a bit won't it?" and emptied my shirt into a big bowl on the table.

Mum's eyes opened wide, "where on earth did that lot come from?" she said.

"Scrumpin' Mum, no problem, no one knows, they got plenty more where that came from. They won't miss 'em. Might go back for more," I said a bit too cockily.

"You'll do nothing of the sort, you'll go and take that lot back," she said sharply.

"Can't do that, it was miles away. Couldn't find it again if we tried," I lied.

Mum spotted that, "thought you said you'd go back for more, don't lie to me now."

"No Mum, don't know really, we won't go back."

"All right then, but don't do it again, you hear," she said.

Phew, I had managed to get out of that one.

I hadn't!

A couple of days later Mum grabbed me by the ear, "I want a word with you. In there now," she said, shoving me roughly into the living room.

"Where did you go scrumpin? No fancy tales now. Where was it?"

"Not here Mum, well away, down Southwood road. What's up?" I stammered, "no one knows."

"I know. I know all right. Down Southwood road for sure. I go to work this morning, cleaning for Mrs Wright and she tells me a right old story. A gang of young thieves, she says, raided her garden, stealing virtually a shop full of prime fruit. She asked me if she should call the police. For god's sake you stupid, stupid little fools, you go and steal apples from the very place I go to work. How do you think I felt?"

"Dunno Mum, sorry, but what happened?" I asked very apprehensively.

"I asked her if she knew or would recognise the boys again."

"Yeah?"

"She said no, she didn't get a good look but they were a nasty looking lot and god only knows what their parents were like."

"I am furious with you, you are weak and easily led. You need to sort yourself out. Those boys are not a good influence on you. Imagine the gall of the boy who went and knocked on the door and just stood there eating a pear. He really needs a good hiding."

Oh boy, I had a choice. I could either let Mum think I was weak and easily led or I could own up to being the boy who needed a good hiding.

I decided weak and easily led was the better option.

I was only young. I had a lifetime to put things right.

The Black-Eye

I was having a spot of bother. It comes to us all at some time or other. Killer Gromshire was only a year older but about three years bigger. I had won a scholarship to Aske's and had to wear a variety of school uniforms depending on the seasons and sporting ability.

Killer took exception to my straw boater. The fact that I didn't like it much either didn't matter to Killer. He had found an excuse to humiliate and bully me.

We were living at just around subsistence level so looking after our clothes was important. Killer didn't care. He was out to destroy my straw boater.

I needed to preserve it so I kept out of his way.

Our gang was on its way to the fields to play Football when we bumped into Killer walking his dog. He was proud of the dog which he swore was a ferocious beast only being restrained by a tough guy like him.

We didn't believe it and thought he was a bit of a pratt but didn't say so to his face as he was so big.

I thought I was safe as I wasn't in school uniform but he didn't want my boater he wanted our ball.

As he grabbed for our ball I grabbed for his dog.

Big mistake.

A huge fist slammed into the side of my face which knocked me flying. I still had hold of the dog's lead so the dog flew with me followed by Killer.

My mates grabbed the ball and ran. Killer grabbed me.

As he yanked me in front of him I yanked his dog in front of me.

The dog was a wimp, not ferocious at all. It was whimpering and whining.

Killer dropped me and I dropped the dog. I ran like hell.

I was away for now but feared for the future.

We had a good game though.

We were heading for home when I remembered something I should have remembered before. It was Saturday and we had relatives coming for tea.

Kids are only good for remembering things they are supposed to forget and forgetting things they were supposed to remember. I was no exception.

I hurtled through the back door trying to appear as though I had come through hell to get there on time.

It didn't work. Dad gave me a smack round the ear for trying too hard. He told me not to think of taking up acting as a career as I was lousy at it.

Mum took a closer look. Trust Mum.

She shrieked and wanted to know what I had done to my eye.

It was multi-coloured and closing fast.

My Aunts, Uncles and Cousins poured into the kitchen to say hello.

They all examined my eye. All had an opinion but I had no explanation. Not one that they believed anyway.

I tried out bumping into a tree, a wall, a bush. I mentioned tent poles and gate posts to no avail. Then just as one Uncle accused me of fighting amidst gasps of horror I had an inspiration.

I was playing football and someone had accidentally elbowed me in the face. This settled things down but an atmosphere of suspicion still hung in the air.

My Uncles and Aunts were all incredible people. They were kind but tough, gentle but durable and had come through two terrible world wars and a massive recession, while growing up and bringing up families along the way. Unlike pathetic self inflicted drug ridden and alcohol ridden celebrities they really had been to hell and back.

I tried to sit down and keep quiet in the presence of my elders and betters.

I managed well for a time in spite of being irritated by my younger brother. He was five years younger and was an expert in irritation. My course of action was limited. Usually a swift punch was enough to stop him but we were under the watchful and reproachful eye of my mum who well knew the trouble that could explode in seconds around us two.

He realised his advantage and was pinching and twisting my skin behind my back. I managed to smile innocently at everyone before shooting him off his chair onto the floor accidentally catching him with my foot as he went.

He wasn't hurt but was very embarrassed as Dad told him to stop acting the fool and go and get a drink of water.

I was determined to try hard to be good as this part of the family had got religion. They were Baptists and organised guitar groups to play religious songs during services. They were not sorrowful sinful moaners but joyfully accepted The Lord and his teachings.

I was acceptable as I was a member of The Boys' Brigade and attended Church Parades and Bible Class. However I felt guilty. I had only joined because I wanted to play in the band, make the football team and chat up the girls in the Girls' Brigade.

I didn't let on though.

Then Mum dropped me in it.

She mentioned that I played in a band. I played the drums.

This went down well at first and should have been left there especially as one maiden Aunt exultantly exclaimed that it was okay as everyone should blow their trumpets to The Lord.

I started the rot by telling her a bit impatiently that I didn't blow drums.

It was all down hill from then on in.

First it emerged that I played drums in a band. A New Orleans Jazz Band.

Then I had to admit that we played pubs and clubs even though I was fifteen years old.

This wasn't the USA with it's ridiculous colour prejudice. It was known as black music but not in a derogatory way. It was a badge of excellence to which we all aspired.

It wasn't just the music but the venues that were regarded as the bad influence.

My goodness one newspaper had investigated and found that teenagers pranced around in a wild dance while others smoked cigarettes underneath the piano. Presumably it was a grand piano!? Such decadence would be the downfall of the younger generation.

My relatives didn't appear shocked. They seemed confused.

How could a son of brother Albert go so wrong.

Brother Albert, my Dad, was even more confused. He was relieved that I had found an interest other than hanging around street corners with gangs.

The afternoon was not a success and my Mum was quite upset as she was sure she would be the one who would be blamed.

She was wrong. Although there was gossip my relatives were more generous hearted than that and mainly attributed my faults to growing pains.

With one crisis hardly safely out of the way I had to face another.

I was told Killer was looking for me.

This was a much bigger problem than kindhearted relatives.

I decided that positive action was required.

Killer liked to let his dog roam around the houses under construction. As the estate grew and matured the building sites had moved further away from the residences and so were very quiet outside of work time.

I had to wait for three or four evenings perched up on the first floor scaffold with a heavy bag of cement until Killer and his dog appeared underneath. I dumped the bag over the top aiming for his head.

It missed and smashed his shoulder.

I heard the crack. He slumped to the floor with the dog running round yapping it's head off.

I climbed down a nearby ladder and ran over. His face was screwed up in pain.

"What happened mate?" I exclaimed, "you look a bit sad. I wouldn't hang around these sites so much. They are bloody dangerous places you know."

"You stupid sod," he groaned, "you might have fucking killed me, you little cunt."

"I was trying to fucking kill you, you stupid big cunt and next time I will," I said.

He tried to look up at me but couldn't manage it.

He asked me to take his dog home while he tried to make it to the doc's.

I dragged the scrawny thing along behind me and told his parents that Bob wasn't feeling so good but would be along later. I was just trying to help out.

They looked more surprised than concerned.

Killer recovered, eventually.

He gave me a wide berth, didn't shove, punch or extort anymore and at times could be viewed as polite.

It just shows that a Colt Revolver is not the only great equaliser and peacemaker. Sometimes a bag of cement will do.

Sex Education

I was comfortably sitting in an armchair besides the fire reading a book when a Sunday newspaper was suddenly dumped in my lap. I looked up to see a red faced embarrassed Dad walking away muttering in my direction, "there's something there for you to read. All right?" and he disappeared hot foot for the kitchen.

"Hey Dad, wait a mo', what is it?" but he had gone, door firmly shut behind him.

I picked up the paper, spread it out and saw the headlines, "Sex Education, every adult and child should read this!" Two full pages of it.

"Yeah," I thought, "just the job, no more sneaking looks at pin up pictures, no more rummaging around to see where Dad had hidden his Micky Spillane Books, no more drooling over the underwear section in Mum's Mail Order Catalogue and no more guess work. I wouldn't have to climb ropes or lamp posts rubbing up tight to get a thrill as I pulled up hard. Kids who couldn't shin up ropes didn't know what they were missing. This article promised the works.

I couldn't wait.

I read it through twice. Big deal.

I went out to the kitchen. Mum and Dad were pretending to concentrate on the washing up.

"Right, you can have the newspaper back now," I said and folded it up on the kitchen table.

Dad looked round and sheepishly said, "you read it already? Understood it? It was good wasn't it?"

"Of course he understood it 'Elb, didn't you Den?" Mum said hopefully.

"Well that's it then, you know all about it now," Dad said, suddenly all positive before I could utter a word.

"Know all about what Dad?" I asked innocently.

"That, that there," said Dad, pointing at the paper as though it would bite him.

"Well it's hardly helpful is it?" I asked, "it's all about birds and bees and flowers an' all that rubbish we did in biology at school."

"See," said Mum, "he knows already 'Elb, told you didn't I?"

"Well of course I know it, I couldn't really miss it could I?" I exclaimed, "blimey Uncle Fred keeps chickens don't 'e'? I see the old cock that Uncle Fred reckons is goin' ta be Christmas dinner this year up at the hens all day long. I know how our cat get's kittens because we have to chuck buckets of water over all the old toms coming round when she's in heat. Dogs are the same and you can't imagine what I see down the stables when we take the horse back after the bread round. Birds and bees for god's sake. No wonder girls get pregnant if that's what you call sex education."

Mum and Dad were stunned.

"Well we've done our bit to tell you," Dad said a bit shirtily, "it's up to you now."

"Right, I'll go out and see if I can do better than that Alsatian dog down the road, perhaps he knows what humans do to make babies because it seems that parents don't. They obviously didn't play doctors and nurses when they were young," I said as I left.

We were all street wise and very few of us ever had shotgun weddings. We would leave that to the posh tarts from the bought houses a mile or so away.

As soon as they were old enough they couldn't get enough.

They were considered too posh to mix with us rough lot and of course that was quite right. We were a sorry lot but we didn't get girls pregnant.

One lovely girl was much desired and on the odd occasion honoured one of us by going for a walk or to the pictures. She was called Alice.

Her mother stepped in and banned us from contact. We could only look longingly from a distance as she walked by with her short arse sailor boyfriend.

We bumped into them one day, chatted for a while and then after looking hard, nudging one another, and escaping with pathetic excuses, we burst out laughing. Alice Robbins was pregnant.

The cat was out of the bag and a bun was in the oven.

Alice was packed off to wherever unmarried pregnant girls went in those days and we didn't see her again.

But we did see her parents—as often as we could.

"Hello Mrs. Robbins, how are you? Alice okay? Has she had the little basta'—sorry, baby yet? Did she marry that bloke, you know, all the nice girls love a sailor? Particularly a little one."

"Too bad, we all liked her you know. You know what we mean?" we said, before walking on swiftly.

They sold up and moved within a year.

Hard times had made ordinary people more prudish and conservative in their ways and attitudes. Decency was all they had left and they took a pride in it.

Boys and girls knew the rules. No sex before marriage. Virtue was an asset and virginity was prized. Abortion was illegal and homosexuality was a crime and most believed that to be correct. There were no before or after contraception pills but there was the 'dutch cap' and the 'rubber johnny', neither of which was easily available to young people. Anyone who went into a shop to buy a packet of contraceptives immediately revealed that they were doing it and doing it was definitely naughty.

If a girl got pregnant she knew she was tainted for life. She had a choice. Marry the father if she knew him or go to a home for unmarried mothers and have the baby adopted. Either way she could then carry on her life as a respectable person as long as no one in the know blabbed their mouth off.

While she was at the maternity home she was treated as a second class bad girl and she fully understood why.

Basically she was viewed as silly, immature and irresponsible. Giving her baby for adoption to a deserving couple was a form of redemption.

Years later many women came forward claiming trauma and sympathy for the way they were treated and according to 21st century mores and morals they were. But they were not living in the 21st century. They well knew the rules at the time concerning respectability and they flaunted them. They were not brave pioneers they were silly, careless young girls who didn't want to pay the price for a lack of control. No one forced them to do it. Simple—good girls said no. The worst crime of all was to bring an innocent child into the world with the stigma of being a bastard for life.

Rape was abhorrent to everyone and rapists viewed as needing their dicks cut off. A referendum would have supported it at the time. God help a rapist if the public got to him before the police.

Society is different today of course, but not better—just different.

'Queers' were banned, period. It was only discussed in hushed terms behind closed doors, if it was discussed at all.

We had all experienced the smarmy guy sitting next to us in the cinema, carelessly throwing a dirty raincoat over his and our laps and then groping around hoping for a quick feel or thrill. He usually got a right smack on the jaw and a call to an attendant which made him beat a hasty retreat to the exit.

They were the butt of ribald jokes, hounded and beaten if discovered, and ridiculed in public places if they dressed 'funny'.

Coming out was not an option, it was a crime.

Dykes were rarely recognised because most people dressed sensible and basic, not fashionable. Certainly a respectable working class woman would go to pick up her kids from school with her pinafore still on and her curlers still in. A woman who went out shopping or picking her kids up from school dressed up and with makeup on was regarded with great suspicion.

"Did you see her, that floozy? Who does she think she is, the Empress of Russia? I bet her husband doesn't know she goes around like that! Where does she get her money from, answer me that then?"

Divorce was horrendous as there had to be a guilty party.

High society staged media exposures with flash photos of supposedly surprised guilty parties in bed in a hotel room caught in the act. This was usually the husband as a wife was thought to be above suspicion and could not have her reputation ruined. It didn't matter to a man because he was automatically deemed to be ruined anyway.

The wife could then get a divorce because of the husband's adultery.

The lower classes generally stayed married.

Kid's were seen and not heard. Their opinions were not required because they knew nothing. Consequently when they were older they were full of them.

Between school and the army I enrolled at Woolwich Polytechnic to go to night school for accountancy. I was glad I did as it cleared up that idea for me. I realised that never in a million years did I want to be a pen pusher for life.

The Poly was good though.

Once a year it had a festival over a bank holiday weekend. Three days of nonstop joy. There were dozens of different activities in separate halls going 24 hrs. a day. Plays, revues, satires, comedians, poetry, dancing and bands. As one set finished at one end of the hall so another started at the other end with impromptu performances all over the place.

We took blankets, thermos flasks and sandwiches and just slept and picnicked in the corridors. When we finished we went back to the fun.

There were no fights, no rapes, no drugs and no harassment. At least not in the Poly but all hell could break loose outside.

Those were the days.

There were no loud campaigns at that time to abolish the death penalty, but fortunately there were no public hangings. We associated public executions with the barbaric countries and regrettably still have to do so. It was thought that if the state had to commit judicial murder then it was preferable to do it in private.

The main excuse was to protect the dignity of the condemned but how it made a difference to the accused whether the neck was broken in public or in semi-privacy was a bit obscure. The guy going for the long drop is probably beyond worrying whether he shits his pants in fear in front of just ten or a couple of hundred people.

Whenever the issue of abolishing capital punishment arose then the front rows of the Tory conferences were filled with ferocious ladies shouting against it, violently waving their programmes, "No abolition! Who cares if an innocent man dies? Hang them all and hang them high." They bore quite a resemblance to the hags who sat knitting before the Guillotines of the French Revolution but they were much better dressed of course. The Tory ladies I mean, not the hags, although I reckon the hags were better looking!

Even at a very young age we roamed the streets for hours. At seven or eight years old I wandered for miles, from high up on the hill in Plumstead, down to Erith marshes, across the Woolwich Free Ferry to the Silvertown docks and all over the Woolwich, Plumstead and Slade Commons and into different woods miles apart and other suburbs. In between times we would play football, cricket, rounders and rough games like aye jimmy knacker one, two, three. We climbed trees, lamp posts and walls and jumped ditches.

I never heard the word tired until bedtime and not one of my generation was overweight.

As long as we turned up for meal times and returned home before dark no one worried.

If we got mouthy or cheeky or misbehaved then we got a clout from any adult handy. The thought of anyone telling your dad of misbehaviour was just too worrying to think about and as for being bad enough to make your mum cry, well that was a real crime. You were no man if you did that.

It never occurred to anybody that you could be kidnapped, violated, robbed or assaulted. We didn't have anything except maybe a few bottle tops, conkers or bits of string. We were scruffy, dirty back street kids, definitely not sex symbols in any shape or form.

There were bullies but they were soon sorted out by big brothers or by a few of us uniting to beat them up. They were not admired and rarely had sucking up cronies. As far as we were concerned the nasty organised cliques only occurred in American movies or English public schools. We were a pale imitation.

We believed that it was because we were never heroic cowboys fighting savage redskins. It was the Wild West that made America what it was.

We didn't rate the American City gangsters. Al Capone looked like a slimy slug and couldn't compare to Gene Autry, Tom Mix and Roy Rogers our cowboy heroes.

In the early days of the war you had to make sure you were close to cover when the air raid warning went but later on we became a bit blase as the German raids slowed and the Allied defences and offences built up.

My Mum came home from visiting an Aunt one day and asked me where my little brother was. I didn't know, did I? He and his little crew were experts at being nuisances, so we avoided them where we could. Not knowing where they were was a great relief.

A neighbour told my Mum he was on the roof of the bombed and burned out school on the corner.

Mum moved like lightning.

There he was with a pal, sitting four stories up, breaking slates and throwing the pieces over the school wall into the street. They were laughing and shoving each other at near misses.

He was three years old.

Mum told me to get up there, get him down and get both of us indoors immediately.

To an adult it was a tricky, dangerous business but to us kids it was normal.

On the way down I banged him a few times for getting me into trouble with Mum but he didn't care because I was in it just as deep as he was. He loved it when the two of us were marched along the street by our ears in front of mates and neighbours, trying to look across at me with a smarmy look on his face.

When we were getting whacked he kept telling Mum it wasn't fair as it was my fault for not looking after him better. He told Mum that we had shoved him away and told him and his friends to clear off. It was true—the little sneak!

So I got whacked by Dad as well later.

We had love affairs of course starting at a young age. Signs of affection from the girls came in the form of spitefully pinching the skin on our arms while we showed our love by pulling their pigtails. The girls ran off shrieking with the boys chasing them.

Superiority was displayed in several different ways. When we had moved beyond the 'my dad is bigger than your dad' bit and 'I knew it first so there' we would go into the school lavatory, the urinal being against a wall in the open air. We would all compete to see who could pee furthest up the wall and one champion was never beaten. He peed right over the top of the wall into the girls toilet. He was expelled but his fame lived on.

Indeed those were the days!

The White Fiver

We were likely lads. Didn't go looking for fights but didn't usually back off if any threatened. Fight, fright or flight generally depended on who the opposition was and how many of them there were. We'd read the books and believed discretion was the better part of valour.

The old crap about 'he who turns and runs away, lives to fight another day' didn't work because if you had to run it meant that the opposition was stronger, bigger and faster than you. Better to stand and try to talk your way out. Street smart kids were good at that.

The fact that we were inclined to be hooligans suited the real gangsters just fine. They used the street kids to cause problems in areas that they weren't bothered about so as to divert the police from their real operations.

We were only occasionally of use to them but when we were they were generous.

One Friday evening we were hanging around at the top of Eltham Hill, near the traffic lights leading to the High Street when two Humber Super Snipe Saloons pulled up.

Wow, it must be the Queen come to show off her nearly new crown.

Windows were wound down and a hand beckoned us over.

"Yes, milord," one of us said deferentially.

"Oi, you taking the piss or something?" said a gruff voice, "you want a good slapping or what? Pay attention for crissakes."

We did.

"Right then, you know the Harp Club down in Deptford?"

We nodded.

"They're all Paddies right?"

We nodded again.

"Okay, now Billy wants you to start a punch up down there at eight o'clock tomorrow. Get it going into a real riot and then scarper. Once them Micks get going they don't care who they bash. The Old Bill just love to bang up a load of Micks on a Saturday night to stop 'em going to confession on Sunday morning. Now that's really evil." he chuckled.

We were there, seven o'clock, as the doors opened.

Oh oh, the place was nearly empty.

Eight o'clock came and it was barely half full.

We took the decision to wait until nine.

By nine fifteen things were livening up and at nine thirty one of our lads walked up to the long bar which was full of noisy hefty navvies on about their fourth or fifth pint of Guinness with a Jamesons chaser.

He pushed through, looked around and asked, "Are you all Catholics here for Christ sakes? Well fuck the Pope then."

He shoved two of them together, knocked one of their beers down the front of another and turned to a third, pointing to the guy wiping himself down and said, "did you hear what he said? Blasphemy if you ask me. Why did you shove him anyway? No need for that."

He whacked another guy on the back of his head and shoved him against the bar telling one bewildered drunk that he shouldn't do that to a mate.

All this took about ten seconds.

They were off. Their faces lit up. Here was a good reason for a good scrap and the evening had hardly started.

"Who you shoving?" asked one belligerently, while shoving back hard, knocking a few more beers over.

"Mind my fucking beer," yelled another while chucking a whisky in someone else's face.

Our lad backed out, excusing himself that it was not his fight.

Fringe crowds looked on, staying neutral until a couple of us at the end of the bar, hidden by the punch up under way, slung bottles of beer at them scoring enough successes to inflame them.

Two more well aimed glasses shattering against the wall behind them convinced them that staying out of it was not an option.

They were in.

It was a good start but no riot. Then the doors burst open and it was time for us to beat it out of the emergency fire exits.

Word had quickly spread to the neighbouring pubs. The Marquis of Granby on the opposite corner was empty in minutes. Nobody could remember why or what it was about and didn't care who was in it—it was a Saturday Night fight. That was enough.

The English, Irish and Scots were like that, but not the Welsh, they'd still be singing or reciting poetry in a language that no one understood any more.

We walked quickly to the tram stop by New Cross Gate Station, got on a number 72 going to Eltham and went upstairs for the front seats.

The tram trundled slowly back past the Harp Club. The police were all over the place, Black Maria's being loaded with drunks still lashing out at each other in between the thumpings from police truncheons. Some were even using the truncheons ripped from constables and others were wearing police helmets. A crowd had gathered cheering everyone on.

We were proud of our success and could hardly wait until the next Friday.

Sure enough the cars drew up.

Down came the windows and we waited eagerly for the praise and money we thought we were due.

"What's a matter with you lot, you deaf or something. A few weeks ago you were too early down at the Green Man in Finsbury Park and we only just scraped by and now we had to wait half the bleedin' night to get started because of you hanging about too long in Deptford. The boss wants a word," and he indicated the car behind.

We went heads down to the other car.

"Nah, you are lovely lads, I love you like my own sons but sometimes I have to chastise them as I might have to chastise you. See Frank in there, well if he chastises you a bit too enthusiastically you would all be hospital cases and we don't want that, do we?"

We shook our heads, we hoped rather convincingly.

"Well then we'll pay you off this time but I don't reckon we will use you again so don't hang around here in hopes anymore."

He nodded to a guy in the front seat who pulled out a wad of fivers.

They were very large notes and very white. They were also a rare commodity to the likes of us. Six quid a week was a top footballers wage in those days.

If you tried to use them for ordinary shopping then you were refused as the shop didn't have enough change in the till. A bank would ask you to sign them and put your address on them and would probably notify the police if we tried to change any. God only knows what my dad would say if I took one home and here I was being offered two of them.

I shook my head, and gave them back.

Billy looked at me intently. I felt his eyes fastening on me from the depths of the back seat.

I stuttered a lot but managed to explain.

"This kid's bright," he said at last, "if he takes 'em anywhere, awkward questions will be asked. If he takes 'em 'ome his old man's going to lead off and take him up to the nick. More awkward questions. Freddie, got any ten bobs, yes, right, give 'im the dosh in ten bob notes. All right now kid?"

I nodded.

"Okay, keep thinking lad, you'll go far, but not with me."

They drove off and we didn't see them again.

We were relieved really but didn't like to show it. We all blamed each other for our failure to be real life gangsters. My mates traded their notes in to one or two shady characters on our estate at a fifty percent discount. I was the only one to have the full amount in my pocket.

My Hobbs of Barbican sports bike got quite a few upgrades.

We decided to leave the real gangster stuff to the nutcases who were never going to go anywhere in their lives except to jail.

There were some real hard cases all around us among our mates.

One family, we called them the 'Hollers' because they were always shouting the odds somewhere to someone, believed in strict rotation.

If one or two came out of the nick then two went in. Somehow they never managed to get them all in or all out at the same time.

My mum, when she heard the nickname, said it should be horrors not hollers. Both were close enough to their real name actually.

One son, when it came to going to the Army medical, took a builders mallet and broke his own leg and ankle. He would suffer a permanent limp and failed the medical. We were horrified, but he was jubilant.

"Don't you read the papers?" he said, "this is nothing to what the enemy can do to you. Me, I'm staying at 'ome."

He didn't. Within six months he was serving time in a Borstal detention centre.

Another of our friends Ted wasn't very big but had a bad temper. He also had a very sexy older sister. We all secretly lusted after her but didn't go public with it because Ted was touchy on that subject.

His sister brought home her boyfriend to show off to the family. He was from the Yorkshire Moors, very tall, fresh faced and healthy. He had ridden horses on his farm and so was serving in the Life Guards and justifiably full of himself.

It was Winter. As this was a special occasion Sister and Boyfriend were allowed to go into the front room. A specially lit coal fire was roaring away making everything very cosy.

Ted decided that he had better keep an eye on this fine fellow so joined them in the front room.

Everything was fine at first until it became obvious that Ted was not going to take the hint and scram.

Big Boyfriend started to take the piss out of the little brother.

The Sister protested but Big Boyfriend had the bit between his teeth.

Ted warned him and then invited him to come outside.

Big Boyfriend roared out laughing, "what's the point, I won't be able to spot you titch, I won't be able to find you will I?"

"Okay," said Ted, "I'd better let you know I'm 'ere then."

He stoked the red hot coals in the fire and then like lightning swept up the glowing poker and rammed it into the Boyfriend's neck.

Luckily the guy passed out from the pain and shock almost immediately. The poker had cut through skin, muscle and blood vessels and would leave a terrible mark for life.

The family called an ambulance who called the police.

Ted couldn't understand what the fuss was about. The guy was a big headed pratt, a country yokel who had threatened him. End of story as far as he was concerned.

The police thought differently.

They arrested Ted—or at least they tried to.

There were two constables standing at his front door blocking the way. Ted punched one in the balls, kicked the other one in the shins with his hobnailed boots and ran for it.

That was bad enough but his mother told the police he was probably armed.

That caused a panic.

It wasn't true actually but his mother later said she had told the story to let Ted get further away. She hadn't thought it through.

There was nothing in place at the time to deal with this. Only real gangsters were armed and even then not all the time.

Several policemen cornered Ted not that far away. They weren't armed but had a lot of guts.

Word spread swiftly.

Ted was going to have a shoot out with the cops.

The few police had to face two ways. One way to make sure Ted was still where he should be and the other way trying to keep back the crowd who couldn't get close enough to the action.

Support between Ted and the cops was about evenly divided.

Cops, "are you armed Ted? Lay down any weapon you have right now. It's not worth hanging for Ted. Come on lad, be sensible."

Ted, "what the fuck are you talking about? You barmy or something?"

Cops, "we know you have a gun Ted, throw it here. At the moment you only have GBH, don't make it worse."

Ted, "you in lala land or something. You been celebrating Christmas early? I'm not bloody Billy the Kid for crissakes."

The cops closed in tentatively, so did the crowd.

Ted picked up a sack lying at his feet. He hadn't been idle. He put his hand inside and pulled it out quickly.

One of the police rushed in and we all flinched as we fully expected to hear a shot being fired.

Instead Ted had half a house brick in his hand which he threw flat out at the advancing copper hitting him on the side of his head. Although he was probably relieved it wasn't a bullet he was unfortunately a patrol car cop. He didn't wear a helmet, he wore a peaked cap. He went down as though poleaxed.

Ted threw two more bricks, which missed but slowed down the advance of both police and crowd.

He had chosen his place well. He was against a tree.

He looked around, couldn't see a way out and so shinned up the tree along with the sack.

He resisted all pleas to come down and give himself up.

Anyone approaching too close was showered with stones from the sack.

By now the place resembled a major disaster scene. Police, fire brigade and ambulance were there swarming all over trying to look busy and important.

They failed.

They were all being held at bay by a teenage kid with a sack full of rocks.

Command of the situation had been taken over by a police Brass Hat. He didn't know what to do either but he did very little very effectively. One tough CID guy provided the very solution which would work but was not allowed.

He suggested bringing up the fire escape ladder, swinging it round and, "let's knock the stupid little bastard out of the tree. Just get it over with."

We all agreed and hoped we'd see it, but it never happened.

Ted finally ran out of rocks. Several police tried to climb up after him but got severely kicked in the head by Ted's hobnailed boots.

We suggested loudly that the Brass Hat should try as it might improve his intelligence.

Even the police grinned at that one.

Mr Whippy's ice cream van turned up, ringing his bell, and did a roaring trade. A couple of mobile kid's merry go rounds arrived and the little ones had a great time going round and round to the music. All that was needed was the fish and chip van and it wasn't very long before it arrived.

Some wag found a few souvenir cardboard policemen's helmets at home and offered them with some chips to the Brass Hat.

He took it well and asked for salt and vinegar. He was relaxing a bit as it was becoming apparent that Ted might be dangerous but he wasn't armed and never had been. Also he couldn't stay up the tree in mid winter with night time approaching.

He started to stand down the emergency team.

All that was left was an ambulance and fire appliance with crews and a dozen policemen.

The crowd however had grown bigger and more boisterous. A couple of enterprising guys had gone to the local off licence at opening time and bought a load of beers which they were selling at a small profit.

The crowd had been well fed and watered and were in party mood. They were encouraging Ted to stay in the tree.

Ted was responding with Churchillian victory signs and singing the National Anthem. When the crowd followed this up with Land of Hope and Glory the Brass Hat decided enough was enough.

He ordered the police to disperse the crowd. There was resistance at first but then the majority started to move away. We were among the last to go entreating Ted to stay the course and telling him that we'd come to see him in the morning.

It never happened.

Without an audience Ted soon got bored, climbed down and quietly gave himself up.

Ted said later that a dozen cops dramatically jumped on him, suddenly full of life, although he offered no resistance. They bundled him into a Black Maria, knocked him about and then reported that he had cut up rough.

He didn't care, he reckoned that they were just getting their revenge for the damage he'd done to their buddies. "Fairs fair," he said.

He was put up before a magistrate in Woolwich the next morning, pleaded guilty, was held in custody for a while and placed on probation subject to a social worker's report.

He was lucky he was tried in a working class area by people who knew the locals and their lives.

If he had been tried in Dartford by the Black Bitch it would have been a different story. The leading magistrate there was a steadfast Tory Dame and called the Black Bitch because we reckoned that if she had been a judge then she would have hanged everybody who wasn't from her white upper class. Judges at the time when presenting the death sentence had a black cap placed on their heads hence her nickname.

Anyway the report stated that although volatile Ted presented no danger to society. The future would prove the report wrong.

We believed, possibly unkindly, that his mum had made the gun call on purpose in order to get him shot. That actually happened later.

Jack was no danger to us, his mates, or to the neighbours. He was a menace to everyone else. In the high street one evening, waiting for a bus home, he saw a group of boys kicking a chewing gum dispenser in frustration as it had taken their money but given out no gum. Jack decided to help out. He did. He kicked and beat the living daylights out of the five guys.

The magistrate wanted a long custodial sentence but apparently the crime didn't merit it. He reckoned Jack was a danger to society and he was right. Jack was fined and put on probation.

Jack was aggrieved and said so. He believed that he was acting in a public spirited way and that if everyone acted like him then there would soon be a lot less crime on the streets!

He did do his national service but took three times longer than most because he kept getting put in the glasshouse. Any time spent in custody in the army is added on to the end of your service.

He was a driver in the RASC and a good one. He was so tough that basic training and discipline were fine by him. Nothing could be harder than living with his old man.

The Armed Forces at that time were replacing all the old lead gas and electric coin meters in the married quarters. Lead had just been discovered as poisonous.

Jack had to collect them and deliver them to a service depot for eventual disposal. Lead, then as now, was expensive and in demand.

Jack had a bright idea. All the meters were stored upright, one on top of the other. Unless lifted up the bottoms were never visible.

Jack cut out the bottoms, sold them and stacked up rest of the meters very neatly. He had to have a driver's mate and that's where the scheme fell down. His mate was demobbed and the new one spilled the beans.

Basically he shit himself when he realised what Jack was up to.

They were arrested. His first mate was all cocky as he had been demobbed but soon found out that he was still in for part time territorial service.

They were tried by an army court, found guilty and sent to Colchester.

Jack survived but his mate cracked. He gained an earlier release by giving up his share of the loot. Laws were different then so Jack had no intention of surrendering his money as that meant being punished with nothing to look forward to afterwards.

After demob Jack set up a small builders business where no one refused to work for him, no one was ever late and nobody refused his estimates. He did do a good job though for a while.

A few years later my Dad told me he had seen Jack and they'd had a little chat together. He proudly showed Dad a hole he had dug for the Local Council, all on his own with no help.

We never saw him again after that.

There were so many decent families being brought up in difficult conditions who didn't stoop to crime or deceit that it would take a book just to name them but one or two do stand out.

There were the Cooksleys and Brandons who were typical solid good English people who took the passage to Australia.

Of those who stayed behind there was one family who were fine in spite of having more than their fair share of disasters. They were the Jenners.

There was a bit of mixed blood in them which made for quite exotic looking kids, especially the girls. To us they were absolutely delicious.

They had lost their mother to disease when they were still very young—five of them. Their father had decided to work and bring them up with no outside help. They would all help themselves and each other.

Consequently there were very often domestic fireworks which overflowed onto the green outside their house.

We kids laughed when young Peter and Valerie sometimes came flying out of the front door followed by a number of pots and pans thrown by an irate father who had discovered that they had skipped their round of chores.

Mum would reprimand us, "that man brings up five kids on his own and goes out to work as well to support them. It's no laughing matter. You lot can think yourself lucky."

We didn't.

Austerity

The war was over. World War Two was becoming history but the suffering was going to continue for a long while. The USA became the focal point of everything desirable, deservedly so, and remained that way into the future but far less deservedly.

Europe was a mess. It had taken the full brunt of the war and was devastated. Money, food, shelter and infrastructure were in short supply. Good ole Uncle Sam stepped in with vast amounts of generous aid as either a gift or a loan. Peculiarly they were not so generous to Britain, their main ally and the only country to have fought the Nazis from beginning to end. On their own the British had taken Italy effectively out of the war, rendered France useless to the Nazis, defeated Germany on sea and in the air and had just defeated the army in North Africa and were rolling them back to the sea. Russia was valiantly slowly relaxing the iron grip that the German Armies had on them when Japan stupidly stabbed Britain in the back and brought America into the war.

After the war the American government piled obstructions in the way of Britain using its colonies to get back on its feet while at the same time introducing their own colonial policy that by its very naiveté was to cause huge problems throughout the 20th and 21st centuries. They believed that if the whole world embraced America and the American way of life then all would be beauty and light. In their ignorance they took no account of civilisations, religion, culture, heritage, style and history that had long predated their corrupt tycoons of the 19th century and the gangsters of the twentieth.

Heroic Britain was shown in a mediocre light while America stole all the glory. They had contributed hugely, there was no doubt of that, and their armed forces behaved superbly under circumstances that would make 21st century men shake in their boots. We shall never see their like again. They carried on carrying on to the end under terrible conditions. Russia, which had performed beyond all reason, and China, which had suffered beyond all reason, had now become the enemies But the USA couldn't see the way to give credit where credit was due.

Britain only just finished off paying the so called generous loan in the early 21st century, more than 70 years later. The USA were not going to allow any rivals on the post war scene.

Germany and Japan were far too soon wondrously transformed into worthy allies. The rest of the more sane world never quite got over that. They should have done, but they didn't.

Holland and Belgium and most particularly France suffered from guilt at rolling over so easily in the face of the German attack which took some years to work its way out and some would say in the case of France it never did.

The armed forces returning to civvy street didn't have to worry about being out of work. There was so much to rebuild along with a government intent on full employment. Britain actually underwent an incredible social revolution the beneficial effects of which would only be felt some years later. There was no shortage of manpower or enthusiasm. There was a vast shortage of money, resources and food.

Wartime rationing continued for years. Food, clothing and luxuries such as sweets could only be obtained on coupons. We finally saw ice cream, oranges and bananas several years after the war. We had to make do with ice lollies which were frozen cordials on a stick. Fruit and meat were available but rare unless you had access to the black market. Most of the population didn't have the money so we queued for hours or got in early if we'd picked up a rumour that certain things were going to be available locally.

Just when it seemed that the long road to recovery was beginning nature hit back. Whenever and wherever humans had been ground down and were slowly lifting their heads then you could bank on nature kicking everyone when they were down. Several of the most severe winters on record occurred in the 1940's. Gas and electricity were already in short supply anyway. The bad winters caused long power cuts at the very time heat and light were most needed.

We huddled as close as possible around coal fires and went to sleep with overcoats piled up on the beds. We stuck newspapers under doors to keep out draughts. Irrespective many died.

Our three story flats were damp due to war damage. Water ran over the ceiling and down the walls and burst pipes were common. We had a gas cooker and lighting paid for on a shilling meter. If you ran out of shillings then you ran out of gas. We lived in the kitchen and all slept in the one bedroom. We hardly ever used the living room in summer and never in winter.

In the kitchen was a galvanised bath which was pulled up to the ceiling on pulleys and lowered on Friday which was bath night. The water was heated on buckets and tipped into the bath. Dad went first followed by us two boys and mum went last. We occasionally topped up with hot water. During the week we washed in the sink in cold water. The kitchen had a coal fired stove, all black, where you could cook in an oven or boil kettles on the top. It also heated the room. This was poverty but years late a similar device "the Arga" became a symbol of wealth. Such is life.

We had one outside toilet, a two seater, for the three flats. It was lit in the evenings by a small oil lamp. Nobody wanted to sit down at the same time as one of my uncles. He always had to leave the door open as even he couldn't stand his own smell.

Then we got lucky.

I had chicken pox and had to be kept out the way because of infection, so I was actually doing a jigsaw puzzle in the living room on my own. Alongside me were our bicycles and clothes drying on a rack.

This was the time when two local council inspectors decided to come round to check on my parent's application for a council house. We had been on the list for four years and had given up hope.

When they saw pale, wan me looking all sorry for myself and my little brother kept away in the kitchen then official forms came out and a load of boxes were ticked. The woman said to my mum, "my dear, you can't bring up children in places like this, how do you cope?"

We coped because women then, as now, were bloody heroes.

Within six months we were rehoused in a brand new house on a brand new council estate.

For the few weeks before we saw the new place we walked around looking at houses that were donkeys years old wondering if ours would be as good with mum getting irritated with our questions. "Mum, mum, like this one mum, good as this one mum, will it have electric mum, what about the bog mum?

Ironically it would be nearly 20 years before the old area was redeveloped.

Dad then got a shock. We were going to be all electric. We had no electric appliances and not much money. It was some time before we could give up toasting bread on forks by the fire and heating up flat irons on the electric stove. We washed clothes in the same sink as we washed the dishes.

We had two toilets and one bathroom. Sheer luxury as one toilet was indoors.

We had three bedrooms, a kitchen, a living room and what was always called the front room. It was called that because it was at the front. Only hotels had a lounge. Front rooms were always kept for that special occasion which never came. My brother and I were warned never to mess up or muck about in the front room.

On the floor we rolled inadequate squares of linoleum and painted the exposed bare floor boards brown. It was ten years before we had any sort of carpets.

I like dozens of school kids earned pocket money by doing paper rounds during the week and helping the milkman and bread man with their deliveries at the weekends.

Those were the days of horses and carts and household deliveries so it was a bit of an adventure to collect and return the horses to the stables. After uncoupling them from the carts we sometimes rode them bareback back to the yard. The horses loved the freedom, knew they were going to be fed and watered and suddenly were transformed from old cart horses into young racehorses.

The electric dillies that came in later didn't have the same attraction.

Getting to my school from the old address needed only one bus with a bit of a walk at either end. The new address needed a bus and a tram and a good walk at either end. Then dad found out about the train. Much quicker and direct but needing one hell of a walk at either end. Not bad in summer, just wet, but in winter it was wet and frozen. Still better than wartime—just.

Then bit by bit rationing was relaxed. Stuff was still in short supply but you could buy what you needed if you could get it and had the money.

We were early teenagers sitting on our bikes chatting when one of our parents came over and told us that as from today, like right now, sweets were no longer on ration. It had just been announced on the news.

We were doubtful at first asking, "does it mean we can go to any sweet shop now without coupons and buy a bar of chocolate?"

The answer came back, "yes. In fact the shop owners would be delighted." We totted up our pocket money. Yep, we had enough.

We would have left even the toughest Tour de France champions behind in our rush to cover the two miles or so to the shops.

We didn't have enough money to stock up so we had to be choosy. Fox's Glacier Mints, Rowntrees Fruit Gums and Smarties were favourites. My little brother who had no money of his own followed me all over the place begging for some. He and his little mates usually avoided us but now we couldn't get rid of them. We gave them some at first but they seemed to swallow them whole and came back for more. Even a smack round the ear didn't deter them. After all what was a bit of pain after years of deprivation if it got you a sweet?

He threatened to tell mum.

"So what," I said, "what are you going to tell her? I didn't give you all my sweets, is that it?"

"No," said the little sneak, "I'm going to tell her you took a girl over the fields and she showed you her knickers. We saw."

What! He and his friends were eight years old.

"Okay, and I'll tell her you never, ever help me with the washing up and cleaning when she's at work, which is true. The knickers bit is a lie."

"'Tis not, I saw you looking at somethin' and it wasn't a daffodil," he said smugly.

"She was stung on the leg by a wasp. Anyway what were you doing spying on me. I'll tell mum about that as well. You know she's worried if you nippers follow us big boys around as we go too far away for you."

"Go on then, and I'll tell mum you beat me up. Beat me up bad, so there," he replied, "and I'll cry, I'll cry when I tell her."

I got hold of him by the ear. "Go and say anything you like, you little rat, but if you do none of us will give you any sweets again. Understand, nothing, zilch and we have the money, you don't. Think about it."

He did. Violence he would risk but the threat of getting no sweets was too much. He backed off.

However he and his little gang took to following us about. At a distance.

Whenever we spun round to catch them they ran off. We used this to run off ourselves and lose them. Most times it worked.

When it didn't us older brothers in our group came in for some stick from the younger brothers. They wanted to know why we didn't bash up our younger brothers the way they got bashed up. They had stopped following their older brothers because they got beat up and had decided that it wasn't worth doing it. It was boring anyway.

Eventually our lot got bored and gave in without the beating up.

Good result.

We were not natural born killers although some were on our estate. We walked and talked tougher than we really were. We made ourselves a nuisance at the local boy's club run by a guy we nicknamed Errol because of his Errol Flynn moustache. We believed we were far too macho for such soft things until we found out the link to a couple of local football teams. We were in but were still a nuisance and viewed as a problem by the other members.

One asked me, "why are you so destructive, when we are so constructive here?"

I was receiving a very good education by any standards but that remark threw me. How could any kid be that dumb and use such big words. To be constructive was to conform, not to rebel. That was adult stuff. Why any moment now we would be Teddy Boys when we were old enough. Our suits were ready in our minds. We were having them made by Alf Harley down on Plumstead Bridge. He made all the suits for the lads no matter how outrageous, the favourite being a gabardine or dog tooth check, finger tip length jacket with a velvet collar and drain pipe trousers. Waistcoats were optional. It was a supposed Edwardian look. We had quiffs on the front of our Brylcreamed hair going into a DA (ducks arse) behind and we wore suede shoes with thick crepe soles. We loved the Slim Jim ties and loved even more the Ted Heath band for writing a dance tune about it and us.

How the hell could we be constructive?

We weren't quite yet Teddy Boys either because parents had the money and their idea of a nice suit was not the same as ours.

They favoured tweed hacking jackets with leather elbows and a fart flap on the back with grey flannel trousers.

We had to wait.

There wasn't a lot for young boys to do from poor backgrounds. Everything we liked seemed to need more fees and subscriptions than we could earn even with two or three early morning and weekend jobs. So we worked on being a nuisance.

In late October we noticed a well advertised bonfire night party organised by the local residents association taking shape. In a field, designated to be a sports field on the edge of our estate, a pile of timber was growing ever higher.

As it grew we started to take notice. The residents association didn't like boys, particularly us boys. We were banned from local parks and amenities until we had learnt how to behave ourselves. They were even running judo classes for women to make them feel safer. They admitted that we hadn't actually attacked anyone outside of rival gangs but we looked as though we could!

So we reckoned we owed them one.

The bonfire was over twelve feet high when finished and had a five foot high Guy Fawkes stuck up on top of that. There were two ladders leaning up against it as they put the finishing touches to a splendid creation. It was the talk and pride of the association.

It was just too tempting.

By ten o'clock at night there was never anyone around, all the admirers had gone off to watch the tele' much earlier.

We had got hold of a load of old newspapers and a half gallon can of petrol that one of our guys had taken off his older brother who had a motorbike. We carried it all in a small sack.

We crept over the field from the back. The bonfire, road and houses were outlined clearly in the street lamps, we were not.

We made a small hole in the back of the wood, spread the newspapers inside and soaked them in petrol.

We loaded grass and straw on top with some other pieces of firewood and soaked them as well along with the sack. We closed up the hole but left a trail of paper running to the inside. We then liberally soaked all the base in what was left of the petrol. We retreated to the road and one ran all the way home to drop the petrol can back. We left behind our fastest runner at the bonfire. He patiently waited ten minutes then lit the paper trail and ran for it.

It was a good job he did because the flame didn't run slowly and gracefully along the trail to the centre. The whole bloody lot went up at almost the same time.

He joined us and we strolled along all unconcerned to the fish shop. We got a few cod and chips with salt and vinegar and decided to see if our handiwork was flourishing. We sauntered back to the fire. It was blazing away, fanned by the wind and roaring like an express train.

We sat on the wall eating our chips and surveyed the scene.

Kid's were crying, adults were screaming and a few were vainly throwing buckets of water. It was as bright as day.

A Noddy Policeman arrived, called a Noddy because he rode a two stroke Velocette with his helmet on, and looked around. He talked to a few locals, decided the blaze was unstoppable but not dangerous, spoke on his radio and then decided to approach us out of the whole crowd.

We seemed unconcerned, after all what did it have to do with us, but were really seething as Mr. Plod had got it right straight away. Sussed us immediately.

"Feeling proud of yourselves are you? These people have been planning this for weeks and you have ruined it in one night. Good nights work is it?"

"Dunno what you're on about, we were coming back from the chip shop, saw the fire, felt cold so came to see what's what. Having a bit of a warm up, 'ennt we? Thought it funny that the party started early."

"Yeah, yeah, funny man eh? Got nothing better to do than cause trouble eh?"

"You're right on it there mate. The nothing to do bit. These shithouses here don't let you breathe."

"Watch your mouth and language, and I'm not your mate. Don't go away, I'm just going to ask around a bit, stay here."

"Oi mate, are you nicking us or what cos if not we're away like."

"No I'm not nicking you. I want to, believe me. You can go but I'm going to keep a close eye on you from now on, so watch it."

"Yeah, so what, join the club. Sad bloody lot, nothing to do but watch us. Go an arrest some real criminals for a change." With that we went off down the road acting as affronted as only the rightly accused guilty can act. Full of innocence. We triumphantly screwed up the empty greasy newspapers that our fish and chips had come in and threw them on the bonfire. We shrugged our shoulders at the glaring cop.

One afternoon, in the Spring, we were sitting on a front wall of a neighbour's house. His garden was his pride and joy. We were just harmlessly mucking about shoving, hitting and laughing for no good reason as boys do on the pavement in front of his place.

He was tending his garden.

"Oi! Clear off!"

We looked around to see who was talking to who.

"Yeah, you lot. A bloody nuisance you are hanging about here. Go some where else. Go on, shove off."

It was him. The Gardner.

We played the innocent. We looked all around with puzzled looks, up and down, round about and scrutinised each other carefully.

"Who's talking? Is it a puppet? Did you see its lips move? Where's the ventriloquist? Is it a monkey on a string or what?" were some of the more enlightened comments which amused us but not him.

We shrugged our shoulders and sat down very deliberately on the wall with our backs to him. We then told dirty jokes in loud voices with him often being clearly identified as the idiot.

"Bloody hell it's raining," we said, jumping up at the same time, "where did that come from?"

Smug laughter from behind us made us turn round.

The Gardner was standing spraying water over us from a hose he used for washing his car.

"Told you to move, didn't I? Who's the idiot now?" he giggled.

We didn't move, we just stood there in the spray looking back at him very intently.

He started to lose confidence, lowered his hose, and stuttered, "I told you to move, you should have listened."

"Now you listen you stupid prick," said Tony, "we weren't hurting anyone, just fooling. We might have moved on anyway if you had asked but you didn't. Cocky sod aren't you? Well cocky sod you will regret this."

"You touch me and I'll have the police on you, you see," he shouted out with a note of panic in his voice.

"Touch you, we wouldn't dirty our hands on an old runt like you," said Tony much to our surprise. We definitely wanted to dirty our hands on him.

"You'd better not, that's all," he said gaining a bit of confidence as we walked away.

"What's that all about Tone?" we asked, "we should do him over."

"Nah," said Tony, "too obvious. We go back in a few nights time and wreck his garden. That'll really do him over."

Brilliant.

Later that week, when all the lights were out, we dug up everything he had, piled up dirt, gnomes, plants and crazy paving against his front door with a big bucket of muddy water on top leaning inwards.

Seven o'clock in the morning he copped the lot. He knew who did it but couldn't prove a thing. We again played the innocent.

People who had no kids were all the same.

Shortly after that I went to Harvest camp working on farms near Basingstoke in Hampshire. When I came back I bought a gabardine mac with my earnings and made down payments on a suit.

I was Teddy Boy at last.

We were coming up to the mid 1950's and Britain was slowly getting back onto its feet again. The Labour Party revolution had worked but they were not allowed to reap the benefit. People were growing tired of year after year of sacrifice. They believed that the Tory Party's promise of live a little now and pay later offered more than Labour who still wanted to sacrifice now and live even better later.

The adults and young people had lived with depression, war and deprivation for years and now wanted to breath a little. The Labour Party leadership became out of touch and took years to recover. The trouble was the Tories relaxed too much too soon and everyone became obsessed with living the good life while doing less work.

Harold MacMillan told everyone, "you've never had it so good," and allowed Britain to take its foot off the pedal just when everyone else was putting their feet down hard. Stop go, boom and bust economics were the order of the day and for years to come.

However Austerity was officially over and free for all 'Laissez Faire' chaos was about to begin.

It was to start and end with the Trade Unions. Apparently, and not unnaturally they believed that getting as big a share of the cake as possible applied to their members as well as everyone else. After all they were the basic producers of the new economy.

Wrong!

The establishment and the Tories regarded the manual worker, skilled or otherwise, with as much condescension and suspicion as before. For years they were to make the Unions the scapegoat for all the economic ills that government policies produced and of course over a period of time the Unions reacted. Properly at first and then badly, and then even worse as legislation reduced their course of legal action.

It became convenient to overlook the fact that so much of the benefits of modern society had been won against fierce opposition from the Tory establishment by the very people and organisations that were being villified on a weekly basis.

Many of us never forsook our basic ideals of a just society even under the extremely, blatantly unfair biased attacks by Ronnie and Maggie. More like the Nightmare Pair than the Dream Team. They placed ideologies before sound economics. Placed dictatorial leadership before democracy. Greed was good?? Just how stupid can you get? Talk about Dumb and Dumber.

Then Clinton and Blair sorted it out. For a while. However they became too infatuated with themselves. They initiated further deregulation in the free market instead of reigning in the excesses which were starting to appear.

When George Dubyar took over the dance of the clowns began.

We still believed even when Tony Blair told us we didn't get it. He obviously didn't get it when he, Brown and his so called brilliant cronies totally ruined a British economy that had previously been going places. Neil Kinnock, you brilliant Welsh twit, what did you do opening the door for this lot to go through?

Between Dubya, George and Tony the world went down ten times faster than before. But for now Austerity was over!

Not so Sweet Sixteen

Boys of sixteen first feel, then act, then think. When they're with girls they leave out the thinking part. Their thoughts are too painful. They are capable of so much yet allowed so little. They are considered to be too young to judge when, where and how to have sex. Oh yeah? Tell that to the testosterone.

Growing up in the early 1950's was so frustrating as good girls didn't do it but good boys wanted it so much.

The boys developed complicated strategies to get as close as possible to touching anywhere on a girl that was in a no go area. It never worked but it was fun trying.

The worst approach was to ask any of your show off friends who boasted of all their conquests to point out a dead cert. Whenever I followed their advice and dated a girl who was supposedly a sure bet and ready for it I ended up by getting nowhere and being taken home to show mum that she had found a nice boy.

Before reaching14 years of age a boy would pretend to be horrified and go aargh when kissed by a girl. Up to sixteen or so he would enjoy pecks and hugs and be sort of embarrassed.

After sixteen the whole thing changed. Just to feel a girl close to was enough to arouse strong feelings and to actually bump up against one could be embarrassing. Mum was still doing the laundry you see.

At eighteen celibacy was unbearable.

A popular trick was to ask a girl to go to the pictures with you and try to get in the back row. This was difficult as it was usually full of randy buggers all after the same thing as you and they weren't going to move if they could help it. If you settled for any other seats you ran the risk of upsetting those behind you, particularly older married couples who had forgotten their youth and weren't getting much themselves.

Once you got seated you didn't make your move straight away, that was disrespectful, so the pair of you looked intently at the screen. You waited for a sign which was usually a sigh, a glance or a move closer. Holding your breathe you slipped an arm round her shoulder and hoped that you would both snuggle a bit. If you did, then slowly, oh so slowly, you moved your arm further round and down, and slipped your hand under her armpit. You stopped then, as though it was not intentional. You acted unconcerned as though the hand did not belong to you.

This was a critical stage. If she made no objection then you waited a while longer before stretching your fingers along the side of her breast and stroked gently. The girl would appear not to notice which was disappointing and exciting at the same time. Then came the tricky moment.

This was as far as you usually got so the girl would sometimes look at you, shake her head and ease off so you could remove your hand. Sometimes she would play it dirty and pull sideways keeping your hand trapped tightly under her arm. Unless you wanted a broken wrist you had to go with it and be dragged up and out of the seat. That always cooled things down.

One time I slipped my hand down a girl's back, stroking her smooth bare skin, trying to locate the erotic zone of her bra strap. It was breathtaking when I found it and tried to loosen it. Then the girl pushed firmly back against the seat. Woah, the only way to avoid being badly damaged was to go with it. I ended up standing, facing the people behind, leaning over in agony, virtually within kissing distance. I apologised, told them I had a disability that caused cramp and ungallantly left the girl to watch the rest of the film alone.

Then depending on how you look at it I got lucky. I had left school at sixteen and a half, got a day job and at night and weekends we were Teddy Boys. These were tough times and, although not soft, I was a bit of a loner and not an out and out street scrapper.

Dance Halls then did not dare play records. We could play records at home for nothing so when we went dancing and paid we demanded a live band. Disco's did not exist.

One night I was actually one of a crowd in a dance at Eltham Baths rather than at our usual haunt above Burton's the Tailors on Eltham Corner. I had just had a double whammy. I had got a cheeky bundle of cards on my eighteenth birthday and also my call up papers for the army.

We were in strange territory so we were trying to keep a low profile and not attract the attention of the local mob. We also didn't want the bouncers to notice us as we were definitely going to Jive to Quicksteps and Creep to Foxtrots hoping to be lost in the crowd when we did so. The Jive and Creep were banned at the time so when we did them and got spotted we would stop and slip into the normal dance and dancers until another opportunity occurred.

It was inevitable that we would eventually get spotted either by the mob or by the bouncers and would have to make a swift exit. By the time that happened we had usually attracted a small bundle of Dolly Birds with their high, short hair, tailored white blouses and tight black pencil skirts. If they couldn't afford stockings then they painted black seams up their legs.

They would slip out with us, giggling and we'd go for a few drinks before the pubs shut. Forget getting your end away with any of these girls. They were too street wise and would crush your balls if you tried. This particular night one of them latched onto me. She was a bit older and smarter than the others.

When it was time to split she pulled me aside and asked me to walk her home. She said it wasn't far.

Yeah I'd heard that one before. A couple of weeks previous I had missed the last bus and had to walk back for two hours. Luckily it didn't rain as that would really have spoilt the thrill of her letting me feel her tits.

Anyway I said okay and we split from the others.

She slipped her arm through mine and I felt her hip occasionally brush my thigh. Ecstasy.

She was almost right—it wasn't too far. She lived on a Council Estate that we were at war with from time to time.

The South London suburbs were full of Council Estates new and old, housing people from inner London slum clearance or who had been bombed out. We young ones had become territorial so had formed gangs for attack and defence. To be caught alone off one's patch was very careless.

I was on shaky ground.

When we arrived at her house she went straight up to the door, unlocked it and waved me in.

What? Well at least I would be safely out of sight but what would her parents say? I looked around nervously for an irate father.

She told me to relax, this was her drum, and no one else was at home. Wow, she must be older than I thought. Don't wait to look at her in the daylight, you might get a shock.

She put on the passage light, took my hand and led me upstairs into a bedroom. She went over and switched on a bedside lamp. It was a double bed.

She asked me how old I was and decided I was old enough. Oh boy, was I?

She completely took over, assuming I was a virgin, which I was, well sort of. She showed me how to slowly undress her, smoothly and sensuously. This took some practice as I was an excited mess. Even more when I saw a real live young naked female emerge in front of me for the first time in my life. She calmed me down and stroked her own body showing me how to do it using her hands over the top of mine.

I came in my pants and apologised.

She wasn't worried. She gently undressed me, running her hands everywhere while telling me to caress her. I was soon as hard as a rock again.

That's one of the benefits of youth, you can't hold it for long but can recover quickly.

She stroked between my legs running her hands around my balls and prick and along to my backside. She pulled my head to her breasts which turned up with nipples that stood out like cherries. She wasn't so old then!

I learned to suck, kiss and roll them with my tongue at the same time as I caressed them from underneath.

Oh no, I came again.

She didn't seem in the least bit perturbed, and after gently caressing my cock she lowered her head. What was this an examination? A close up? What was she doing? She slipped it into her mouth. I nearly screamed. I went rock hard once more.

She reached over to the bedside cabinet, took out a packet, stripped it and unfolded a condom.

She made me lay on my back and slipped the rubber Johnny over my cock. I nearly came but she soothed me, took my mind off it by making a few jokes and then slid down on top of me slipping my prick right up inside her.

I had never felt anything like it in my life. I didn't know where I was. She moved slowly up and down, stopping when she sensed I was close.

She played me until she started to move faster, shaking and groaning. I was worried in case I was hurting her or she was having a fit or something. She wasn't, she was coming. Oh boy did she come, great thundering shudders and then she carried on until she came again even bigger than before. She rolled me over, got me on top and urged me to push. I needed no urging. I shoved inside as hard and as fast as I could. She screamed at me to come inside her and oh boy I did just that and more. I heaved and bucked, pushing so far up inside her then absolutely blew my top. She was yelling and screaming, biting my arms and scratching my back as she reached her climax just after me.

We collapsed side by side.

I felt the need to show off. I was not just a man, I was **the** man!

I had a grin all over my face and wanted to talk to her about it but something in the expression on her face stopped me.

She looked at me and quietly but firmly told me not to talk about her, nor tell anyone. This would be our secret. If I blabbed or boasted then we wouldn't do it again. That was encouraging. It would be difficult not to show off to the boys but it sounded as though we were going to do it again. I would definitely like that so I would shut up, hope and enjoy.

We did do it again on a weekly basis for a few months. It was like a sex tutorial. This girl did not worry about the missionary position or any other position. She was not still long enough. She was in constant motion. She taught me so much that in the end I could hold on until we were both ready to come and finish it. She trained me so that I knew that the more pleasure I gave the girl the more pleasure and satisfaction I would get.

This was real stuff, no way was I ever going to be a poof! What freak would ever want to stick it to a guy when you could have a woman like that?

Then one night she showed me to the door and told me not to come again and that if I ever saw her I was not to recognise her. It was all over, don't make a fuss, we'd both had a good time, so keep quiet and go.

I was stunned and shattered. I wasn't just in love, I was mesmerised. I had found paradise at an early age and wanted it and her forever.

She told me not to be daft and difficult, grow up, forget her and go away.

So I did but I was so miserable for a while that my mum asked what was wrong with me. This was not something you could tell your mum so I thought I'd better buck up and get over it.

I did, or so I thought.

Some months later I was out with an ex-school mate of mine, who lived locally, called David. We had been to the flicks and dived into the nearest pub. There at the bar was a fella I'd had a run in with a few weeks before.

He had manhandled an ordinary couple one night in Eltham High Street right in front of me. Two of his mates held the guy back while he fiddled with a very upset girl. His name was Kenny.

I didn't like it, went over and told him to knock it off. He looked at me as though I was barmy, shoved me aside, and carried on.

I pulled his arm and as he turned round I let loose with a left uppercut which connected with his chin perfectly. It was a lucky shot. He went down as though poleaxed.

His mates let go of the guy and dropped down to help their friend on the ground. He was coming round but still well away. I grabbed the guy and girl, stuck them together and shoved them down the street. I decided that I had better beat it myself and walked off in the other direction with the deadly trio yelling after me that I would see them again.

And there they were in the bar. Kenny up front looking evil.

I got ready for trouble by checking how far away from the door I was when he told me to get a drink and not go away.

Stupidly I did and I didn't.

A few minutes later in walked a minor gang leader with a lot of his family and friends. He had just come out of jail after serving three years and was celebrating. The family had seven boys and only three beds as most of the men were in jail most of the time. He was bad news but it was none of my business or so I thought.

Then behind him I saw my enemy and he was pointing me out. He was assuring Danny, as he was called, that I was definitely the one. I thought that it was wimpish if he had to get someone else to fight for him and that it had nothing to do with me or Danny.

Wrong!

I was dragged struggling by four or five guys into the toilet along with my mate who naturally was looking very worried and bewildered.

They shoved me beside one of the old fashioned urinals with Danny in front of me and two others standing either side. I was held by two more. I caught sight of David in a similar situation further along.

What the hell was this about?

I soon found out.

Danny told me that he had heard that someone had been taking care of his missus while he had been inside and that the someone was me.

I replied that I thought that was nice, and hoped that she had been happy to have the company?

Danny grinned a bit unpleasantly I thought and told me that it didn't matter whether she liked it or not, the point was he didn't like it.

I tried to be a smart arse by saying, well there you go.

His reply was along the lines of, no it wasn't, it was where I was going to go.

I was smashed with a tremendous blow on the side of my head which rocked me and the beating began and went on for a bit.

I was determined not to go down and risk a severe stomping so I hooked my arm through the toilet flush pipe and hung on.

Eventually the hammering stopped. They suggested that as it had been such a good fight I should buy them a drink out of gratitude. I was well out it but I did and they left. At one stage I thought I had been rescued when the toilet door opened and a heavily built man had tried to come in but he was told to beat it and he did.

I disentangled myself from the pipe. I found I could stand but not see very well. My wrist need surgery sometime later but the rest of me would heal well enough. However I had to get home first and it would have to be a long walk. No way could we take a bus in this state.

I heard a groan and remembered my mate.

I couldn't focus very well so I took hold of him, held him up and we staggered out through the pub with everyone looking the other way. I heard Danny and the others laughing but didn't stop to hear what the joke was. I could guess.

We staggered home with David telling me he was worried about his eye as seeing through it was difficult and I regret to say I told him to shut up as I could hardly bloody well see anything at all.

We got back to our homes without bothering to say goodnight. We were just glad to get there.

As I went in through the back door my dad had just turned out the kitchen light.

He was surprised to see me and said, "hello, you're early, good that. You must have smelled the tea. I'll pour you a cup and come in and see mum."

He went to switch on the light.

I told him that it wasn't a good move but he did it anyway.

When he saw me he went apeshit.

He swiped me round the ear, shoved me up against the sink, wet a cloth and started to roughly clean me up, taking a slap at me every so often, telling me never to start a fight I couldn't finish.

Yeah great Dad, except I didn't start this one and the guy who did knew how to finish it.

Dad was not impressed and told me to go to bed so mum wouldn't see me in such a state. I did.

Dad made an excuse for me.

I slept well into the next morning which was a Sunday.

Mum came in and it was her turn to go apeshit.

I obviously didn't look so good.

She insisted I go to the doctor's surgery.

On a Sunday.

No way.

So it had to wait till Monday and I had to claim sick leave from work.

The Doctors on Council Estates had to be young and tolerant. Ours was a young, energetic guy, with a Doctor wife practising with him. They were fresh out of medical school and eager to serve.

The problems they were faced with would stand them in good stead for later in life when they went to more enlightened areas of the country. A Council Estate was a great place to start but a bad place to finish.

He had dealt with homemade gun wounds and managed to get the guns confiscated without anyone being arrested. He had helped pregnant young girls to avoid illegal abortions and have their babies adopted anonymously and reduced some of the youthful lawlessness in the area.

He showed me no sympathy.

He examined me, told me I had no severe injuries, only very sore superficial ones and that I would recover well in a few days. He told me he had treated on Sunday the boy I had a fight with and had to stitch back a large layer of skin hanging down over one eye. It needed 17 stitches.

I told him that he wasn't the one I had a fight with. He was my mate. We had been done over by a mob and he was on my side.

The Doc laughed and told me that the next time I got into a fight then he would make sure he wasn't on my side.

Poor old Peter had suffered more than me. At least I had experienced the pleasure as well as the pain. For me the pain was worth it. Years after the pain was forgotten the pleasure remained.

Soon after that I was called up for military service, never went back and never saw them again.

I don't think they missed me.

Bye, bye Baby Boy Blues.

BOOK TWO

"Big Boy Blues"

"Gone for a soldier, fightin' god knows who,
Gone for a soldier fightin' god knows who.
Bye bye baby, lost those baby boy, big boy blues."

Soldier things
Gay Parade?

My breath froze as soon as it left my lungs. It was 7am in January 1955. It was vaguely early dawn and was freezing. Salisbury Plain was covered in ice and snow and so was everyone in the British Army Infantry Training Battalion lined up in companies on the depot parade ground. I was standing stiffly to attention along with my rookie colleagues wondering what the hell this was all about.

Salisbury plain is bleak enough in Summer. In Winter it is bloody murderous.

The British Army carefully choses it's training locations with a purpose. Worse is better.

Every day in training is very tough and serious but this looked more serious than serious.

We didn't dare move or blink an eyelid. To do so would immediately catch the eye of one of the NCO's and there would be more trouble than you would want to handle.

Standing out front was Company Sergeant Major Jenkins, Taffy Jenkins to some but not to us and definitely not "sir" which applied only to officers.

Taffy was one of those professional soldiers dedicated to Queen and Country, in that order and no messing. For a recruit to be noticed by Taffy was usually a bad thing. He never praised, aways criticised and more than enough effort was generally thought to be too little.

He had more medals than chest and all had been bravely earned. The legend said that he had always volunteered for the toughest fights in the toughest places and had been rewarded with wires in his left arm, a plate in his head and parts of two fingers missing on one hand.

He was awaiting promotion to Warrant Officer 1st Class and an appointment as Regimental Sergeant Major.

Much against his will he had been viewed as unfit for further combat so had opted for a move to take on raw recruits in infantry training units and although he seemed to love his job he seemed to despise us.

No wonder. It didn't matter how strong you thought you were and how much you fancied yourself, the army was a thousand times tougher.

Everyone found this out the hard way. There was no easy way.

So what was going on?

Rumours had been circulating during breakfast and bullshine, ranging from a recruit going to be shot before our eyes for desertion, to a War Office Enquiry into the number of suicides amongst recruits unable to take the strain. Others more hopeful were sure that National Service was to be terminated and we would all be sent home.

One smart arse spread panic by insisting that war had been declared and we were all going to be shipped off to fight for England and defend Germany.

None of it was true at the time.

Out of the corner of my eye I caught sight of some vehicles approaching. As they came nearer I could see that they were Military Police Land Rovers.

Two Officers were standing up in the back of the second Land Rover and a recruit was standing up in the front.

They slowed right down as they came up to us and the recruit and all the Police personnel studied the ranks carefully. They kept going until much further along when suddenly the recruit gestured towards someone and the vehicles jerked to a stop. The recruit stayed where he was but Redcaps from all three vehicles jumped down, shot in amongst the rows of Squaddies and reappeared dragging a struggling soldier along between them.

Nothing happened for a while until a military police lock up truck came along. The two soldiers were shoved roughly in the back and the doors were barred.

The convoy moved away and disappeared.

We were marched off and told to take a NAAFI break.

This was extraordinary, totally unknown, so what was that all about.

We reported back to our barrack room, received the order stand by your beds and lined up accordingly.

In came Sergeant Rodgers, the Provost Sergeant, followed by a number of other NCO's. They were visiting each barrack room in turn.

All this was incredible exposure to corporals, sergeants and sergeant majors. Recruits were deemed as being too low be on the same planet as these gods. We even had to stand to attention before normal troops and call them "Trained Soldier." We were dirt and repeatedly called worse.

"Right," screamed Rodgers, sergeants in training always screamed, "what you have seen today is what happens if you are caught fucking a man. Men fuck women, or get fucked up by them, that is normal. They do not fuck other men which is not normal. Washrooms are for cleanliness not for filthy queers.

We are not toffs. Toffs are upper class poofs who go around and bugger people. They have buggered the working class for years. They prey on young guardsmen so you can be thankful you are in the proper fuckin' infantry and won't be mounting guard at Buckingham Palace. Mounting guard has a different meaning there. That's why the Guards march slower than anyone else. Any questions?"

"What will happen to them sergeant?" asked one brave soul.

"Those fucking fairies will be court martialled, that's what will happen. They'll get a few years in the Glasshouse, that's what they'll get, and then they'll know what it is to be really fucked. Then they'll get a dishonourable discharge. Be on their records for ever.

We don't tolerate arse 'ole bandits in the army. What we going to do, attack the enemy skipping like mincing girlies, sprinkling flowers in front of us?

Next thing you know we'll be sending butch birds into battle like those fucking ignorant Russkies. Not on my fucking watch we won't. Right that's it, carry on corporal."

We carried on all right.

We had to make up for the time that the army thought we had lost by having it easy for a few hours. We had it hard right into the night.

Jankers

J ankers are what you get if you misbehave. They are to be avoided. Everyday existence in training is deliberately designed to be unbearable so it is not a good idea to add to the burden.

One day I did.

I was lined up at the cookhouse after breakfast washing my eating irons in the boiling water in the deep galvanised tank by the door. A rookie, still in civvies, was looking lost. He looked at me a bit plaintively. I thought that maybe I had a rare chance to show off a bit.

He had dropped his fork in the water. This was something only a rookie would be careless enough to do. The water was kept flowing at constant boiling point and even a touch on the end of your fingers was enough to make you jump.

I outlined his options.

I told him that for the barrack room corporal to find out that he was a fork short at morning inspection was to be charged with neglect of army property.

He would be up on a charge in front of CSM Jenkins before he had a chance to breathe. He had to get it out without burning himself otherwise he would be charged with attempting to avoid duties by deliberately harming himself and malingering. A worse charge than loosing the fork.

He could tell the cookhouse sergeant who would tell the general duties detail when cleaning out the tank to save the fork and hand it over the next day but this was a long shot and not to be contemplated.

So what to do?

I told him that I had a handkerchief that he could soak in cold water, wrap it round his hand, and dive in and grab like mad.

I put my hand in my pocket to take out the handkerchief.

That was my first mistake of the day.

A corporal appeared out of nowhere, bearing down on me screaming his head off.

"You there, that man there. Yes you with your hand in your pocket playing with yourself. Stand to attention, name and number."

I smartly gave the last four digits of my number, followed by rank and name.

"What do you think you are doing? Hands in pockets? Look at me when I'm talking to you."

Second mistake of the day—it was a trap. I looked down on him as he was a short arse. The loudest ones always are.

"Take your fuckin' stupid face out of mine," he screamed, "who told you to look at me, look straight ahead."

"You told me to corporal, and it was only one hand," I said too smartly.

That was the third mistake and the fourth was about to follow.

He spread his hand over my face, shoved it away, and one of his fingers poked me in the eye. "Shut your stupid mouth and get your ugly face out of mine," he shouted, almost out of control.

That was it. I swung a left hook and caught him flush on the jaw as he was shoving his head forward at me.

He landed smack on his backside in the snow.

He was not flat on his back but he wasn't all there either.

It took a few seconds for me to give the handkerchief to the rookie, who wet it, retrieved his fork and beat it.

I started to walk away when I heard an hysterical roar coming from behind me.

"Hold that man, detain him, arrest him, send to the guardhouse for the RP's, careful, he's dangerous, he's assaulted an NCO," all blurted out at once.

Of course no one was going to side with the NCO'S in a training depot so everyone looked around with deliberate puzzled looks on their faces. We were called stupid every hour of every day so why not act it?

However I had already given my name and number so there was no point in walking away. I just stood there but he didn't get up. He wanted to add to the drama.

A few of my mates nodded which I took to mean I could rely on them to give a fair account if and when witnesses were asked for.

The Regimental Police arrived, handcuffed my hands behind my back, almost lifted me off the ground and frog marched me to the guardhouse.

The Provost Corporal booked me, asked me my intake, unit and company and then dumped me in a cell.

I had just settled down when Atkins, my barrack room Lance Corporal, arrived.

His red face appeared in the small window in the door and asked me what the fuck had happened.

I told him.

He was not pleased. He was normally not pleased anyway.

He was also a hypocrite. He professed amazement that the NCO had hit me first.

Jesus, they were all at it. Every training officer and NCO wanted to have the Champion Platoon on the Passing Out Parade so from the very first day they began a weeding out campaign against those they thought could lose them the title. Violence, bullying, mental and physical torture were the methods. They usually worked.

Recruits frequently surrendered physically and went to a PT school to be built up. Those who had mental breakdowns got moved to service units, (we irreverently believed it was the Intelligence Corps), some managed a medical discharge but some regrettably committed suicide.

During my sixteen weeks basic training there were two in our depot and one more during overseas training.

Although officially deploring it, frankly the army regarded this as natural wastage so that only the toughest went to war.

The weed in our platoon was called Eady. He would have to be wouldn't he?

One morning, at inspection, he was getting the usual going over when one of the trained soldiers assisting the lance jack suggested taking him down to the latrines.

Previously the whole platoon of thirty recruits had decided that enough was enough and that if Eady was picked on anymore we would all step forward and offer to take his place.

Suddenly the fracas around Eady was brought to a halt. There was a crashing of hard army boots on the wooden floor as the whole platoon stepped forward.

Except they didn't.

There were only two of us. My friend Mike, also from London's Dockland, and myself. We felt very alone.

We expected all hell to break loose but it didn't.

The corporal just told us to step back in line.

We didn't.

He came up close to us together with his sucking up cronies and demanded to know why we were standing where we were standing.

We told him we were standing by our barrack room colleague and would take his place.

"This is not the fucking United Nations you pair of pricks, this is the army," he shouted. "Do you fancy your chances then against us lot?" he sniggered.

"No Corporal, but we'd do better than him," we said, indicating Eady.

"Of course you bloody well would, you all would, that's the whole point, that's why he has to go," he bawled, "now step back in line, you too Eady."

He turned and they all left but we knew it was nowhere near over.

And now I was in the cooler charged with striking an NCO. Oh boy!

Outside the cell door I could hear the RP's discussing me in overloud voices.

They were wondering if I had seen the blood on the walls and floor where previous inmates had been beaten up or smashed their heads in pain and frustration. Clearly in the view through my little window I could see them doing pull ups on the roof supports supposedly popping their muscles in anticipation of doing me over.

For goodness sake I was a streetwise kid from the working class streets of London so all that crap was not going to work on me.

But I was worried about going in front of Jenkins.

I was made to sweat nearly all day.

Eventually I was marched to my barrack room and made to bull up as though for inspection. My mates looked on in awe but nobody came near. I was dangerous.

I was then marched at the double to the company office. I was in 24 platoon, B Company.

I had to stand to attention and watch a parade of witnesses, including the injured corporal march into the room to be interrogated by Company Sergeant Major Jenkins.

The Regimental Police escorts beside me kept telling me that I was in such serious trouble and they said it so seriously that I was starting to believe them.

At last it was my turn.

"ATTENSHUN, LEF RI, LEF RI, LEF RI, LEF WHEEL, LEF RI LEF RI, PRISONER HALT. RI TURN. STAND STEADY FOR CRISSAKES, THERE'S NO WIND BLOWING."

My number, rank and name was shouted out to the sarn't major.

There I was standing squarely in front of Jenkins. He was sitting at his desk with a Staff Sergeant on one side and Atkins and B Company Sergeant Rolfe on the other. None spoke and nobody acknowledged my presence for some time. They all stared at bits of paper.

At last Jenkins looked up, followed by the others. All studied me intently.

"You do realise you are in serious trouble son," he said quietly.

Oh god, not again, but this time as it came from Jenkins I became more anxious.

"This could be a court martial offense, and if it goes before the 'Old Man' (meaning the Colonel) then it would have to be. However I don't want that, it would be hard on the corporal who is a regular and a married man. As he struck you first then you could insist on taking this further. You hit him, which was against regulations but you could make out a case for self defence."

I held my breath. It was not me who was in the more serious trouble but I was still in it. I knew enough not to move or say a word.

"Now it's up to you son. You are fully entitled to go before the Colonel and take your chances but if you take my advice you won't. You don't understand it all but it will be on your record and I wouldn't want to be in your shoes for the remainder of your term."

"Now I will tell you what I propose and I want to hear only three words from you, three words only, when I ask you just one question. Those words are,' yes Sergeant Major.' Do you understand?"

I immediately said, "yes Sergeant Major."

The Provost Sergeant suddenly bellowed in my ear, "that's not the question you fucking imbecile, wait for it!"

Jenkins actually smiled and the others followed suite.

"This is the question,—Soldier, do you freely agree that you will accept my decision and my punishment on the understanding this will not go any further and will not appear on your record?"

"Yes Sergeant Major."

The whole room seemed to relax.

"Right," said Jenkins, "three nights shiners starting tomorrow at 6 am. You will report to the guardroom each morning at 6. That's it. Dismissed."

"PRISONER SHUN, RIGHT TURN, LEF RI, LEF RI, RIGHT WHEEL, LEF RI LEF RI LEF RI, PRISONER HALT, STAND AT EASE, STAND EASY."

I was just going to relax and ask a few pertinent questions when suddenly, "COMPANY SHUN, COLONEL ON PARADE," and in swept the Colonel followed by the Adjutant, a Major. They went directly into Jenkins' office.

We all remained strictly to attention.

After about ten minutes the Colonel came out and amazingly stopped in front of me. He looked at the Provost Sergeant, while I stared fixedly into space above his head, still rigidly to attention.

"Is this the man Sergeant?" he asked.

"Yes Colonel," came the reply.

"He made a good decision but he'll have to be ten times the soldier to survive for a while. We need lads like him, full of spirit. Will he make it?"

"We'll make sure he does sir," replied the Provost, making it sound like a threat.

The Colonel was too lofty to speak to me directly but all around got the message including me.

After the Colonel disappeared Atkins and Rolfe came out and told me that Jenkins was impressed. Although I'd said nothing the impression given was that this was a one off and I had no wish to be a problem soldier.

They told me that although it was no business of mine the full corporal had lost three years seniority, been busted to lance corporal and was being transferred to an active military unit. They said that I had better watch myself because although the guy couldn't touch me his wife wanted to kill me as he had lost pay and privileges. They told me that I was lucky that the corporal had made such a public show of it which had worked against him. He should have kept quiet, called the corporal's mess, and they would all have come and nearly beat me to death!

I then stupidly relaxed a little and asked them that if the army liked spirit why did it do its best to kill it.

Bad move. All was back to business and I never got to ask my important question. Basically what the hell was night shiners?

I found out next morning.

At wake up call I dressed, rushed down to the guardroom and got a bollocking for turning up unshaved, unwashed and not properly dressed.

I asked them how I could do that and be there at 6 o'clock.

Simple, I had to get up earlier, before Reveille.

I was given a rusty chain in a bucket of water and a varnished chair. My early morning job for the next three days was to clean the chain with sand and strip the chair down to its bare wood using a scraper. Failure to complete the tasks would mean an extension of the punishment.

I was given thirty minutes to rush to breakfast, wash and shave, clean my kit and get ready to stand by my bed for eight o'clock inspection.

It wasn't done well so the inspecting corporal made me throws everything through the window and do it again before parade.

This wasn't good and it would get worse.

After the day's training and our evening meal I had to report to one of the giant drill sheds. Three corporals were waiting for me. After verbally abusing me in colourful army speak they sent me away to report back in fifteen minutes in full field service marching order.

I came complete in battle dress, greatcoat, back packs, ammunition packs, water bottle, and survival material along with rifle, bayonet and steel helmet.

They then had me running around the drill shed with rifle held above my head and when one got tired another took over. There was no rest for me.

When they got bored they ripped off all my equipment, kicked it around until filthy and then gave it back to me accusing me of turning up in a non military condition. They ordered me to clean it and report back in thirty minutes. I did and they started over again until just before Lights Out.

I then had a few minutes to try and get ready for the morning's inspection. I had to take a chance and continue after Lights Out. Earlier I had checked with one of the Security Picket to wake me up on his rounds before Reveille.

He did it for two packets of cigarettes which I felt was a bargain because I didn't smoke.

Oh boy, did they get their revenge!

I did all the tasks, took all they threw at me and I did become ten times the soldier I would have been.

Even so I wasn't that hot, but stuff you anyway, you bastards.

Injections

During training it was necessary to be injected for anything and everything.

Usually all at the same time. The words "lethal cocktail" in medicine did not exist then. Neither had Post Traumatic Stress Disorder been invented. You were either up to it or you weren't. Men were up for it, cissies weren't. Life was simple. Everyone had it hard so don't make a fuss, just get on and get over it.

The same approach was taken with respect to injections.

We changed into PT kit and rolled up the sleeves on both arms.

We were marched to the medical centre.

Very few of us had ever seen it because in the army you had to be very fit to report sick. You had to appear in full kit for sick parade an hour before normal parade and stand for inspection in the freezing cold for ages. If you made it as far as the doctor, god help you if he decided that you weren't really ill and close to death.

Almost right outside his door were two RP's who checked his diagnosis. If you had no light duties or prescriptions then you were arrested and charged with malingering.

Not even the sick reported sick, they just waited until they collapsed.

We were ushered into a long corridor with open doors along its entire length.

We filed slowly down it.

Suddenly hands shot out from the first door and grabbed the left arm of the leading man, swabbed his upper arm with iodine and jabbed a needle in as though playing a game of darts. The needle was withdrawn, dumped in a bowl of disinfectant, shaken and filled to be used on the next man. The same hands reached out and shoved the first man onwards to the open door on the right. Here he was grabbed by his other arm and he was injected again.

Further along another door got him on the left and finally he ended up being stabbed once more on the right.

This process was repeated on us all and heaven help the last lot who got a blunt needle.

We had tetanus, TAB, cholera and yellow fever and later had to have a few boosters and others along with some disinfectant and iodine.

Our arms were sore in places, unbearable to touch in others and we all suffered from nausea and hot and cold sweats. We were officially put on 48 hour light duties.

This meant GD's. General Duties. We scoured scum out of field Dixie's until our hands were raw, delivered sacks of coal to married quarters until our backs were breaking, cleaned latrines scraping embedded shit and piss off walls with razor blades and stood by baths maintaining the heat for hours for NCO's who never took them.

No wonder British soldiers fought so well. After training you were ready to kill anyone out of sheer frustration.

The best however was to come.

Just before breakfast we were marched into the camp cinema. Wow, now this was more like it—"light duties" for sure.

We all groaned as the doctor ambled onto the stage, with an almost sympathetic look on his face. Was this going to be a mass inoculation or hypnosis or something?

He explained that we were about to see a film on health and cleanliness as a healthy army was a fit to fight army. Yeah, he was telling this to us when we had been tortured for weeks and were feeling like shit. He did not have a receptive audience.

The lights dimmed, planes dive bombed, tanks exploded, infantry charged and ships sank accompanied by martial music. We were bored. We felt sleepy.

Suddenly the screen was filled by a giant penis, covered in sores and exuding pus.

That got our attention. We were wide awake.

The headline was Venereal Diseases.

Every detail was covered including the umbrella treatment which is still too painful for me to think about even many years later.

The images were stark and totally over the top.

We got the message but just in case it hadn't sunk in we were served a breakfast of sausage, runny fried egg, baked beans and tomatoes.

The cooks thought this hilarious.

We didn't.

We were glad to get back to normal training. Light duties were far too tiring.

Dear John

Even though I came from a very downmarket area of South London I had never experienced total illiteracy. Violence, ignorance, prejudice and poverty for sure but even the most hard-case morons could read and write to some degree.

So it came as a shock to me to find that out of the one hundred or so B Company recruits a number were only semi-literate and five of them were totally illiterate.

That seemed bad but a buddy thought that well we were just infantry after all. We were the dispensable gun fodder. However I wasn't convinced, I thought they belonged in the Pioneer Corps but I reckon I'd seen worse in the Education and Intelligence Corps.

I liked the infantry—they were the real soldiers.

However I let it all slide and took no further notice until they skipped off some training to do school a few days a week. Hey they weren't so dumb after all.

We normal guys were resentful so when we got our chance at revenge we took it.

One of them had two letters, one from his mum and the other from his girlfriend. He couldn't read or write.

He wanted to tell his mum he was fine, learning to read and write, and was a good soldier.

He wanted to tell his girlfriend that he loved her and would always be true.

We told him to leave it all in our hands.

Basically we told his mum that he had a girl from the NAAFI who let him do it up against the drill shed wall.

She was pregnant but don't tell his girlfriend.

We told his girlfriend the same but said don't tell his mum.

The poor guy was so excited he recommended us to everyone.

The illiterate guys queued up to get their letters read and written by us.

The first one was comparatively lucky. We warmed to our task and really stitched them all up. Our imagination ran riot.

Some bright spark hit on the idea of helping out the agony aunts in the newspapers.

The questions and situations we sent were outrageous and complicated and we split our sides at the answers and solutions.

However we got a bit too carried away and the aunties cottoned on.

Fortunately for us the illiterates were transferred for further training before the inevitable repercussions.

Then we got hit.

We fell one after the other like dominoes.

We got "Dear John" letters.

They were all so alike that we wondered if there was a service for lonely girlfriends wishing to unload their absent soldier boyfriends.

Dear Tom, Dick, Harry or Fred, I do miss you and love you so much. I will honestly love you for ever and never forget you.

But—although I will never forget you I can't remember what you look like now. Your army photo just didn't look like you at all. I think you must have changed.

I haven't changed but Joey from down the road has been so kind. You remember Joey don't you?

Well he has been very thoughtful and looked out for me and I am confused about my feelings.

It is so difficult for me not having anyone except Joey to turn to. It's easy for you, you are in the army, leaving me here.

So I think it better to be fair to you and break up with you.

It's the best for both of us.

Please don't blame Joey and beat him up when you come home on leave, he's only being helpful.

Mum and Dad send their best.

Your ever loving girlfriend (wife, fiancee, etc).

Oh boy how the rats play when the cat's away. How is it that the Joeys of this world never seem to get drafted?

The ordinary civilian has no conception of what home and stability means to conscripts, particularly when overseas. Everything is heightened and has an exaggerated value. Whenever I was returning from home leave overnight to my unit and the train was passing through the North London suburbs I would look at the lights in the windows of flats and houses. I would imagine going to bed normally and wonder if I would survive to do the journey again.

So when a girl dumped you it was hard.

There was nothing we could do about it. A few fellas were really upset and went AWOL but got nowhere with the girls and ended up with punishment from the army. Those few who did manage to patch it up just received a second Dear John letter a few weeks later.

In the army you got punished for failure whether in love or war.

Camp Concerts

The army operated on a need to know basis. The theory being that the less anyone knew the better it was for them. Consequently rumours circulated everywhere and the more outrageous they were the more they were believed.

We were bulling our kit one evening when L/Cpl. Atkins charged out of his room, shot down the barrack room shouting, "stand by your beds."

We did so, wondering "what next?"

"Full battledress in fifteen minutes, properly turned out. Don't look fucking in a daze, you're in the army. When you get the shout you jump."

We had been shouted and screamed at every minute of every day, insulted, abused and accused so shouts and screams had lost most of their impact.

The NCO's in training camps never worked that out.

However in ten minutes we were standing by our beds looking good but of course being asked what bloody well took us so long.

We were curious. This was eight o'clock at night in mid-winter and we were not carrying capes or wearing greatcoats.

We assembled outside, lined up and marched smartly off.

After weeks of training we could do that and could look good.

We marched out of the camp, past the guardhouse, and along the main road.

The road was wet and slippery, ice starting to form so we used the studs on the bottom of our boots to dig.

As we marched the NCO's would often break into the standard left, right, left to keep up the pace but would also shout, dig, dig, dig.

A Royal Army Service Corps Officer approached so we got the order,

"Company, eyes left." We did so and the NCO's smartly saluted.

The Officer asked, "Cpl. how long have these men been in the army/"

"Ten weeks, sir."

"Fine body of men, Cpl. well done."

"Yessir! Infantry sir."

The Officer had the trace of a smile on his face as he passed by—he got the message.

He didn't know that the next day we would have to pay for his compliment.

For the moment though this was further outside the camp than we had been except for runs and route marches.

After a further twenty minutes we were halted outside another training camp.

We had heard of it but didn't know it and didn't want to know it. It was the Military Police Training Centre.

One of our wags reckoned we were going to arrest them all and another suggested we were going to teach them about honesty.

We laughed when another said that no one knew anything about honesty in the army, especially the officers and the higher the rank the higher the level of bullshit.

We were screamed at to shut our traps or we would all be put on a charge.

We did but didn't stop grinning though.

We eventually marched through the gates, past the piercing, accusing eyes of their Provost and stopped outside a huge drill shed.

There was one hell of a din coming from inside.

We were marched in single file to rows of chairs and benches. We occupied the vacant ones behind hundreds of other recruits and the empty ones behind us were soon filled.

Way in the distance was a stage and floodlights.

Somewhere down there a band was playing a mixture of British Big Band stuff from Ted Heath, Ken Mackintosh, Jack Parnell and Eric Delaney. They would also work in brilliant material from Count Basie, Duke Ellington, Woody Herman and Stan Kenton.

Wow!

Then there was a big drum roll, down went our lights, up went the stage lights and a presenter bounded on to the stage.

My god! It was Ted Ray, the Radio Comedian.

He cracked some risque jokes to warm up and then concentrated on the one's that soldiers everywhere loved. Jokes about the officers and sergeant majors.

Squaddies were on their feet yelling approval.

After telling the Regimental Sergeant Major of a paratroop training section to get a haircut, assuring a captain in the Womens Royal Army Corps that the CO of the Royal Hampshires was cheating on her but only with the doctor's wife and that the Adjutant of the Gloucesters had a stutter, he was our hero for life.

Ted was followed by the girl pop duet The Tanner Sisters. They may or may not have been beautiful but to thousands of hyper fit sex starved soldiers deprived of female comfort for weeks they looked gorgeous.

Then came Max Wall with his drole, self-effacing humour that had us splitting our sides. Singers included the glamorous Beverley Sisters, and others.

Top of the bill was Max Miller, the "Cheeky Chappie." He had made his name around all the shady clubs of Soho and came close to being banned from Radio many times.

His jokes always deliberately seemed to be headed for disaster but he managed to change the last line each time just avoiding total obscenity and substituting innuendo instead.

Here, in front of soldiers he had no inhibitions.

He revealed the punch line to one of his favourites.

"When babies are young they are ready for crying,

When birds grow up they are ready for flying,

When chickens are ripe they are ready for plucking,

When girls are sixteen they are ready for—good night ladies and gentleman."

This time he supplied the last word and received a roar of approval but serious frowns from the WRACs.

The officers noting this also changed their laughter to disapproval.

An announcer told us that Max had been reprimanded but couldn't explain as he was drowned by choruses of boos.

Max came on with a cheeky grin, slapped his own wrist, apologised and then slapped his backside in the direction of the WRACs. We loved him.

We roared for ages for encores and got several.

Those entertainers could never know what their performances meant to us youngsters from lower class backgrounds separated from our families.

We respected them all our lives but sadly many lost their music hall and radio careers because of television.

They never made the transition.

Those that did went on to even greater fame and fortune and we could bore people for years by telling them that we saw them for free in the army.

The next day we were brought down to earth.

Morning inspection brought on the onslaught. Word had gone round the NCO's of the compliment by the RASC Officer.

"A fine body of fucking men are you? Is that what you are? An RASC Officer has the Queen's Commission and has to be respected but it was fucking dark and he was probably pissed. We think you are shit heads, useless and have not earned the title of men. We will have to bring you up to that "fine body of men" standard, but first you have to earn it and you start now."

It did. Double drills, double assault course and double route march.

We could never look an RASC officer in the eye again.

Basics

In those days you volunteered for nothing. You applied for nothing. You didn't have to.

The three services had all the top grade material they needed. You were selected then told you had volunteered.

So your army life could be basic training, overseas training, NCO's Cadre and posting to a unit.

You could be selected for more specialist training which would be very tough.

At any stage you could fail, not shape up, be deselected and posted to a unit.

You had no choice of units unless relatives had served in them before.

Or maybe your passage would be very different. Only a few were commando material.

If you moved up and on then you got your second stripe—a full Corporal.

You could even make Sergeant but that was very rare for National Servicemen. Most conscripts were privates for their full term.

Basic training however was similar all over.

Brutal.

The army worked to the lowest common denominator. Everything was dumbed down and even that was difficult for some.

Everyone at whatever level of fitness went through the same routine. We were all viewed as having dirty habits so we had to initially be supervised when washing, shaving and shitting. Everyone had to sign the shit book. Failure to do so meant you were constipated and had to be treated. The treatment was enough to make you shit bricks.

We frequently had to line up, stand on stools and peer into some poor sods ears, shouting out, "yes they're filthy corporal."

We had haircuts that left a small stubble on top. Baldness was against regulations we were told.

We were examined for piles, fleas and other contagious diseases and the humiliation that followed any discovery of such a thing was worse than the cure.

We started out doing everything in PT kit slowly building up distances, challenges and clothing as our fitness improved.

We looked on the guys who did guard duty as gods. We were still in scruffy GD's, the army's version of overalls, rarely appearing in uniform, while they had been in for ten weeks. They looked and acted like soldiers. You could comb your hair in the reflection of the mirror finish on their best boots. Their greatcoats, trousers, and BD's had knife edge irremovable creases in them and their packs, rifles and slings were immaculate. They looked fit, smart, capable and confident.

We felt inferior—by miles. How could we ever look like them especially as even they weren't ready for their Passing Out Parade.

But slowly and surely the army worked its magic.

They had been doing this for centuries and knew just how to turn out fine fighting men in spite of everything.

When I had my first 36 hr pass after six weeks I wanted to tell my Mum about the terrible things the army had done to her lovely son. However the sores had healed, the sweats had passed, aches and pains and the bruises had gone. Fresh air, regular food and hyper activity had done the trick. She could not stop looking at me and kept asking how they had done it.

I wanted to tell her, "torture Mum, ask me what they've done to your son Mum," but she wasn't listening. The cocky teenage slob who had left home had gone. In its place was a self sufficient young man who stood upright, did not slouch with hands in pockets, was alert, paid attention, made his own bed, cooked his own breakfast and tidied his own clothes. And the Army had only just started on me. Mum was impressed, not at all distressed. I was very disappointed in my Mum.

I decided that weekend passes home were bad for you.

The training was practical. Nothing was left to theory.

We were issued with gas masks.

So we had to test them.

We changed into PT kit and were marched off to an underground bunker. We filed in and the doors clanged shut behind us.

The bunker filled with a yellow coloured gas.

The NCO's instructed us to breathe deeply and run around. So we did.

"Wait a minute," I thought, "I didn't really see what I did really see, did I?"

I did.

The NCO's were tearing off our gas masks.

Were they mad or what?

No way, so were were dodging, ducking and diving.

It didn't matter. When the doors were opened those who had had their masks taken off first were the first out the door. Others were held back so that we were all given equal exposure and were all bent over heaving and gasping, with tears streaming from our eyes. Our throats, noses and eyes were burning. Some were vomiting.

"Right," screamed the corporals, who had of course kept their masks on almost until the end, "that's what it's like to survive a gas attack but you haven't survived yet. You need to clear your lungs and the best way is to take deep breaths and the best way to do that is to run."

"Oh yeah," we thought, "good joke."

No joke.

"Come on, move you idle bastards, move, move move, get those legs working. You'll feel better sooner so move, bloody well move!"

We started on a shambling run, peering through watery red eyes, stumbling along while being screamed at to pick up the pace.

Eventually we did.

We never experienced an enemy gas attack. Only that one from our own side which veterans from the First World War assured us was about par for the course.

We were getting so fit we used to set our own challenges in the barrack room.

Obviously we were brain washed.

We would do sit ups. We would do the first with one rifle behind our heads, complete with magazine, bolt, sling and bayonet. Then we would do two with two rifles and so on. At first we had to strip down some of the added rifles but eventually the only restriction on performance was how many rifles we could accommodate behind our heads.

The route marches became longer, faster and over tougher terrain. We eventually tackled them in full field service marching order on the double. We did them during the day and at night with the favourite being the dawn patrol. We only broke step to go over bridges so that the uniform vibrations of normal marching did not weaken the structure.

There were trucks following behind during the really tough ones to pick up those who collapsed or to take the kit off those who could struggle on with a lighter load.

After the march we had to take our boots off and lay on our beds for foot inspection. This was carried out by the medical officer who declared everyone fit for duty even if they had raw blisters.

We always reckoned that Army Medical Officers would declare everyone fit even if they were dying from plague. They never got close enough to know any different.

Bullshit was as always just bullshit. In Winter you had to paint coal white to match the snow and make it black again in the Spring. The barrack room had a black coke stove and flue in the middle, a single wash basin with brass taps at one end and a galvanised dustbin at the other end. God help you if you used them.

They had to be kept immaculate at all times.

Kit inspection was a daily hazard. Someone always copped it and one day you knew it would be your turn.

No one escaped.

Boots in general use had to be cleaned but best boots had to be something else. First the toe caps had to be gently ironed to smooth out the welts and then spit and polish applied for hours to achieve a mirror finish. Soles had to be blackened and the studs shined. They were a work of art.

Bedding, socks and clothing were folded in specific ways and cardboarded to achieve smooth finishes. Mugs, eating irons, toothbrushes, soaps, flannels all had to appear unused and the only way to do this was to have a spare set.

We bought them from the NAAFI but it was against training rules so we had to make special hiding places which the Drill Corporals well knew about but chose to ignore until it was time to pick on you.

Folding chairs had to be raw wood sandpapered clean, lined up with string besides the beds along the whole room. Everything placed on the chairs had to be lined up in the same way.

When it was your time you could have done the best job in the world but it would make no difference. You had to take two paces forward, not one. You didn't dare look round or anywhere at all except for a space in the far distance slightly higher than your eye level. The Corporal would be screaming in your ear and ripping apart everything you had taken hours to prepare. You had to about turn, pick up all your rubbished gear in your arms and throw it through the window.

"I don't want to see you walk, run, fly or crawl I just want you to disappear and re-appear again with all your bedding in the right fucking order," he screamed, "do I make myself crystal clear, you fucking useless moron."

I moved like lightning with the Corporal following me around the windows hurling abuse through them.

I got back in seconds.

To be greeted with, "Where the fuck you been, on 48hrs leave or something?"

He was on his knees looking underneath my bed.

"Get down here, you useless blockhead, look at all this dust. It's filthy, look at this finger."

I looked, there was a microscopic piece of fluff barely visible on the tip of his finger.

"Look at it, look at it, full of filth, I have to live with you amongst all this filth. Get down and clean it now," he bawled, "wait a minute why is your bedding a mess? Jesus Christ you are fucking idle, get it sorted. Report for cookhouse duty in the morning. Fucking useless!"

The assault courses were always the ultimate. They varied from the achievable to the almost bloody impossible. In the end you could do them all and then it became a case of racing against the clock.

Frequently the Cpl. or Sergeant would ask you as you finished whether you found it difficult or easy. Either answer was wrong.

If you said easy then the camp fire brigade was called. Everywhere and everything was soaked in water, allowed to freeze, except in certain places, and you had to go through it again.

If you said difficult then you were not fit enough and had to do it two or three times more.

The live range assault course was a nervy trial as all rounds were fired by recruits who could use their initiative up to a certain point.

They were often willing to risk a bollocking by using their initiative and going beyond that certain point.

I found out that the sandbagged grenade throwing area was not just to protect you from the outside blast of the thrown grenade but also from the one's dropped in panic on the inside.

During most training sessions you would see men throwing themselves over the top of the sandbags from the inside hoping to land swiftly and safely on the outside. Most did.

Everyone has seen a dumb cluck recruit on the firing point turning around with a jammed weapon only to see everyone throwing themselves flat on the ground trying to dig a hole with the armourer sergeant screaming his head off at him. The guy usually said plaintively that his gun had stuck.

One of our men who did this had to stand on a box in the barrack room with his trousers round his ankles, rifle in one hand and his dick in the other.

He had to recite countless times that, "this is my rifle, this is my gun, this is for firing and this is for fun."

It apparently was the standard punishment.

We were all taught to count out loud in exact time together so as to complete all orders and manoeuvres in complete unison. When this was achieved we had to count it silently, just to ourselves. Then we performed pre-learned rifle and drill routines operated to perfection without any verbal orders being given.

We could shoot rapid fire, learned to strip down a variety of weapons speedily and in total darkness and mainly hit what we were aiming at.

Maggie's Draws did not appear as much as they used to and local farmers relaxed as training progressed.

Some of us became first class shots and went further.

We went on manoeuvres and once attacked a local RAF camp capturing it successfully after a short fight.

We were celebrating when we were asked abruptly to leave by the Union Leader of the Civil Servants employed on the camp and the Flying Officer in charge because we had interrupted their tea break.

Britain was already changing and not for the better.

However before I could consult with our officer one of our lance jacks came up and confirmed that the Civil Servants were going to lodge a formal complaint.

"What, because we interrupted a cup of tea for crissakes?"

"Not just that sarge, Scottie and Scouse got a bit carried away. They herded them all up and threatened to shoot them as spies and traitors because of their moaning and groaning."

"Oh Jesus, this is one for the 'Ole Man' to sort out."

Fortunately he did.

We learned to charge into battle with and against heavy artillery fire, running behind and riding on the backs of tanks, digging in and surviving mortar fire and taking cover against aircraft bombing attacks.

We had to survive tropics and arctics. I couldn't believe it when we had to remove our gloves in freezing temperatures and fire our weapons. If our hands froze on the metals parts we were charged with attempting to mutilate ourselves. We had to learn how to fight no matter what the circumstances. None of it made sense but then if you had any you wouldn't join the army.

It was dangerous.

After what seemed an eternity we finally reached the status of guard duty.

We were ready.

We were the new gods.

Finally came the Passing Out Parade.

We were the Champion Platoon.

We headed up all the companies on the march past.

Such was the standard that one of our guys was very ill but was determined to complete the Pass Out. He nearly did pass out. He didn't really know what he was doing but we arranged for him to punch the back of the guy in front while marching to keep him on track. While standing still he had to sort himself out somehow. He just survived but was later hospitalised with severe pneumonia.

Parents were invited to watch and we all went for lunch in the food hall.

Officers circulated trying to appear part of the normal human race instead of privileged beings and even the Colonel put in an appearance. He came to our table and I immediately jumped up.

"No, no," he said, "stay sitting."

Oh yeah, as if.

He looked at Dad, said, "unpromising start, good finish, good soldier, carry on."

I breathed a sigh of relief. Dad was okay, but only slightly impressed. It took a lot to impress Dad.

The RSM and the CSM's did not bend at all. They had trained us as soldiers and we had to act accordingly all the time.

They were the most impressive men on the planet.

Well they had trained us shower of shit hadn't they?

Because of those absolute bastards we had earned the right to be called Trained Soldiers.

Yeah.

Black, Brown and White

We were just starting the noisy evening bullshit routine in our barrack room after Grubtime when suddenly the hubbub died down. The few voices that carried on soon petered out.

I followed the direction of most of the eyes towards the door.

A black guy, in a strange uniform, was dragging a huge kitbag along the floor accompanied by a regimental police sergeant.

He was shown to a bed space left vacant by a colleague who had been sent back for extra physical training.

Before he could look at anyone he was ushered out again, returning in half an hour with bedding and other equipment.

He didn't say a word to anybody and nobody said a word to him. We were all dying of curiosity but didn't want to make the first move in case it was a wrong one.

We had been in training for a couple of months and knew better than to stick our noses in anywhere uninvited.

No worry. In came CSM Jenkins with his usual entourage of staff.

We jumped to attention and stood by our beds.

"Right," shouted Jenkins, in his sing song Welsh lilt, "at ease, this 'ere is Samuels, private Samuels, but on 'is way to becoming an officer in the Nigerian Army. 'E is going to train with us to toughen 'im up like. You are the chosen ones. Aren't you lucky? You are going to make 'im welcome and set a good example. A very good example because if you don't you will all be in deep shit. The War Office, no less, is watching this one."

"The black blokes have not previously had a very good record in the British Army due to a tendency to run, unfortunately rarely in the direction of the enemy. That is why you won't often see one."

"Yes, what is it?" asked Jenkins of one brave soul who felt the need to say something.

"What about the Indian Army and the Gurkhas, They're brave aren't they? They don't run do they?" he asked.

"Are you fucking blind or something son, they're brown aren't they? For Christ's sake wake up lad. Samuels won't be 'ere for long, 'e needs to study our training from the inside so 'e can pass it on in his own country. Right carry on!"

He and his aides swept out the door.

We all converged on Samuels. Most of the lads had never seen a black guy except for the Robertson's Jam label and the Black and White Minstrel Show on BBC TV. Samuels was no fake stereotype, he was the real thing.

He was quite a guy. His father was a chieftain and he had the facial tribal cut marks that were given to him on achieving adolescence.

In spite of the culture he was Christian which convinced our local Pastor of the value of devoted missionaries. He was disappointed that not one us volunteered.

He tried hard enough. His Sunday sermons featured poor old Samuels, seated right at the front, as an example of the benefits of Empire and the Baptist Church. He was so on fire and wound up that he barely flinched when Samuels told him that his father and grandfather had fought the British for Independence and that they were Catholics.

Samuels was a novelty that soon wore off. He had to hack it like the rest of us but for him it was temporary. After a few weeks he would be off to Sandhurst Military Academy and learn to be an officer along with a number of other ex colonials training to take up positions of responsibility in the armies of their own country.

Unlike the British Army which was used to protect the country and its people too many of the ex colonial armies became armies of oppression and were used against their own population. Tragically so many other of the poor or underdeveloped countries trod the same route. We weren't surprised at them as they hadn't had the benefits of the British civilising influence. It never occurred to us at all as to whether our influence had been beneficial or not. Of course it had.

Most of our lads could not get used to him.

Country Yokel in all seriousness informed us, "at 'ome we thinks a foreigner comes from another town a few miles away. Aaarh oi knows that even those who lived in our village for ten years are still strangers. They's all of 'em white though. Dunno 'bout a black." He scratched his head. Well we had no hair.

The idea of coming from or going to another far off land was remote. Being British we probably had a better idea of the world than most because we were born and raised in the time of the British Empire and were all conversant with the map of the world showing huge areas in red. Getting there was another matter.

That was where National Service came in. Thousands were shipped overseas and most were unable to repeat the experience in civvy street until years later.

Continental travel was for the rich. The rest of us travelled by bus to work and spent two weeks at the seaside if we were lucky.

Some of us living in dock areas were used to seeing foreigners on a daily basis but most were not. Attitudes were fixed.

Two guys from Birmingham, who had never got further than Walsall, offered their opinions, "they're funny though aren't they, these foreigners?" one of them said, "I mean Mediterranean people are greasy ain't they because of all that Olive Oil and they stink of Garlic."

"I mean look at it, those Frenchies eat frogs legs, snails and horse meat. Not surprising that no one trusts them. The bloody Germans and the Dutch eat stodgy pudding which makes them fat with no sense of humour and the rest don't count anyway, do they?"

"Nah, nothing in the world can beat Fish 'n Chips and Roast Beef with Yorkshire Pudding," said his mate, "makes us what we are, true British."

Everyone nodded knowledgeably in agreement.

The wonderful invasion of immigrants from the West Indies with their relaxation, colour and music was just beginning and the influx of Indians from East Africa and Chinese from Hong Kong with their devotion to hard work, education and fabulous food was just still in the future.

A new style of Great Britain was to burst out in the middle Sixties but unfortunately the quality of immigrants would slowly deteriorate over the years.

Later inflows would be more reluctant to blend in and enjoy the freedom they claimed to want. They would focus more on the material giveaways provided by a benevolent society which would have to rethink the whole set up. Few brought benefits like the originals. Instead they brought baggage and fixed ideas. A great pity.

Guard Duty

At last I had achieved the dream or more truthfully the nightmare of being a rookie good enough to mount guard. After ten weeks of basic training there I was lined up for inspection as part of the incoming new guard facing the outgoing old guard.

All of us were in mint condition, perfectly turned out.

The orderly sergeant was not from our unit. We had to pass his test which was an unknown to us.

He was in a hunting mood.

My eyes followed him just slightly.

"That man, I saw his eyes move. Why are they moving about? Fix your fucking eyes on a point just above the man's head in front of you," he screamed, "if you can't manage that then I'll bloody well remove you and stick you up on a charge. All of you, stand fucking still. I don't want the orderly officer to see a bleedin' bunch of nig nogs blowing in the wind."

"The officer hasn't got to stand here all morning has he?" muttered a voice close by.

Immediately the face of a furious orderly sergeant was stuck in front of me.

"Was it you, was it you talking when standing to attention in the ranks? Answer me you piece of shit?" he bawled, "WHO WAS IT?"

"Don't know sergeant, can't see can I? My eyes are fixed on a point above the man's head in front of me," I said smartly.

"It's not your fucking eyes I'm asking about, it's your ears, you moron" he shouted frantically.

"I wasn't listening sergeant, I was paying attention to your orders," I said.

"Well pay attention to this then. If I have any more insubordination from this shambles that calls itself a guard I will personally order your arrest by the old guard and you will get to know the guardroom from the inside of a cell. Do I make myself clear?"

"Yes sergeant," we all shouted out together.

The orderly officer arrived and was satisfied. The new guard was on and the old guard marched off in relief it seemed at not having an orderly sergeant like ours.

There was no such thing as a kind sergeant, they were all bastards, but some were real bastards and one of them had found us.

We were marched into the guardroom where we were briefed by the Provost Sergeant.

"Right then, the guardroom is your base but the front gate is not. The only people liable to come in that way are presumed to be friendly, drunk or daft.

They will be handled as usual by the Regimental Police. Your job is to patrol all the rest of the base, inside and out, to make sure the unfriendly chaps do not get in anywhere. If you find drunks trying to climb the wire tonight then you will not beat them up. You will inform us and we will beat them up. They are usually ours but if they are so drunk that they belong elsewhere then we hold them overnight, hand them over in the morning and their police can beat them up."

"If you see anything suspicious you will shout, 'halt, who goes there, friend or foe'? If the answer is friend then you will say 'step forward friend and be recognised' but if the—? Who's that sniggering, you, you there what's so funny?"

We stayed silent but there's always one!

"We don't really have to say that do we provo sergeant? I mean you're taking the piss right? Whatever he is he isn't going to say foe, is he? If he did he'd be a nutter wouldn't he? But if he did he's going to say foe and then bang bang you're dead, en'e? So much for guard duty. All over 'ennit?"

There was dead silence.

Then.

"There will be no two hours on and four hours off for this guard. Smart asses the lot of you. So you will be on alert the whole 24 hours. I will disappear from time to time and jump out in front of you when you least expect it and god 'elp the man who doesn't shout, 'halt, who goes there, friend or foe,' because I will personally take his bayonet and stick it up his arse," he said quite calmly but menacingly, "are you clear?"

"Yes Provo Sergeant," we answered giving our mouthy colleague filthy looks at the same time.

Our orderly sergeant looked absolutely pleased with the situation.

"Right, in order for you to stay alert you will need to be occupied. I will be finding comfortable little jobs for you to do such as cleaning the regimental police shit houses and emptying the prisoners slop buckets at frequent intervals. That will achieve two things. It will piss you and the prisoners off at the same time.

The posh people use smelling salts to wake up feeble ladies, the army uses the stink of shit houses to wake up fucking useless squaddies. One tip by the way. If you see an officer doing something he shouldn't in the wrong place you will challenge him even though he may be known to you. It is an alertness test."

"More like a stupidity test," murmured my neighbour, "how the fucking hell did we ever win wars?"

We survived the guard duty and many more and found out that things were done very differently in the real army to what they were in the training camp.

We also found out that alertness saved lives.

Many governments thought that only the best was good enough for their soldiers. The British government always had it the other way round. Only the worst was bad enough. They thought it built character, resentment and meanness. It did but then you couldn't be critical if you turned it loose and sometimes a bad result happened. This is what occurred in Northern Ireland when they let loose the paras onto a demonstration behind which the cowards of the Provisional IRA were hiding, as usual. Of course the stone throwing, brick and petrol bomb throwing crowd made the usual propaganda protests when the army retaliated and the gullible media lapped it up as always. But turning the paras loose was way over the top.

The British Army is tough enough but you certainly don't mess with the paras, marines or commandos.

They are not a police force they are a fighting force.

The paras should have been reprimanded, not condemned, the commander who gave the order was the person responsible and in the wrong. The demonstrators, in all fairness, should also share some responsibility but heaven forbid that would ever happen.

It reminded me of Malaya when after the location of a terrorist camp was identified the CO gave the order to go in to the British captain of a company of Ghurkas. The captain hesitated. The CO asked what was wrong, wouldn't his men go?

Oh they'll go alright, but they'll get all fired up and I'm not sure when I can get the little buggers back, was the reply.

The paras are like the Ghurkas, don't let 'em loose unless you are prepared for a big result.

Alertness on its own doesn't always pay off. It should be accompanied by intelligence. Stories abound of men on guard duty shooting at shadows, cows and birds, absolutely certain of being under attack. One incident led to a patrol in Kenya, under temporary canvass in the bush, being roused out in the middle of the night scampering to safety leaving their weapons behind in the panic. They regained their courage, charged back bravely into their camp to overpower the enemy and recover their weapons only to find it occupied by a herdsman driving his wandering cows back to the pastures where they belonged. This incident should have remained buried and unknown except that a couple of the lads let it out in the NAAFI later over a few too many beers. Maybe just a drunk's story.

We did guard depots in the UK which had been identified as possible targets by the IRA and others. In these circumstances we were issued with five live rounds but were under orders not to fire unless instructed to do so by an officer. We were supposed to be re-assured by the fact that we were re-enforced by a security picket armed with pickaxe handles.

Can you just imagine being attacked by intruders, asking them to hang on while you looked for an officer, who would then wait for a guy with a pickaxe handle to turn up? Yeah!

Now the Provisional IRA were cowardly sods, not real fighters, just assassins and murderers, mainly of innocent unarmed people but they weren't stupid. Far from it.

Theirs was not the old heroic justified fight for Irish freedom that had gone before but a cynical slide into a peaceful protest made justifiably against protestant stupidity, stubbornness and prejudice in the north.

They knew and took advantage of the fact that Britain zealously guarded its law of not allowing the general ownership of weapons, nor the carrying of them in public. So they knew that by and large Britain was barren territory if they wanted to secretly stock up on weapons and ammo in a big way.

They usually went elsewhere.

Mainly to the gullible Americans who were suckers for the soft sell and whose government's foreign policy seemed to have been for years to support the mass murderers ruling underdeveloped countries.

The IRA got from the Americans funding and support to enable them to continue murdering innocent men, women and children who were supposed to be their long term friends and allies.

Some friends.

Now the world faces new enemies who employ the same tactics.

The same murders, provocations and demonstrations resulting in retaliation is almost always condemned by the same old gullible media who only ever scratch the surface before moving on to the latest headlines.

Guerrilla warfare against a superior enemy army is understandable. Intentional cowardly attacks on innocent civilians is not.

To paraphrase the words of the song :-

"Where have all the young men gone,

Gone for soldiers, every one,

Where have all the flowers gone long time passing

When will they ever learn, when will they ever learn."

Perhaps they have learnt.

Because they use unmanned drones. These are terribly unpopular with the enemy. They are not regarded as sporting or fair by an enemy who doesn't know the meaning of the words, who employ tactics of making people feel unsafe but moan when made to feel unsafe themselves. There is a huge difference between employing tactics against an enemy in which there may be accidental civilian casualties and deliberately targeting innocent men, women and children in order to spread terror.

Yet again the media seem ignorant of the fact.

Who would want to be on guard duty?

Friendship

We were into overseas training. We had completed basics, passed out and were now being brought up to combat fitness. This was to last for four weeks.

Whatever had gone before was kid's stuff. Everything was done at the double, even going to meals or the lavatory.

Route Marches were much longer and done on the run, assault courses were more formidable and were timed. We had to accurately map read and assess the terrain.

We were made to abseil down cliff faces and haul ourselves up again with packs on our backs loaded with house bricks.

We learnt street by street and house to house clearance.

We assaulted beaches from every kind of craft imaginable, dumped into quite deep water and were expected to scramble out fully loaded under fire.

We learned to go without sleep, go hungry and thirsty without any drop in performance. We snatched sleep where we could and grabbed food at every opportunity. It was a bad idea to be distracted when there was food about. If you didn't keep your hands and eyes on it then it would swiftly disappear.

We conducted rookies on their training route marches, running up and down the columns, carrying their kit or assisting the exhausted into trucks and then running back up to the front again. Those that still managed to keep their wits about them looked on us as though we came from outer space. It was all they could do to survive and there we were acting as though it was child's play.

It didn't help to tell them that we were the same as them just a few short months ago. They were horrified to think what they had to do to get like us!?

We were doing miles on the road or over rough country either in disciplined formations or attacking supposed enemy positions.

We learned to keep moving under shell fire and not to be too disturbed by the concussions from the explosions. Although not directly fired at we had to try to ignore the weapons going off around us in all directions so as not to get disorientated.

We passed out comfortably and were relaxing in the NAAFI waiting to receive our leave passes and further orders the next day.

Two of our mates from Newcastle were playing snooker and we all had small private bets on the outcome. We should have been relaxed but the training had really wound us up.

There was a dispute over a foul shot and fists were flying. That was bad enough but the two Newcastle Lads started on each other with the snooker cues. When the RP's sorted it out one had lost an eye and the other had been so badly jabbed in the throat he couldn't talk.

They were both medically discharged after coming so far. What a tragic waste of time and training.

Hot and Cold

We had done the land, sea and air bit when some bright spark in the war office decided we should do hot and cold as well.

The hot part was not performed in a hothouse in Kew Gardens neither was the cold bit done by swimming in the North Sea.

We were given a strong dose of the real thing.

We soon found out that hot and cold were more dangerous than land, sea and air.

The jungle was a strange place. It had a life of it's own that countless natives and animals had blended into over hundreds of years learning to survive in spite of each other. Life was not idyllic. Disease and danger were rampant, women in labour and young children being especially susceptible. There seemed to have been agreement that differences should be settled, maybe with a great deal of noise and menace, but certainly with as little actual bloodshed as possible. It would take civilisation to change all that.

We were civilised.

We had more and more injections and took more and more tablets. Compulsory were salt tablets. Nobody died of blood pressure because of them!

Jesus we leaked sweat like buckets. We drank beer, the officers had their gin and tonics. We had to avoid dehydration and they had to protect themselves from malaria. Whatever the reason none of us actually caught it.

We were bitten though, so much that sometimes it was difficult to see our dirty white skin under the masses of red bumps. Perhaps they all cancelled each other out.

We learned to hack it, crack it and fight barely visible targets at close quarters amidst chaos.

We got foot rot, gut rot and any other kind of rot going. When we finished we were shagged out and we hadn't even had to fight an enemy.

We longed for the cold.

Big mistake.

We weren't going to play snowballs or make cute friendly snowmen.

We were going to where it was cold enough to freeze the balls off those brass monkeys.

Somehow we managed to hang onto our balls but only just. It was so cold that nothing moved, except us.

We crossed country on skis, shuffling along in white camouflage, and shot at targets miles away. We weren't too much in love with our skis until we fell flat on our faces with snow shoes.

The army had it's own way of making a point.

They had to be sure that we really understood that it was cold.

We were on the range in sub zero conditions, wearing white thermal clothing, gloves and dark glasses. Our kit was ultra protected as we were.

Suddenly the order came to remove our gloves.

No one moved. We weren't crazy.

But the army was.

Off came our gloves so that we could feel how bad it would be if we lost them.

Right, got that.

Then came the order to fire five rapid rounds at the target. The quicker the better so that gloves could go back on.

We respectfully pointed out that the metal on our weapons was freezing so that our hands could freeze and stick to it.

We were told that as we were geniuses enough to work that out then we would certainly be clever enough to work out a way round it. If we didn't and we suffered injury then we would not only fail but would be charged with self mutilation!

We did work out how to fire by somehow grasping the wood stock only but we were not very accurate and we had battered shoulders from the recoil.

We passed.

After that none of us complained about the weather in Britain.

Well not for a while anyway.

The NAAFI

We were taking a bit of time out on maneouvres when we were assembled and marched into a large tent and told to sit down and shut up.

As usual the rumours spread immediately.

This was not an exercise but the real thing as the Russians had really invaded. We were going to be briefed on a top secret overseas mission, that's why we were in a tent out in the wilds. We were going to get a bollocking as we were crap under fire and last but not least the evergreen. National Service was over and we were being sent home.

The mystery only intensified when two stiff upper lipped gentlemen in civilian clothes took their places up front. My god, we thought, it was MI5. Who was the spy amongst us? We all looked at each other suspiciously.

The Colonel entered. We stood up and sprang to attention.

We were told to sit at ease.

One or two took that too literally and got shouted at for slovenly behaviour.

The Colonel nodded to the Adjutant.

"Men," he said seriously, "the Army takes care of its own and the NAAFI takes care of the Army. This is Mr. Lewis of the NAAFI to tell you all about it."

Mr. Lewis coughed, smiled, and said in an over articulated upper class accent, "The NAAFI is a nonprofit making organisation. We provide support of everyday needs to all the services no matter where they may be. Whatever you want, be sure the NAAFI will have it." Here he paused and chuckled.

No one else did.

He coughed and carried on.

We'd all been to the NAAFI, knew what it was and did. We also knew how desperate we were for women because most of us had tried to chat up the NAAFI shop girls. Even though they were a rough lot we didn't get anywhere. They always said that they were saving themselves for the officers or senior NCO's.

Whatever it was they were saving we didn't think it was worth it!

The man droned on. We didn't even notice when the other guy took over in an attempt to liven up the proceedings.

He failed but we wanted him to carry on as sitting comfortably being bored in a tent was preferable to charging around pretending to be dead.

None of us were impressed. The NAAFI shops operated normal retailers hours which were nine to six on weekdays, half day Thursday and closed on Sunday. This was as much use to us as a hole in the head because we were on the go in training from six in the morning to eleven at night every day. The bar and recreation room was open late but we never made it.

The only ones of us who saw the inside of the NAAFI were those who lived too far away to take a 36hr pass. We used them to get necessary stocks of toothpaste and boot polish etc. for us.

What really tickled us was the fact that this presentation was made while we were on maneouvres. No matter what hour or in what state we finished anywhere in the world there was the Salvation Army van providing tea, buns, warmth and comfort. No signs of the NAAFI.

All of us have had the greatest respect for the Sally Ann ever since.

They really are incredible people. They are gentle, soft and naive yet go into the roughest toughest places to help and sell their Watch Tower news sheet yet never try to convert or preach unless invited.

In my day anyone who offered a threat to a Salvation Army girl put his life in jeopardy. I am told that times have changed.

Maybe one day they will change for the better.

Over the years the organisation of the NAAFI underwent a transformation. It became big business. The old shops became more like supermarkets and department stores and their buyers became quite important players in the market. During the years of my active employment I came into contact with NAAFI executives and found them to be as dedicated and professional as most others.

They had definitely lost their stiff upper lip Old Public Schoolboy amateur approach.

What their role is in today's shrinking military expenditure with so much more competition I just don't know. My military service years are long, long gone.

A Question of Identity

Ladysmith Barracks, Ashton-u-Lyne, was just down the road about ten or twelve miles from Manchester. It was the training depot for the Manchester Regiment, the main Regimental Office being in Ardwick Green not far from Manchester City centre and London Road Railway Station.

The Barracks were old. The outside appearance was like a castle complete with moat and drawbridge, except the drawbridge had long been replaced by a sturdy immovable structure.

Just inside the gate on one side was the guardroom and on the other side were the quarters of the Regimental Police. The R.P.'s. A door and corridor inside led through to the cells.

Immediately past the gate was the large rectangular parade ground with a rostrum and flagpole on one of the long sides.

Surrounding the parade ground were a number of three story barrack rooms. One of the barrack rooms was reserved for the medics and the medical centre.

The whole lot was built in local greystone found all over the moors and gave everything a forbidding appearance even in Summer.

A turreted wall inside the moat encircled the lot.

There weren't too many of the regiment around, most of them were serving in Malaya. Those who were around were on the parade ground for an Identity Parade.

They were in three ranks spread two paces apart.

This particular day I was Orderly Sergeant so it was my job to host three young ladies, one pushing a pram and two highly pregnant, and escort them along the lines of apprehensive Squaddies.

These were the days before DNA so establishing parenthood was done on the basis of opportunity, resemblances, and blood group. Very hit and miss.

The Troops had good reason to be worried especially as one of the women was the camp bike.

I asked the girls if they wanted to go individually but they preferred to go in a group.

We set off. Having done a number of these parades I knew what was going to come.

The one pushing the pram had only gone a few paces when she stopped, pointed, and said, "it's 'im, defnally 'im. It's 'im awlrite."

I signalled to one of our RP's.

He came over and I told him to escort the lady outside the barracks.

"Sorry love," I said, "but this man has just come back from two years service in the Far East. Good try but goodbye."

She started to protest, demanding a second try!!??

No way, these woman weren't interested in finding the father who was usually a shiftless wanderer but just wanted to snap up a decent bloke with a long term job.

The two pregnant ones looked and learned. They put on serious expressions, giving the impression that they were focusing on the job in hand and would genuinely spot the "Daddy."

We proceeded with the farce.

One of the girls stopped in the second row. We at least had got that far which was unusual as they generally ran out of patience and made their pitch well before that.

She had picked out a fresh faced young man.

She was doubly sure it was him. Clever try as he had obviously not been in the Far East for two years. She was five months pregnant.

But he was a new recruit in training and had only come into Ashton seven weeks ago from Carlisle, miles away. Hadn't even had a leave yet.

Good try and again goodbye.

This left the camp bike.

Now I was nervous.

She was nicknamed Machine Gun Myrtle because she spit out men faster than bullets.

One of the Regimental Police came over and asked for a word.

He had recently been transferred from North Western Command in Chester and had been on inspection teams around the North. He must have been the only one who didn't know Myrtle personally.

However he had seen her—frequently.

He told me she had tried this same thing on at the East Lancashire Regimental Depot and even the Seaforth Highlanders and lately at the Military Police Camp at Mellonsfield. At each place she had named around a dozen possibilities before being asked to leave.

I went and told her the game was up and she couldn't waste any more of the Army's time.

She shrugged and asked if she could at least make a few dates before she left. Oh boy, what a gal!

Many years later I decided to take my family on a trip to see some of Dad's Army places. We managed to find our way out of Manchester on the right road after heading first for Rusholme, realising we were wrong, backtracking to Droylsden, finally getting it right and eventually crossing Ashton and climbing the hill towards Ladysmith.

I had an MGB sports car with a hard Bermuda top. I was crammed in it with my wife and three children. We were squashed but felt a sense of adventure. I couldn't wait to reach the guardroom. I roared across the bridge, through the gate, slowed for the guard, kept going and stopped on the parade ground.

The place was a deserted building sight.

After a few minutes workmen appeared out of a few holes in what had once been barrack rooms. I looked around. Almost the only things still standing were the walls and the gate. The guys looked at the hairy hippie and his family in amazement particularly when we all spoke with London accents.

I roared out laughing and shouted out, "where were you lot nearly twenty years ago, bloody hell we would have bought you some bevvies then? You really would have been popular."

They got it in one. They were all too young or had failed for different reasons to have served in the forces but were locals and really interested in what I knew. They remembered the parades by the regiment through Ashton on Remembrance Sunday.

No more unfortunately. The Manchesters had been absorbed into other units and Ladysmith was due to become a housing estate. I never went back to have another look. Some government cuts ran too deep.

After the end of the Second World War successive governments had committed to an economy guaranteeing full employment. At the same time they made conscription in the armed forces compulsory for two years full time and three years part time. This took a huge chunk out of the workforce which could not be filled by women who were able to find more and more lucrative positions allowing a degree of less rigid hours.

They no longer wanted to work in the archaic conditions in the mills of Lancashire.

So the owners brought in foreign workers. Many of them were women refugees from Eastern Europe and were very happy and grateful to be in England. They were used to a war torn and devastated Europe so found even a dismal recovering 1950's England quite a good place to be. They were accommodated in blocks of flats with subsidised rents and got regular pay packets every week.

They were not overpaid but they were oversexed. Well they seemed like it to us. Our girls rarely gave you any whereas they couldn't stop.

Consequently our healthy, fit, sex starved army lads gave them plenty of attention.

Too much it seemed. Nearly half the girls were pregnant. Some found husbands but most did not.

The mill owners complained to the Local Council who complained to the North Western Command Headquarters.

The orders came down from above. The women workers quarters were off limits and out of bounds to all military personnel.

The main job of handling it fell to the Military Police. They were overwhelmed by the task. They didn't have enough manpower to handle it on their own.

There were still dozens of Squaddies pouring in and out of the women's flats who had posted their own sentries to warn of the Police approach.

The MP's could not maintain round the clock enforcement so employed the tactic of surprise raids on different days at different times. The number of arrests increased but unfortunately so did the number of pregnancies. It was obvious that as they felt more insecure and harassed the lads and lasses dispensed with the delays involved in birth control. So the MP's enlisted the aid of our Regimental Police and also our security guard pickets.

When Orderly Sergeant I sometimes attended the raids.

This maneuver backfired. Alerting the security picket in the barracks was as good as letting the whole world know.

Of course there were few domestic telephones and no handphones in those days but somehow word always got through usually just as we arrived. As soon as we were cordoning off the area and the blocks of flats, doors, windows and gates flew open and men appeared all over the place. They were running like mad, some dressed, some not, and some trying to get into their trousers urged on by shouts of encouragement from their girlfriends who managed to hurl insults at us at the same time.

Those who were sensible had girlfriends on the ground floor. They usually escaped. Those on the higher floors got caught unless they took the chance and jumped, risking injury, or had escape ropes to slip down.

Whether we caught a lot or not didn't really matter to us. We loved the spectacle which gave a new meaning to coitus interuptus.

Eventually we slowed down the pregnancies and the owners later moved the girls to another district.

Spoilsports!

However we heard that the girls were happy as they could trap more husbands among the civilian population than they could from the army.

Orderly Orders

I was convalescing in a recruitment camp in the north of England. That was how the army gave you a rest after combat duties, wounds and injuries. As it had a substantial guardhouse and prison cells it also served as a holding unit for prisoners awaiting court martial. Most of the prisoners were really hard guys without a shred of conscience or decency. Probably ideal military material if controlled but the lot we got were well beyond control. They needed a spell in the Glasshouse in Colchester to slow them down. No one came out of Colchester the same no matter how many Elstree Studio films were made about the heroic rebellious prisoners.

As Orderly Sergeant the prisoners were one of your many responsibilities for 24 hours. The day commenced with the changing of the guard, always a big performance, followed by meal inspections, hospital visits and checks on the general running, security and cleanliness of the camp.

The first problem was the Orderly Officer. We all dreaded the Hooray Henry Rupert type or a second lieutenant. Especially a National Service one who always looked and felt like a fish out of water.

Give us a seasoned captain any time.

The Ruperts and 2nd Looeys were so inexperienced, self conscious, intense and serious and demanded no deviance from the book.

At meal times we went around tables asking for comments or complaints with us naturally standing behind the officer making negative faces to discourage any would be moaners. A captain would make sure we were standing in his line of sight. This lost me a few extra breakfasts at the cookhouse.

Still we were well fed and pampered in the Mess.

This particular day, a Sunday, started badly. The Orderly Officer was a young eager beaver, a newly graduated Sandhurst Military Academy Graduate indoctrinated with the firm belief that he was born to lead. I was already pissed of enough as it was drawing a weekend guard duty but to have a duff officer as well was just about the limit.

He interfered with the inspection of the new guard as I prepared them for his walk around. He referred to the men as chaps, was overbearing and patronising, and told them in a Hooray Henry voice that they had better shape up. I noticed the change in body language and expressions of the guard and thought oh oh. He thought I was too insulting and used unnecessary violent language. I deferred to him of course.

However I told the corporal that I would see to him later for presenting the officer with an inferior turned out guard.

After the breakfast inspection and camp patrol, we checked on the set up of the security pickets, fire pickets and general duties. I told the errant corporal that he was taking charge of the security picket night watch.

Then came the guardhouse, regimental police and the prisoners.

Everything seemed in order but the Provost Marshall was jumpy. While the officer was showing off relating to the RP "chaps" he took me on one side and told me that he was worried about this batch of prisoners.

There was apparently a multiple murderer, several hardened criminals, two deserters and a subversive barrack room lawyer. That was the current opinion anyway. Whether they were actually guilty of all that goodness only knows.

So far it had been okay because the previous two Orderly Officers had been Captains accompanied by tough sergeants.

He was worried about my officer. So was I!

We went to check on the prisoners. The first few were routine, "Attention! Orderly Officer present. Any complaints? Everything in order? Treatment and food acceptable? Right, carry on, at ease."

Next up was the murderer.

He was chained. Able to move but shackled to the wall.

As soon as the cell door was opened I saw horror on the face of the second lieutenant.

"This is barbaric, positively mediaeval," he exclaimed obviously outraged.

"So is the prisoner sir," I explained.

"Who ordered this, tell me that?" he asked.

"The CO sir," I replied.

His jaw dropped, was about to accuse me, thought better of it, and instead sensibly asked, "do you know why?"

"The Colonel doesn't want an incident on this base while holding such a dangerous man sir. Orders have come through that this man must be shackled and watched 24 hours a day as he has escaped twice and caused grievous bodily harm while on the loose. Frankly sir I wouldn't just chain him, I'd break his legs as well, that'd slow him down."

He looked at me with some disdain and attempted to regain control.

"Tell me, you there, have you any complaints?"

"Yes General, this lot 'ere won't let me have my regulation exercise, they don't know nuthin." he moaned.

"Sergeant, this man must have exercise, why hasn't he had exercise?"

"Because he's chained up sir," I said as patiently as I could, "and I cannot go against CO's orders sir."

This stopped him, he shrugged, muttered, "jolly bad show," and we moved on, but not before I threw the prisoner a glance that said I will be back to see to you later.

The next guy who was charged with multiple bigamy, theft and violence complained that he was High Church Anglican and we wouldn't let him go to Church.

"See to it sergeant," said my officer.

Oh I would see to it all right.

I asked the guard corporal to find out the times of all the services at the nearest High Church.

The barrack room lawyer knew his rights sure enough. He was a Communist who had been recruiting military personnel to apply to go and serve in Germany and then defect to Russia. In the 1950's this was very bad timing. He complained that his cell was too small, his mattress uncomfortable and the heating was too low. He was cold all the time.

Okay, we could fix that.

"What next?" I thought.

It wasn't long in coming.

We opened up the next cell to find the prisoner holding his stomach and moaning.

"Right," I shouted, "I've had enough with you lot. I'm up to my eyes in bullshit. Stand up and stand to attention in front of an officer."

"Can't sir, it's me stomach I'm afraid. I need a special diet 'cos of me religion. The cookhouse grubs not good for me," he said, grimacing all the time. I looked at the officer and said very respectfully, "do you mind if I have a word in private with this prisoner sir? I just want to get a few medical details and they might be unsavoury."

The officer looked a bit puzzled but went along with it.

I told the Provost to shut the door, I would be out shortly.

The Provost said afterwards that he had heard quite a rumpus going on before I came out again.

I emerged with a sympathetic look on my face.

"What's happened sergeant, how is he?" asked the 2nd Looey.

"He's okay sir, just wanted to make sure he had stomach trouble and needed a Doctor."

"And does he?"

"He certainly does now sir. We'll call one right away."

We moved on to the last but one occupied cell.

"This one's a slimy shit sir. He goes with prostitutes, leads them on, beats them up and steals their money. When he was arrested he asked the girls to be witnesses in his defence!"

"Good lord, let's take a look at him," said the lieutenant.

We did.

He jumped up to attention.

"Right then my man, everything tickety boo with you, no complaints I gather."

"No sir."

"Right good, carry on, at ease."

"Just one thing sir,"

"Oh right, yes. What is it?"

"I could do with more exercise, it gets boring just walking round and round this cell all day, every day," he said in a persecuted tone.

I rolled my eyes up, surely even this rookie officer would realise that he's taking the piss.

"See to it sergeant, that's what the army thrives on, fresh air and exercise."

"Right sir, will do. Have you noted everything down orderly corporal?"

"Yes I have orderly sergeant," I wasn't worried about the last inmate. He was trying to work his ticket by virtue of insanity and it wasn't working so he was almost genuinely going barmy trying to convince the doctors that he was really off his rocker.

We opened up.

I shouted, "Attention! Orderly Officer present."

He didn't move.

I rushed over and bellowed in his ear at the top of my voice, "on your bloody feet now you stupid git."

That got him up.

"Was that necessary sergeant," asked the officer doubtfully.

"Yes sir, he acts daft but he ain't deaf as you can see. He never wants anything, just to get out of the Kate. Seems to me sir that we're the mad ones to stay in and he's the sane one to want out."

"Hermmmm, yes well, I don't know about that I'm sure," said the officer uncomfortably, "is that the lot? Have you noted everything sergeant? I'll leave it all in your capable hands."

"Fine, we'll action everything after we finish off the rounds here. Are you done sir?"

"Yes Sergeant, jolly good show, carry on. I will check up later."

He went.

I ran like blazes to the Sergeants mess. It was a Sunday and luckily only a few were on leave. I got as many as possible rounded up at the Guardhouse.

First off was the Anglican. He was escorted handcuffed between two guards to every service the church held including the Young Mothers Counselling Group and the kid's Sunday School. We rotated the guards as we didn't want them to get soft with too much religion.

By Evensong he was begging to be let off and by Midnight Mass he was screaming for mercy. He had not had time for food and he had not had a minutes peace as all the Church goers were sure that they could make him repent.

He repented all right. He was sorry he had ever opened his mouth.

He wasn't the only one.

The barrack room lawyer was given an extra mattress that we told him had not been deloused and the heating was turned up so high that he stripped down to his vest and shorts and was still sweating. He didn't stop scratching for days even though the mattress was perfectly clean.

The guy with the stomach problem wisely declined medical aid and we gave the slimy joe so much exercise that he collapsed.

We had him running round the drill square for an hour. If he slackened off we told him he would just have to stay out longer until he had completed the number of laps we had in mind. We didn't tell him what we had in mind.

We let him settle down in his cell for a short while then just as he was about to sleep or relax we would barge in shouting, "regulation exercise," and off he would go again.

I showed the accused murderer that he could get an amazing amount of exercise while still chained up when trying to dodge my kicks.

By the next day the camp had got the message.

When there are seasoned sergeants around don't take the piss out of junior officers.

We were in the local pub one evening when an elderly well dressed man came up and asked if we were from the base.

He told us that for our information one of our officers was in a spot of bother. Not acting correctly or something. This guy owned several service stations and repair shops and the officer owned a spritely red MGA sports car. Did we know him?

We did.

He told us to tell the officer to remove his bloody car from his workshop and pay his bills, it was not a bloody corporation car park. The car had been there for five weeks.

We explained we were mere minnows and couldn't tell an officer anything. They were supposed to know it all already.

Apparently it didn't matter as the man was a member of the local town council liaison committee and had met our Colonel and the Adjutant recently. A short while later the officer was transferred.

The Officer was on his bike complete with MG sports car.

He was the Second Lieutenant Hooray Henry with a double barrel name and his arrogant ignorance stood out a mile.

A couple of months later it was the turn of the Sergeants' Mess to entertain the Officers' Mess. The Officers enjoyed this twice yearly event rather than when they entertained us as they could let their hair down more when playing away. Besides which they always claimed that the Sergeant's wives were prettier and funnier than their own. It was obviously a part of Sandhurst training to try and knock off other ranks wives if possible.

They were just being ultra polite as some of the wives were indeed pretty but others were right old battle axes.

I was a member of a small group chatting away to the CO and the Adjutant when the Adjutant looked at me and asked, "by the way, was it you Hayes who said that we were the mad ones to stay in and he was the sane one to want out?"

We all knew straight away what he was talking about.

I replied hesitantly, "yes sir, guilty I'm afraid."

"And is that the prevailing philosophy in the sergeants mess these days?" he smiled.

"Of course Major,"

"Thank god for that," exclaimed the Colonel, "good to know that all is still well in the mess."

The Crime of the Century
(The case of the Brewer's tray)

Ashton-under-Lyne was not a hot bed of crime. Nearly 100% were solid, decent, ordinary people so the local police force was hardly stretched.

A few rowdies after closing time on weekends was as near as it would get to hooliganism, you could walk the streets in safety and most doors were unlocked.

The lads in the Manchester Regiment were mostly locals and didn't want to tear up the town.

We were in a local pub one night when I got lucky. A girl actually fancied me and wanted me to walk her home.

I went.

I left two of my mates behind.

I was not there to witness the crime of the century.

It was part of the culture to collect suitable mementos for the sergeants mess and Barry had taken a shine to a tin tray, covered in Brewer's adverts. Just the job he thought.

We were in civvies so as he was leaving he stuffed it inside his raincoat and on the walk back to the barracks he wrapped his arms around it from the outside. It was a cold night.

All went well until he was crossing the main square. He rounded a corner and nearly bumped into a police sergeant on patrol with a policewoman.

"Whoops," said Barry, and opened up his arms to apologise.

The tin tray clattered to the ground.

Barry bent down, picked it up, stuffed it inside his coat again, looked a bit sheepish, nodded and walked on.

"Ello, ello, ello, wot 've we 'ere then? came the voice of the police sergeant behind him. Mr. Plod sensed he was on the trail of a master criminal.

Barry was detained, taken to the police station, charged and asked to make a statement. He did and asked for me.

A phone call to the guardroom got me scurrying down to the cop shop.

My walk home had been just that. A walk home, a quick snog and then her mum's loud voice telling her to get inside.

I was received most politely by the desk sergeant and asked to wait. I did.

I took up a position close to two policewomen who were discussing the latest military case in hushed awed voices. I leaned closer. What top secret military case was this? Ladysmith Barracks would be agog if I could get hold of this bit of juicy gossip.

Then it slowly dawned on me. They were talking about Barry and the tin tray.

I couldn't help it. I burst out laughing, pointing at the two women and indicating to the desk sergeant that I couldn't believe my ears.

They had been saying that Barry had smuggled out stolen goods and tried to sneak them past a police crime patrol.

If this was how it was being over dramatically presented now what would it look like in the morning if the local press got hold of it?

This was ridiculous.

I asked Dixon of Dock Green to come over and sort out these two birds.

Before he could do so the publican came in, saw me and said, "what's all this about then? Someone saying I was serving you after hours or what?"

"No Dave, Barry took a fancy to one of your Brewers trays, liked the decoration, thought it would look good in the Sergeants Mess and volunteered it for military service."

"Oh great, looks good does it?" he asked with a grin.

"It never got that far, he dropped it in front of what they're trying to make out was a regional crime squad patrol. They reckon it's worth a tenner and he stole it. They're charging him." I declared.

"What! It's a freebie from the Brewery, no value, they replace 'em after a while anyway and we just chuck away the old'uns. Great that it was finding a home." he said.

"Well it's not, it's stuck 'ere," I told him, "it's evidence."

"Look officers," Dave said sternly, "I served in the Manchesters. If anything of mine finds a place in the Sergeants Mess then it's fine by me. It's a gift. Barry didn't have to ask, so can we all go home to bed now? He probably dropped it because he'd had a few over the top."

The police looked dumbstruck. It seemed as if the arch criminal Barry was going to slip through their fingers.

They were rescued when a uniformed Inspector arrived.

He bustled in full of self importance, stick in one hand and a note in the other.

We listened as he waved the note around demanding details.

After listening intently, he turned round, looked us up and down, asked what we were doing there and came to the conclusion that we should leave.

No way, Dave and I were not budging.

He appeared shocked. Someone was disputing his authority. He tried to invoke the full majesty of the law.

Dave told him to get off his fucking high horse and show a grain of commonsense. If he persisted in spite of Dave's statement then the police would look absolute pratts in court.

Inspector Clueless didn't care.

Barry was going to court.

He was represented by the Regiment's Adjutant.

Dave was great. He gave his evidence clearly and fairly. The Adjutant claimed that Barry was a bit hazy from the booze and merely took the tray before permission was given and would have returned it if Dave had objected.

The magistrates concluded that there was no real case to answer and reprimanded the police for wasting the court's time and public money.

There had been two burglaries that night, one close to the main square that were still unsolved probably because the police were concerned with more trivial matters. The magistrates were not amused.

They told Barry to behave himself in the future and dismissed the case.

The police did look like pratts which is what always happens when common sense and discretion fly out of the window and egos take over.

We were told later by some mates in the Manchester Police that if it had happened in their city then they would have given Barry a lift home complete with tray after a few pints in compensation.

Self-Defence

Self defence is a much overstated art form. It is not possible to catch bullets in your mouth, dodge them or knock them aside when fired from a weapon outside of movies. Those who believed it died.

Humans cannot run up the side of buildings, leap across roofs or hang upside down from ceilings. Those who tried fell flat on their backs or damaged other vulnerable parts.

Unarmed combat, and bayonet practice are little use against a machine gun.

To survive you don't just need skill and experience you need luck. A lot of it no matter how tough you are.

I read about a judo champion who boasted that he feared nothing nor no one.

There was one very stupid person.

If you were a sergeant then you had to enforce discipline and that meant that your actions were sure to arouse resentment somewhere along the way. Sometimes that resentment festered into a craving for revenge.

If the aggrieved was smart he would wait with four or five of his mates until one night when you were a bit pissed and alone walking in a deserted area.

It would happen but not often.

When jumped like that you just knew you were in for a right seeing to no matter how good you were.

The most you could do was put up a fight and get in a bit of punishment and do some damage to the opposition while being done over.

But! Being a sergeant had its advantages. Sergeants took parade every morning.

The trick was to rip an ear, split a nose and tear a mouth as severely as possible. No bruises or black eyes, those could easily be explained away and didn't need medical treatment.

The other injuries did and would stand out next morning on parade. Gotcha!

A real going over in the guardroom worked wonders.

The word soon got around.

Reputation was the best form of self defence.

On Leave

A 36hrs leave pass was barely long enough to put your bag down, say hello to Mum and Dad, have a cup of Ovaltine, sleep, enjoy a breakfast and say goodbye.

Consequently a 48hrs pass seemed like heaven.

Home by Friday night, out with the lads on Saturday. No problem.

Except there was.

You weren't on the circuit anymore.

Parents and neighbours were fine.

Your old mates were not. They had forgotten you, had got used to being without you.

So you had to go around humbly investigating and asking to be included.

Hardly the actions of a returning hero.

Embarrassing actually.

You were glad to be out of uniform and wear some of your old clothes from your wardrobe.

The first question you were asked was why you weren't in uniform, the second was why were you nearly bald.

One guy had been watching too much tele and said in what he thought was a Sergeant Major's voice, "am I hurting you laddie, I should be. I'm standing on your hair?" They all roared out laughing and wondered why I didn't join in.

If only they knew.

I couldn't tell them that it was a very old joke and no soldier would think it funny anyway.

One or two did ask how I was and how it was in the Kate (Kate Karney—Cockney rhyming slang for army) but started talking to some one else before I could answer.

They weren't interested. Those who failed the medical felt guilty and those who were waiting to go in did not want to hear the horror stories. They would find out soon enough. Nothing could describe it anyway.

We were sitting in the local pub, getting a few in, and sinking a few more, when one of the girls in the group noted that I wasn't saying much and appeared out of it.

She came over, wriggled herself in beside me and introduced herself.

She said quietly, "I'm not pushing but you don't fit. I haven't seen you around. Are you new or something?"

"No, I'm not new, I'm local but I'm army." I replied.

"Where's your girlfriend then, I bet you've got one?" she probed.

"Nah, no one in the Army has a girlfriend, we all got letters. You can't trust a silly young girl, out of sight out of mind. As soon as you've gone so have they. Bye bye Johnny bye bye." I said harshly.

She was taken aback, leaned her head on one side and said, "oh, I see, sorry" I spoke, and moved away in a huff.

Man oh man I could certainly pull a bird all right, pull them completely the wrong way.

She spoke to a couple of friends who looked over at me, then looked down and away. Not a good sign I thought.

A little while later one of the other girls came across, shooed away my friend sitting next to me and sat down very close. She looked at me intently and gently.

"Oh oh, here comes the sympathy vote," I thought, "do I want sympathy or what? Yeah, I do. Okay then give it to me."

She did.

She was very curvy, almost chubby, but not quite. She had a round open face, lightly made up and short brown hair showing traces of red. She was wearing a blue blouse, the same colour as her eyes, with a ruffle down the front hiding the buttons.

"Damn," I thought, "if I get lucky that ruffle is going to make me bungle the smooth move I'd love to make on her tits. Where the hell are the buttons?"

I lost a bit of her conversation worrying about that.

She was sorry to hear of my bad experience. "Not all girls are like that. Most are steady, want a boyfriend and hope to get married and have a baby."

"In that order?" I thought.

"Slow down girl," I said, "most of the fellas I know met some one else's girlfriend, made her pregnant and were marched down the aisle by her family. Married, game set and match. Like an Indian arranged marriage really. They got to know one another later."

She giggled. She was great. She had a sense of humour.

We talked.

She had a brother in the army.

"Wow, great, where is he stationed?"

"Colchester!"

Silence.

"Yeah? So? What is he there, is he an MP, a guard or what?"

"No, he deserted. He did a runner while in Germany. He thought he was running to Switzerland but ended up in Denmark. He was sentenced to three years in the Glasshouse."

I winced and went, "ooomph."

"Why? Is that bad? Is it bad in there?" she asked tentatively.

I thought for a while. How to handle this.

It was bad to get on the wrong side of the army for a start but to end up in Colchester was the baddest side of bad.

I had escorted prisoners on two occasions to Colchester. They were real hard cases but even they were nervous about going and at the hand over they looked back at me almost pleadingly.

Just standing in the receiving areas made your hair stand on end. You felt apprehensive and wanted to leave as quick as possible.

One Provost looked at me and said, "right you are, sergeant, we know all about this one, he's been here before. He's ours now. We'll make sure he won't be back again."

He was trying to be friendly but it didn't come across. He was a hard, hard man handling the toughest of the tough and he was never going to lose.

How could I even begin to explain it to this girl who would tell her family the bad news and who were all naturally already worried stiff.

I told her that although it would be tough her brother would be okay if he was mentally strong and would come out a different person. Oh boy, he would be a different person for sure.

I told her that being in the army was a hard life but a fair one.

I lied!

She asked me what I did. I told her I was a sergeant who bossed people around.

That seemed to be it. I had served my purpose. She lost interest.

That was how it was when you only made it home occasionally.

However as we were making a move she came over and said that it was early, she didn't fancy dancing, but wouldn't mind if I took her to the pictures.

We didn't call them movies, that was American and we didn't say cinema because that was upper class.

The main Picture Palaces were the Odeon, Granada, Gaumont and the ABC. The rest we called the Bug Hutch. They really were built like Grand Palaces, regrettably doomed because of the TV revolution growing ever larger over the years. They ended their lives as Bingo Halls delighting hordes of old women with nothing else to do except yell out "bingo, house or line" and win a bit of cash.

The Palace of dreams turned into The End of all Hope.

We went to the Odeon to see John Wayne and joined the queue for the *one and nines. (one shilling and ninepence)*. This was for the upstairs seats and we would always go there when showing off to a bird. When you were with your mates you used to go downstairs for a *bob. (one shilling seats)*.

The girl kept on snuggling in and felt soft, warm and comfortable. That is until she turned round and moved in full frontal, pressing real close.

She was still soft, warm and comfortable but I wasn't. Peter had sprung smartly to attention and was boring a hole through my trousers and digging well into her skirt in exactly the right place between her thighs. She felt it all right and pressed back strongly.

I couldn't wait to get inside. I meant the cinema of course.

When we did we were groping and gasping all over the place completely oblivious of the tut tuts and oh dears from the people around us.

We left early. Probably just before being thrown out for going too far.

We were more or less in control on the bus but when we got off we were at it again.

It was summer and warm for a change so there weren't too many clothes in the way.

There was a small wood nearby so we headed for the trees. Once hidden from the road we threw caution to the winds. This was turning out to be an unbelievable leave. Definitely one to boast of in the mess over a few pints.

Her blouse was open, breasts kissed, fondled and bitten. Skirt was up and knickers were down. Peter was grasped in her hand being pulled and pushed all over the place. I loved it. She was wet and open.

She pulled me closer and breathed, "put him in, put him me in now."

I was nearly a goner when I pulled back.

"I can't," I said sadly, "I don't have a rubber johnny."

"That's all right, don't stop now, do it, do it, do it!" she cried out desperately.

There I was, in a wet dream situation without a durex.

"No, you'll get pregnant for sure, look at that, that's a baby maker," I said with weakening resolve, pointing to my rampant cock, on the verge of giving way.

Then she said it. She murmured, "don't worry, we can always get married, me mum won't mind."

Whoops, wrong answer.

I cooled off very quickly.

Peter drooped.

"Oh no, look at that, I've come already, I'm so so sorry." I said pulling my pants up before she could check.

She was stunned for a minute or two, then started to sort herself out. She didn't say a word.

We walked hand in hand in silence to her front door.

She looked at me and said, "when will I see you again? What are you doing tomorrow? You could buy a packet of johnnies and we could. You know??"

No way. This girl was very, very dangerous. She was capable of sabotaging the best that Durex had to offer.

I told her that I had to go back to my unit but I would see her on my next leave. We kissed and left it at that.

With the way the overseas wars were going my next leave was liable to be a long way off.

I then found I had a two hour walk home.

It was worth it though.

Marksmanship

All infantrymen had to qualify at least to the level of second class shots twice a year.

It meant frequent visits to the armorer and the shooting range.

I was left handed so I had a choice. Either I learned to handle weapons right handed or else I had to fire a rifle or sten gun left handed with a complicated over arm maneuver to action the bolt for reloading. This would take far too long a time to reload particularly with the enemy charging down on you.

I learnt to fire right handed!

The armorer worked on improving the accuracy of battle sights and adjustable sights on the rifles. This should have put everyone in with a shot of qualifying but unfortunately some could not hit what they were aiming at and others found it difficult to hit anything legitimate even at 100 yards.

If you were any good the final test was the 1,000 yard run down firing at a stationary target.

You fired five shots from the prone position at 1,000 yards then ran down to 500 yards, reloading as you ran. The standard issue .303 Lee Enfield Service Rifle took a five round magazine. It had the kick of a mule.

At 500 yards you fired another five shots from the prone position and ran down to 200 yards, reloading as you ran. Up to then you had used the adjustable sights. While running you switched to the basic battle sight and on reaching the 200 yards firing point you fixed your bayonet. This was to extend the focal length of your rifle and improve it's accuracy.

At 200 yards you fired five shots from the kneeling position and then finally at 100 yards you fired five shots standing up. That's if you could stand up when you reached there. Just trying to hold the weapon steady was difficult. It waved around all over the place. It was always a safe bet to stand well behind the person on the firing point.

After this came the bandit. These were a series of life size, life like cutouts of camouflaged enemy soldiers spread around the terrain who would pop up either singly or in pairs at irregular intervals. From 200 yards you had to hit them preferably in the kill zone.

Last of all were the sten gun for close range targets and also the Bren Gun (LMG—light machine gun) for longer range targets.

The sten gun was semi-automatic, you had to cock it first, but a bastard to use. It overheated, jammed and misfired regularly. You always seemed to be stripping it down rather than firing it.

The Bren was a stunner but difficult to judge your skill. It was so fast and accurate that you could easily put four or five shots through the same hole. Spraying your fire was difficult so it became an exercise in restraint. Squeeze and release was the order of the day.

When I was close to my demob date rumours circulated that a new foreign rifle was being tested to replace the Lee Enfield. It was an automatic and word was that it was the Belgium FN.

Before a shot was fired priorities had to be established, the main one being could the Guards Regiments drill with it outside Buckingham Palace.

Naturally we all found this to be ridiculous but it was typical of government and war department attitudes that have frankly lasted through to today. There are always genuine attempts and intentions to equip our troops with the best weapons but weird priorities frequently get in the way.

We were also amused that ordinary squaddies were subject to rationing when it came to the issuing of ammo, even on active service. This was difficult enough with single shot weapons. God only knows how it would work with automatic, rapid fire ones.

You could not and did not have unused live ammunition lying around anywhere. When it came to distribution the rounds were handed out as though they were gold dust and at the end of any action spare ammo had to be handed in, rifles opened for inspection and a declaration made that no rounds remained in your possession.

This seems ridiculous now when you see newsreel pictures of irregulars shooting dozens of rounds into the sky to show off in front of the camera.

Even so you never see disciplined troops doing such a thing.

We would have fought tooth and nail to get our hands on even half of the equipment that the modern soldier carries today but we probably would never have known what to do with it.

One thing for sure is we really did know our weapons. None of this fairy story stuff of commandos strolling in to a shed, deciding it was a Kalashnikov day, selecting that and various other bits and pieces and ambling over to a jeep that roars off spilling people all over the place who manage at the same time to wave smarmily to pretty girls.

If we had had a radio operator on active service who didn't know the correct co-ordinates and wavelengths and cocked up we would have shot him.

If we had been allowed to land on the wrong side of an island and lose lives plus a helicopter then heads would have rolled.

If intelligence had landed us in the wrong place at the wrong time with false information then they wouldn't have been viewed as intelligent for long.

There is just too much film and TV coverage that glamourizes and sensationalizes mundane activity and excuses poor performance.

We weren't the supermen of Book and TV legend, we were soldiers.

I virtually slept with my weapons and greatly prized the crossed rifles of markmanship on my sleeve plus other qualifications sewed on my uniform that I regrettably had to remove on promotion to sergeant.

The hand gun I was trained on and issued with was the Webley Revolver which we fired sideways on with the arm fully extended. There was no turret position then. We did present a smaller target but if hit then it was usually fatal. The most impressive handgun I fired over short distances was the .38 Smith and Wesson Police Special. Well the Yanks knew a thing or two about weapons didn't they?

I did develop tremendous respect for the old marksmen who fired those ancient flintlocks and percussion rifles. I fired one at Bisley, the mecca of British shooting, one day. I had to laugh at what appeared to be an age between squeezing the trigger and the round leaving the barrel. You could almost follow the passage of the ball down the range.

Those old guys not only hit what they aimed at but were amazingly accurate.

It is hard enough to hit a moving target at distance with a single shot high velocity rifle today but they could do it regularly with what we would regard as inferior weapons.

Respect is due.

Our bayonets were round spikes. They were more efficient when being removed from a body. The shape reduced the suction on withdrawal. This did not sound reassuring to us when we compared the relative lengths of enemy bayonets to ours but we were told that a few seconds could save our lives.

We could get ours in 'em and out of 'em that much quicker than they could and they didn't like it in 'em for a start. Neither did we actually but thought it better not to say so.

If you qualified as a high level marksman then you could be issued with a lighter weight Lee Enfield .303 calibre rifle which you were expected to love and cherish. It was always a bolt action single shot with a telescopic sight.

Sighting in was a very necessary performance. A tripod was hammered into the ground on the firing point and the rifle was clamped firmly and tightly in.

The range was 200 yards. Battle sights were the first to be tested. Test shots were fired and the armourer would adjust the foresight accordingly until the weapon fired true. The adjustable sights followed.

We were moved back to 500 yards and the telescopic sight was zeroed in.

The main sight was always narrow angle so that you had to have a smaller wider angle one set on top in order to search out the target area before fastening on the actual target itself.

After all that performance god help the person who either dropped or banged his weapon in any way.

Ammo could be special also. Powder would be weighed exactly, bullets would be pressed into perfect shape and detonators would come from the same production group.

This type of prowess could well be rewarded with a few extra beers in the mess.

Most sergeants would have several excellent platoons in a company, good tough soldiers who would stand firm and not panic. They could drill, achieve superb fitness and fight but there were always a few who could never qualify as 2nd class shots.

Just by coincidence we would always be practising on the range when a company was due to qualify and just by coincidence a few bulls would appear on a previously untouched target. The coincidences would be just enough to give qualification to some fortunate lads and would be just enough to get me a few extra pints from a grateful sergeant.

On one occasion a visiting officer told me not to push my luck. Our own officers would happily turn a blind eye.

Many of us developed additional specialist skills and had experiences which we had to put behind us when we went back into civvy street.

This took a bit of time.

Because my rehabilitation was interrupted by Suez and not completed it caused amusement and teasing later in life because if ever I became objectionable in any way it was attributed to my lack of retraining or detraining at the end of my full time service.

Respect

The Quartermaster Sergeant was an old WO 2 serving out his time. His name was Mcleod, a Scot.

He had served in the Second World War in the Far East.

He had two General Duty assistants, both were Geordies. They were just about fit for this but not much else. They were regulars, not conscripts, and so were entitled to higher rates of pay and privileges. This was a bone of contention with us and the two guys knew it.

They tried to take it out on Q Mcleod.

They would get things confused, get in a muddle and then blame it on what they called their poor instructions. Sometimes they were in the right because Q was very often confused himself.

Consequently the company stores were not well run.

It was inevitable that it would come to the attention of the Colonel even though loyal attempts were made in the Sergeants Mess to cover up and put things right.

The "Old Man" called in Regimental Sergeant Major Josephs and told him to get a grip. The RSM was not happy at that and if the RSM was not happy then for sure he was going to make everyone else unhappy.

He called a meeting of the Mess.

"For god's sake jock, what's going on?" he started in straight off, "this is not bloody funny. When it's so bad that it get's to the Old Man then we're up shit's creek. We should have stopped this before."

"Sorry John," said Mcleod, "it's those two wankers you gave me. Couldn't organise a piss up in a brewery. I need better support."

"Right, let's get 'em in to the office then," said the RSM.

They were ushered into the regimental office by a sergeant. They were looking very sheepish and overawed, There were two CSM's, five sergeants, Q McLeod and the RSM in attendance. It did have the appearance of a kangaroo court and they were right to be nervous.

"Right," said Josephs, "what gives with you two? Funny men are you? You think the army is some sort of comedy show or something? I've had my eyes on you two for some time. Shit skivers you two are. You get a soft number and cock it up."

"Sorry sir," said one of them," we'll put it right."

"I don't want you putting it right, I want you out. You've had your chance and you've blown it. I know Q is a bit old and slow but he's served the army well. He should be shown a bit of respect. In the war he was captured by the Japanese and severely tortured and beaten. What do you say to that?"

"It must have been on the fuckin' head sir!" said the Geordie.

Best Blues

W
e had returned from a week's leave after finishing some more specialist training. This time on leave I had taken a couple of mates from the sergeant's mess home with me. We had dressed in our best blues. I had taken a bit of illegal licence with the peak cap by sewing the sides down a little so as to give it more of a German Army Desert Officer's look. I was lucky to get past the Provost Sergeant Major at the guardhouse but I suppose a sergeant was entitled to a few favours and privileges.

We looked good, felt good and milked it for all it was worth.

On the train down to London people made way for us and at the bar where we spent most of our time. We had priority service.

One old guy, with twinkling eyes, saluted us, but we were brought down to earth when he told us we looked like Italian bus conductors. He told us it was a compliment as even Italian ticket collectors dressed in General's uniforms.

We told him it was style but he said it was bullshit.

We had taken an early train so that we intentionally arrived in broad daylight at Euston. On the London Underground and the Southern Railway commuter line we pretended nonchalance but soaked up the admiring looks. Well why not? We had been through some difficult combat. We didn't want to evoke the crap Hollywood sentimental scenes. That was for the Americans with their sweethearts, mom and apple pie. We were modest British soldiers but that didn't stop us showing off a bit or a lot if the truth be known.

We were young, fit and battle scarred. Apparently we were also smart enough to rival the Italian ticket collectors.

Mum closely examined me and appeared satisfied. Good job she hadn't seen me a couple of months earlier. In fact she hadn't seen me for months nor known where I was. A BAOP address was not much of a giveaway. Fortunately I was far too old for her to bathe me so she wouldn't see the scars. At that time they were still a little raw and sore.

There were two new pubs on the Council estate. There hadn't been any when I joined up. One of my mates came from Northumberland, a Geordie, and the other came from Guildford in Surrey. The Guildford guy had been a fairground booth fighter in civilian life but had volunteered for the regular army thinking it was a less dangerous profession. After Malaya, Kenya and Cyprus he wasn't so sure?!! We called him the gentle giant but in a fight he wasn't so gentle.

The Geordie was a steel worker, a conscript like me. Unlike me, when he was demobbed, he had had enough excitement so went suburban, married for life, stayed in the same job and lived in the same house.

In comparison I was a disturbed character, looking for change, taking risks, unsettled and experimenting with marriages. Well it takes all sorts.

We went to the local.

Again, unlike American films where the good old boys either hugged each other and sunk beers while checking their hunting rifles, or immediately started slugging it out in a king of the heap style fight, we knew nobody and nobody knew us.

European films are always an anti-climax compared to Hollywood.

We moved on.

Another local. Another dead loss.

We caught the bus to Eltham High Street.

My god when you've been away all over the place in the army, for months on end, home life seems so flat and boring. Some would say comfortable but I did not.

I didn't know it then but I was only destined to be home with my parents for a matter of a few months after I left the army.

We met up at last with a few of my old mates but the conversation was a bit stilted. They went to work each day, collected their wage packets, watched TV (early days black and white) had a few beers and chased girls. They had two weeks holiday in Margate and maybe a night out in Southend at the Kursaal. Wow!

They didn't really want to hear about our adventures in foreign lands and we didn't really want to tell them. We didn't know where to start. If we actually tried, and I had once or twice before, they thought we were showing off so it was best to let it lay. We pretended enthusiasm going along with their tales of macho daring do with some of the local "tarts" as they called them. They thought being exciting was drinking too much, falling over sick and getting into the odd punch up.

Yeah well! Pathetic.

Booth Fighter, however, warmed a bit to their tales of yah boo fights and just had to tell them of one Saturday night at Belle Vue Dance Hall. The band was Bill Edge and his boys. That night we had a scouser with us, called Pat of course, who had a rather dangerous sense of humour. We had warned him before setting out that we wanted a quiet night out with no trouble. If he didn't understand that then we would leave him behind. He re-assured us in all seriousness that he would be polite and agreeable.

All went well until a gang of local Teddy boys arrived. They were noisy and full of themselves, dressed a bit over the top, but not really troublesome.

Pat kept looking and wandering towards them but we kept heading him off.

Eventually he escaped us, went over to their leader and said very politely and agreeably, "hello darling, can I have the next dance?" He then equally politely and agreeably stepped back in surprise and said, "oh dear I am sorry I thought you were a girl." He then calmly walked away.

All seemed well for a while until we noticed that the gang had been strongly re-enforced and had blocked off the exits.

We were heavily outnumbered. We were certainly a lot tougher but there were not enough of us.

They moved towards us in force. We were not in the mood for negotiation and neither were they. We resented their unforgiving attitude and they wanted revenge.

We retreated and climbed up onto the stage. We motioned to the band to keep playing. We lined up. When they got close, Pat yelled, "Geronimo," at the top of his voice and we threw ourselves off the stage on top of the Teds.

It was an absolute shambles with everyone punching everyone else while we worked our way sideways to the fire exits. The band played on. A lot of the ordinary locals resented the Teddy Boys and had taken the opportunity to even a few scores.

By the time the police arrived we were long gone. The military police who had also been notified were mystified as the Teds were sure the army was involved but apparently no squaddies were there. We were sinking a few pints in a pub in nearby Longsight with Pat telling us every few minutes that he couldn't understand what all the fuss was about as he had gone out of his way to be polite and agreeable. Pat had one more furore at the Tower Ballroom in Blackpool which went terribly wrong for him when the bouncers became involved. When he came out of hospital he was posted overseas for safety.

I smiled across expectantly at my friends who had gone quiet. Nothing!!

So Geordie started to tell them of Asian brothels with luscious girls who really loved you and everyone else and could boom boom all night long. Then he really got going with his story of one of our sergeants who had just been demoted to the ranks yet again.

He had fallen in love with a Hong Kong night club hostess, a real beauty and couldn't stay away. The problem was she gave him a dose of syphillus. He was demoted while being cured, re-promoted afterwards but kept going back again and being re-infected. This time he had not only been demoted but posted back to the UK. He had deserted and was arrested in Liverpool trying to work a passage back to Hong Kong.

He was busted to private and was receiving psychiatric treatment as well as a cure for the clap.

He was up for re-evaluation as he had told the military psychiatrist that he would be insane if he didn't try to get back to Hong Kong. The girl may have been diseased but she was the most fantastic fuck ever.

He was due for a medical discharge. There was a rumour that the medical report stated that he should be discharged as it was better he wasted his own time and money on this fantastic fuck rather than the Army's.

My mates were open mouthed. Nothing like that happened on Council Estates. They were uncomfortable and we had lost them.

We decided to talk about the new television soap opera called Coronation Street. We didn't think much of it and were all convinced it wouldn't last very long. Obviously we were never going to be television critics.

My old mates left and didn't suggest we join them so we didn't.

We chatted up a group of girls who were warming up for a hen party later. We suggested we should join them as we had been a bit short on parties lately which made them giggle and they said we were funny.

They all said they loved men in uniforms which bucked us up no end until one of the best looking ones asked if we were RAF pilots as they thought they were the real heroes. At least they didn't say we looked like ticket collectors because we were getting a bit of a phobia about them.

We told them that we mostly had our feet on the ground which didn't interest them very much until the booth fighter in a flash of pure genius mentioned parachutes. That got 'em.

Geordie nearly mucked it up by getting carried away with technical details but booth fighter soon retrieved the passion by talking about broken legs, roman candles and dead bodies. We overdid it by telling them of fast low level deployment under fire and had to recover by telling them humorous stories of misplaced landings and of me jumping in training and counting the free fall seconds the wrong way round and getting one hell of a bollocking. They loved the fools better than the supermen.

They decided to take us to the hen party.

It didn't turn out too well. The young girls were indifferent but the mums went frantic and they were soon into smothering us not mothering us.

Some of them were attractive real sports so we obliged them with a number of knee tremblers up against the side of the pub wall. We couldn't do all of them satisfactorily but we did our best. It seemed to be good enough.

The young girls were shocked at the behaviour of their mothers until one of the ladies said that just because their father didn't often use it, it didn't mean it had been closed up and shut down.

She said, with a slurred voice, "if I don't use it soon I may as well wear lint drawers and let it heal up." She lurched sideways, grabbed me by the belt and said, "right soldier boy, come to mama and do what papa should do."

That did it. The girls thought that we were disgusting doing it to their mothers and reacted badly to our suggestion that they should take their place. We told them it would be okay as we were already warmed up.

After that the hen party was over for us.

We were chuffed. We had drunk free beer, had a few packets of crisps and had shags unlimited.

My mates wanted to come on leave with me again.

Women in Uniform

The Royal Marines All Arms Course was a very tough one. Most failed.

However that wasn't the reason we were called together in the main lecture hall. It was packed.

An elderly Major in the Royal Marines strode in through a side door and climbed onto the podium. We recognised him as one of the very tough ones who had risen through the ranks.

He carried no papers and didn't need any microphones. His voice carried all around the hall.

"You may have noticed that the armed forces contain many females. It is organised so that the ladies become officers and women occupy the other ranks," he started off saying, "All the Ladies carry the Queen's Commission and must be treated accordingly by all ranks. When approached by those of a lower rank they accept and return the regulation salute. The salute should be given smartly and seriously."

He then raised his voice considerably, "This is not being carried out to the letter on this base but it will be in future. Do you understand?"

He did not wait for a response.

"Officers in the WRACS, WRENS and QARANCS have complained that they are being given half hearted salutes by men with smirks on their faces."

He raised his voice again above the hubbub of muted protests, "don't bullshit me, it is going on and it will stop. Right now, do you understand? Any infringement will be severely dealt with."

He paused, "Women are not the same as men, and I don't mean in the way of the dirty minded lot at the back of the hall. I mean they complain about things we would not notice. I am told by my wife that this is because of the monthly curse and the baggage it brings with it. They get impatient and irritable for reasons that we don't understand so you will go out of your way to show respect. They are fit to be drivers, nurses and pen pushers and so release valuable men for active duty. Heaven forbid they will ever be given any real responsibility. A woman officer will of course not interfere in the main course of the military but holds a commission that you will respect. Do I make myself clear?"

Clear as mud.

Strike up the Band

At school I had decided to become musical. I asked my mum and dad if I could take violin lessons. The music teacher enabled me to buy a second hand fiddle. I was twelve years old.

Carrying the instrument was great. I could carry it to school feeling like a maestro and believing I looked like one. The reality of lessons was something else. There were three of us in the class.

I had to look at where I put my fingers all the time and no matter how much I practised there always seemed a long period of time between the notes. This may have been viewed as some sort of progress except that the sound that eventually came out sounded like something between a cat wailing and a primeval scream.

My tutor, eager to show signs of improvement, used to frantically resin the bow every few seconds from which the only benefit was to gain a short respite from the torture. The other two students made reasonable progress.

I knew I wasn't doing well by the look on my parents faces when I brought them up to date on my prowess.

Most loving parents will smile benignly and proudly at the most god awful performances by their kids. Not mine. They screwed their faces up in agony, and my dad, always short on praise, shouted out, "for goodness sake Den either sell the damn thing back to the teacher or I will dump it in the dustbin."

I was that good.

The recommendation from the teacher was, "give him something to bash."

I joined the Boys' Brigade. This was a great organisation, devoted more towards working class kids than the Boy Scouts and encouraged true Christian Manliness in their motto. We didn't sing silly songs around a campfire thinking we were pioneers. "In gang gooley, gooley watcha, ing gang goo ing gang goo," what was that? Men and women, boys and girls singing stupid stuff like that thinking they were having fun. Not for us. Bloody hell the boys still wore short trousers.

Even at school things had changed. The school magazine reported that the refined strains of Beethoven and Mozart were no longer to be heard coming from the sixth form common room. Instead the raucous sounds of raw blues from Muddy Waters were more usual.

I joined for the band, drill and football. My mates joined for the gym, drill and football. We all joined to get close to the girls in the Girls' Brigade. I learnt the drum, fife and bugle. I loved it and soon became solo drummer. After a couple of false starts I became a star turn.

Once a month was parade. We would march with band, colours and full company through the streets of the local council estates, trying to attract recruits, ending up at the local chapel in time for normal Sunday morning services. The Girls' Brigade didn't march but were lined up as a receiving Guard of Honour. As we marched past them the band of course were the heroes.

We knew the performance backwards as the colours were marched off, then the company was led into church with the girls following on. They had to pass close to the band so that with a succession of nods, winks and suggestive motions we managed to sort out who was going to wiggle a seat next to who.

The Officers of both girls and boys were well aware what was going on and did their best to thwart it but were always going to lose more than they won. Estrogen and testosterone have been fighting to get together ever since life began and will find a way around the most difficult obstacles. We won more than we lost.

I did manage a girlfriend from the Girls' Brigade who was a year older than me. She was quite luscious and often rubbed up against me sensually asking me if I minded that she was a bad girl. I was Steadfast just like the motto and told her that I didn't mind as long as she behaved herself with me. She didn't stay with me for long after that. What a stupid prick I was then.

Sometimes I was rented out to the Salvation Army, usually when they wanted to parade. For other occasions such as Easter or Christmas I was rejected as I couldn't resist jazzing everything up. I told them I was adding a sparkle but they told me they had fireworks for that.

However the experience shot me forwards and I became Drum Major of the 6th City of London Regiment, Royal Fusiliers Army Cadet Drum, Bugle and Fife Band. Field Marshal Lord William Slim inspected us on two occasions and I played in competitions in The Royal Albert Hall with the Fusiliers and the Boys' Brigade, winning two championships.

We worshipped all types of jazz, blues and rock and roll. We joined the queue at record shops to get the latest releases of legends like Louis Armstrong, Kid Ory, Bunk Johnson, Johnny Dodds and the later Charlie Parker, Dizzy Gillespie and so many others. Big bands were also favourite. Black, Brown or White were no odds to us. We were colour blind. Blues and Rock stars we regarded as geniuses. Oh boy did we love Chuck Berry, Little Richard, Fats Domino and Bo Diddley. Elvis and most of the white guys we left to the girls to swoon over except for Jerry Lee Lewis and Carl Perkins.

Before the days of visiting blues packages I managed to catch the immortal Big Bill Broonzy in concert a couple of years before he died. He sang the song, 'Black, Brown and White, with the punch line of 'If you'se white you're all right, if your brown stick aroun' but if you're black oh brother get back, get back, get back. He told us he didn't dare sing that in the States. He also said that he didn't draw any distinctions between types of music. For instance why call something 'Folk Music' when you don't ever see horses doing it??

The man really did have a rooster crow in his voice.

We would walk down the road working through the big band arrangements. One of our favourites we had off pat was Tommy Dorsey's On the Sunny Side of the Street.

Benny Goodman we admired. He was one of the first to put black and white musicians playing public engagements together on stage. When he was told he could never go to the South and do that he replied that it was their loss not his.

On Sunday nights we would go to the cinema which was given over to live British Big Band Concerts. We saw the best of British which was Ted Heath, Jack Parnell and Ken Mackintosh.

We were turned off the American pop stars very quickly after we saw them live at the London Palladium. Well we sort of saw them. They were so small that the microphones of the day hid them from sight. We were not impressed.

At sixteen I was playing drums in a New Orleans Traditional Jazz Band. I reckoned I was the greatest drummer ever as I had a collection of Gene Krupa records and I could play anything. To me it was easy. Give me any tune, tell me if it was fast or slow and then I would play it.

Of course it was played basically the same way but if it was fast, then it was fast and if it was slow, then it was slow.

I could mama dada roll, I could paradiddle, I could drag or flam, play in 2/4; 3/4 or 6/8 time, I had a seed box and cow bell attached to the kit and could even play the washboard. I was king.

Until!!

I was convalescing in an army unit recovering well from a serious condition.

Fortunately I had been WIA and not KIA or MIA. Not good though.

I joined the dance band. Great at first, we really shook the joint. Our St. Louis Blues at mid tempo with a three chorus intro by piano and drums brought the house down. It was a mix of Benny Goodman and Glenn Miller—well that's what we thought. Then in came an officer from the Intelligence Corps. We always felt that to be the most misnamed unit in the British Army, second only to the Education Corps.

He promoted himself to Musical Director. I was in trouble.

He introduced written arrangements with modern jazz pop songs such as George Shearing's Lullaby of the Leaves along with a singer who did her best to sound like Ella Fitzgerald. No one could sound like Ella but at least she tried like a lot of others. Thank god she didn't think she was Billy Holiday.

Anyway she gave me some very funny looks when I hit the cowbell or seed box which I was inclined to do when I got carried away which was often. I played with great enthusiasm and power, after all I was a Gene Krupa fan.

The director called a band meeting. They told me that the singer had a problem with me.

"Got it," I said, "she doesn't fit, does she, when does she go?"

"Not her, you," came the reply from the director.

"I want less head arrangements and more written ones. I want the discipline that goes with it. I have a drummer lined up who reads music."

"What!" I cried, "what respectable drummer actually reads music. You are insulting my jazz integrity." Then realising that the world's greatest was about to be sacked with loss of face and that a brave soldier couldn't cry or plead I followed up with, "so give me a break guys, what instrument haven't we got?"

My mate the piano player said that we were short in the rhythm section and I should learn the guitar.

"Hmmm, what about the banjo?" I asked.

"Why the banjo for goodness sake, this is a modern band not a hoochie coochie ensemble?" laughed my friend.

"Well a banjo has got five strings and I've only got five fingers. A guitar has six strings so what do I do with the one left over?" I said seriously.

My mate graciously took the two base strings off and showed me four string guitar cords which got me by for a while until I finally graduated to six later on.

When I was returned to normal service I left the band and sad to say they didn't seem to miss me.

We were not in the United States Army Hollywood style. They always seemed to have a guitar or blues harp player at hand from out of nowhere and someone who could sing like Frank Sinatra or play the trumpet like Harry James. We didn't.

We were not settled, often on the move, allowed very little in the way of personal property. The only continuously worn article we had belonged to the army—the stainless steel dog tags. We never took them off even when sleeping or bathing. We started out as 28 bob a week men less deductions. That was 1. 8s. 6p. less 3s. 6p. and for that we were treated like dirt. Even so I sent 2s 6p. home to my mum. I soon saw the advantages of promotion. When I made sergeant life changed for the better. I got extra leave, waiters in the sergeants mess serving better food, higher pay and for the last six months I was viewed as the same as a regular soldier.

Before I was posted yet again to another unit Louis Armstrong came on tour. He made it to Bellevue in Manchester. We went to see him. It wasn't a jazz fest it was a love fest. The critics declared it to be one of the worst bands that he had ever played with but no one cared. All he had to do was stand there.

It was so good to see him.

I would eventually see the Basie and Ellington Bands and most of the blues artists but Big Bill and Louis were my first.

Shortly after demob I went to see Muddy Waters who appeared with his own blues band along with Chris Barber. It was at St. Pancras Town Hall in London over which the Communist local council was flying the Red Flag.

I was amused by the irony of a communist council going against the British musicians' union who had decreed that American artists could only perform in the UK if there was an exchange British performer going to the States. So much for solidarity with the workers. Just the usual hypocrisy.

Muddy Waters invented electricity. Well at least for the blues guitar. Chris Barber's band was a really excellent British Jazz Band but they sounded even better when accompanying Muddy.

Years later I returned to the guitar and drums but I never felt good enough to really make a living at it. I was never offered much of a chance either. I was undiscovered.

The music however has given me and many others a great deal of pleasure.

Demob

Every conscript kept a demob chart virtually from the first day he was in. Seven hundred and thirty days calendar style stuck up on the inside of the locker door along with scantily dressed fantasy girls.

The unlucky one's included a leap year.

Every day was meticulously ticked off.

The favourite expression of those nearing the end of their term, when talking to newer arrivals, was, "Get some in."

As we were trained and had served in some nasty places we were viewed as unfit to rejoin civilised society. We were more than a bit uncouth for sure. So we were sent to a rehabilitation centre six weeks before our demob date to learn how to become useful citizens again. We had one weeks leave before and one weeks leave after.

I had the usual thoroughly organised piss up at my leaving do, being bundled onto a truck with my gear, leaving behind most of the sergeant's and corporal's mess in shambles. There had been songs, speeches, laughter, vomit, fights and collapses galore. A total success.

I was nearly comatose. They dumped me in the Guard's Van of the London train. I would be well looked after as the guard would take care of me and wake me up with a cup of tea before arriving in London Euston Station.

Society was different then. It was only ten years after the end of the Second World War and most had "done their bit," many in the armed forces and there had been numerous conflicts since.

We were carrying on the tradition.

We old soldiers from those days find the modern attitude completely bewildering.

If you join the army then surely you expect to fight, even if you don't fancy it too much. You don't just parade around. It is tragic if your son joins the army and you lose him. It is totally devastating but you can't complain to the generals if he gets killed while fighting. He joined the army didn't he?

There are no such thing as just wars—only necessary ones.

I still have my weapons training manual which states 'your weapons are given you to kill the enemy'. No doubt expressed there is there?

One mother complained that the army had killed her son but didn't he join the army knowing he may one day kill another mother's son?

We have some fine soldiers, great young guys who should be respected.

Not so sure about that Navy lot who ran into a spot of bother with the Iranian Republican Guards in the Gulf. No shame, no fight and no guts—hardly in the best traditions of the Navy. Afterwards instead of sensibly hiding away they actually courted publicity and wanted payment.

One officer unbelievably assisted the Iranian propaganda on TV. In my time he would probably have been tried for treason and aiding and abetting the enemy.

If you're looking for truth then you won't find it in war. Everyone lies—some more than others. Grow up for God's sake.

We had no choice, we were conscripted. The Queen was very insistent that we serve her, we were not volunteers. If we didn't turn up then the Military Police arrived smartly dressed in red caps, arrested you, and took you away. Not a good start.

I was comfortably into my rehabilitation course, which was a good skive. We were actually regarded as human and almost treated that way but not quite. The Army doesn't really do nice.

Then I was recalled to my unit.

Suez had happened.

I received my orders, travelled to Euston, went to the RTO at the station and collected further orders and my rail travel voucher.

On the way back on the train I was sitting in a carriage on a seat away from the corridor. The other window seat opposite was occupied by a woman in her thirties.

We were alone.

Shortly after leaving the station a rowdy group of young men, a few in USAF uniforms barged along the corridor, shouting and shoving. They slung open our door, peered around inside, discussed the situation in high pitched, loud voices, then charged away giggling.

Blissful silence.

I looked at the woman who smiled.

I said, "I wonder what they think of Suez. They're in the forces."

"They are Americans, they don't even know where it is," she replied.

"But you sound American yourself," I said.

"Oh no, I'm Canadian, there's a big difference. The Americans think we're slow but in fact we're just more mature. Americans couldn't recognise that if it was put up in neon lights."

Ouch—end of conversation for a while.

Within a short time our carriage filled up as more recalled Squaddies came along looking for seats. We were a real mixed bunch from various regiments, but none of us talked about Suez or where we could end up. We talked about the sad little bastards in pop music who had pulled strings to keep out of the army so as to not spoil their shitty careers. Elvis was our hero, he served his full time in the ranks. There you go Elvis.

This was the overnight train leaving Euston at midnight and arriving at 6.30 in the morning in Manchester.

We had a well rehearsed drill for sleeping. Bags were removed from luggage racks and a guy shinned up and stretched out in each. The person by the window put legs up on the seat opposite as did the one by the door and this left a space between along the seats where two people could curl up. One more snuggled up between the bags on the floor. Seven people down for kip for the night, not greatly comfortable, but accommodated.

Then those up in the luggage rack took out the light bulbs and others pulled down the window blinds.

The only disturbance came from the ticket collector doing his rounds.

This time a lady was present. We explained the system but said if she objected then we wouldn't do it.

She was great and said that we were English and she had no worry as she was in good hands.

She was actually.

What a pity the English have changed—or have they?

I only learned years later that Suez was a stitch up. Yes we were worried about Nasser and the Canal but the British and French governments suckered the Israelis into a war with Egypt without involving the USA.

The idea was to start the war, then stop the war, while at the same time "securing the safety of shipping in the Canal" by invading and re-occupying the Canal Zone.

We occupied and secured right enough but the Yanks lost their balls and screamed. They threatened a number of economic measures which they well knew would cripple the UK.

We were no sooner in than we were out.

A right bloody fiasco.

Whatever the rights and wrongs, and there were many, Europe and later many others learnt a lesson. The world had to dance to the all American Song Book.

This was to cause immense resentment over the years with mixed results.

With a lot more maturity the USA could have lead the world by example rather than by coercion. Their cock ups have been legion and the backlash has been severe and tragic.

Anyway I was demobbed nearly on time and had the luxury of getting everyone totally pissed a second time. Way to go to win a popularity contest.

Day Tripper

I t was a present from my fiancee for my 21st birthday. I don't think it was a making up present, I liked to think it was a genuine treat. She had dumped me shortly after I was conscripted and we had only just made up again. It was probably just a young girls virus that struck them all when their boyfriends went off to the modern version of war and peace. It affected their memories. After a couple of months they couldn't remember what we looked like, they got confused, and we got 'Dear John' letters. Then when we were due home, after a couple of years away, their memories miraculously returned and the confusion disappeared. We then got 'oh my darling forgive me, I've missed you so much' type letters. Oh Yeah!

Never mind. We were going on a day trip to France. No passports necessary as we weren't staying. Just a card from the post office valid for 24-48 hours.

We were sailing on the Royal Daffodil from Margate to Boulogne. The Royal Daffodil was one of two old paddle steamers, gaudily decked out with two high stack funnels. They both sailed to France and back on Sundays. One to Calais the other to Boulogne. During the week they sailed the Thames complete with dance bands and parties.

They had proved their worth at Dunkirk assisting in the rescue of thousands of Allied troops from the beleaguered beaches in 1940. They proudly displayed the memorial plaques that commemorated the event as did so many of the heroic small ships who responded to the call.

That was fifteen or more years before. They were old ladies of the sea then in the forties so they looked well ropey and out of date in the fifties to most people.

Not to us though.

We were excited and up for it.

The band was playing corny songs that were outdated even back then. This was the hey day of Rock and Roll so that 'Oh we do like to be beside the sea side' and 'life on the ocean waves' did not add to the excitement. I personally hoped that if that was the best the band could do then please let them be seasick very early on.

The ship was tied up to one of the dock arms with two narrow gangplanks, with a rope hand rail on one side, leading on board fore and aft. We filed on sedately and in good order. There was a small crowd of early morning holiday makers to see us off. It was the end of June and the day promised to be a scorcher.

The ship sounded it's siren, a warning to get on board right away. A few minutes later the ropes were cast off, gang planks removed, bells rang, engines roared and paddles thrashed the water.

We chugged away from the dock leaving onlookers behind waving. We waved back as though leaving England for ever. There were also a few others waving frantically on shore, jumping up and down and running flat out along the dock pier. They were late comers left behind.

The captain came on over the public address system asking if we minded going back for them. We were in an adventurous party mood, felt sorry for them and shouted yes.

We turned back and picked them up and immediately lost all sympathy for them.

As soon as they got on board they were yelling the odds about nearly being left behind.

A couple of burly dockers went over to them, told them to shut their fucking stupid gobs and enjoy the day or else they would chuck 'em over the side and they could swim back home.

They shut up but when they thought they were out of sight they carried on muttering quietly for a while.

We had breakfast. We watched the white cliffs disappear on one side of the Channel and soon after appear on the other side. We had lunch just before we landed.

Boulogne was very quiet. It was Sunday and the locals had finished church and would be having lunch. We took a coach trip to Wimereaux a short journey along the coast. There was a fair bit of mediaeval English history around and we did the full tour.

Half of us had joined the tour, the other half had stayed behind in town.

We arrived back in town about an hour before the ship sailed for home.

What a difference a day makes.

The square before the dock was a mass of staggering English. They had taken the advantage of the fact that there were no licensing hours in

France, the bars were open all day and half the night, and the booze was cheap.

If they had bothered to eat anything then it wasn't apparent.

Most were legless and those who weren't were well on the way.

More than a few were roaming around asking the locals the way to the ship which was actually in full view only metres away.

The locals were ever helpful but spoke in French. Slowly it dawned on us. The surrounding areas were full of locals, some of whom had brought folding chairs in order to see the spectacle. The spectacle was the weekend amusement of seeing the drunken English trying to get back on board the Royal Daffodil.

Was it really worth it we thought?

It was.

The fun started early.

Those few who were left with a small amount of functioning brain decided to take up the challenge before the crowd started to board.

They linked arms and took a lurching zig zag path towards the gangplanks. The ships crew and the locals leaned forwards expectantly.

They were not disappointed.

By the time they reached the gangplanks only a little over half were still standing. The rest were being part dragged, part pushed and part pulled along. They stood no chance of hitting the gangplanks. They teetered on the edge of the dock for a few moments and then started pitching over into the water. Every time one went in the local crowd shouted 'ole'. The rot quickly spread as those falling in clutched at those who were next to them causing a domino effect.

One in, all in.

There was only a narrow space between dock and ship and the tide was in so they didn't fall far. They were soon being fished out by ships crew and dock workers using bill hooks. They were dumped on the dockside floundering and spluttering but not in the least bit sobered up by their ducking.

Other drunks decided they were far more capable than the pioneers, pointed at them, lurched onto the gangplank, laughed triumphantly and promptly fell in.

More than a few decided to take a run at the gangplanks trusting to the momentum to get them up, over and on board. One or two actually made it.

Others leaped on the gangplank but then sheered off sharply to right or left, while the remainder missed entirely.

Those who had made it on board leaped up on to the side of the ship doing a victory dance. Two lucky ones fell backwards, and were unconscious most of the way home, while the others tipped forwards and fell in.

The local crowd was in hysterics. This was why they came from miles around.

Eventually all the half drowned drunks were loaded and we were able to board.

The gangplanks were ready to be removed and the ropes cast off so why were the locals still there waiting just as expectantly as before?

A cheer went up. There came the latecomers, a mixture of drunk and sober.

They were rushing into the square as though pursued by a herd of bulls.

The actions of the ships departure didn't stop.

Bells were ringing, whistles sounding, funnels belching smoke and paddles starting to turn.

Some made the gangplanks which were being removed, charging up them regardless and some made it on board. Others didn't. Now it was dangerous because of the paddles. One or two were clinging and swinging along the ropes still hanging on even when the ropes were thrown off the bollards on shore and were being hauled aboard. A number were diving headfirst into the water which was widening all the time between ship and shore.

We looked back and saw why they had run pellmell into the square. The local police had gone into the bars further into the town and chased them out. Those who didn't make it were arrested, spent the night in jail and had to pay their own fare home the next day on the normal ferry. They also had a great deal of explaining to do to immigration and customs officials on both sides of the Channel.

The ship was well under way, pulling along the dock wall on it's way out of the harbour.

We couldn't believe our eyes.

There were still one or two racing along the wall, diving into the sea and swimming like mad to the ship hoping to be pulled on board.

They were disappointed as they were rescued by coastguards and taken back to shore.

We watched the locals slowly wandering away. The show was over for another week.

Nobody waved.

A few of the crew were standing nearby tidying up.

"To think we rescued them from fucking Dunkirk for this," said one tanned wizened older man, "should 'ave let the bastards drown there. A bloody disgrace that's what they are."

"Come on pops, they bloody well earned it, give 'em a break," said a young one, smiling.

"Break their fucking necks, more like," said the man.

When we arrived back at Margate we were all tired and subdued but happy. Many were walking wounded with dreadful hangovers worsened by the sun.

There were a number of ambulances for those whose day didn't turn out quite as expected.

We went home happy and contented.

Brotherhood

After being demobbed from the army I couldn't live at home so I got married.

My ex-fiancee, who had dumped me while I was away suddenly realised she couldn't live without me once I'd come back. Well we were young then with a lot to learn.

My brother was five years younger than me and so missed National Service. It was over. Britain no longer ruled the world and didn't need a large standing army anymore.

He would have been deferred anyway as he was an apprentice in a metal print company. A good job and a good potential career. He was a steady stay at home, predictable, nice sort of guy, a bit chubby and healthy.

Me, I was always the runt of the family, pushy and fidgety, never knowing what I was going to get into next.

We'd been married a while and were expecting our first baby.

My wife took a phone call one morning, looked upset and told me we had better get over to my Mum and Dad's place.

On the way over she was seriously quiet and wouldn't say much.

Just for a change I managed to take the hint and shut up with my mind working overtime praying that nothing had happened to my Mum and Dad.

It hadn't, it was my brother.

As soon as we walked through the back door the sadness was tangible. The atmosphere was awful.

Several neighbours were making tea and dramatically hurrying about and pointed me to the front room. Use of the front room meant it was serious.

My Mum and Dad were old school, stiff upper lip British. Never wash your dirty linen in public, never let your emotions show in case people thought you were soft and soppy, and never let anyone know your business.

That was all gone.

I had never seen my parents so shattered. They were sitting on our best settee, holding on to one another sobbing their hearts out.

I knelt in front of them but they couldn't look at me. They were ashamed to appear like this in front of me. Their pride prevented them.

I just sat there on the carpet for a while until a friend attempting to be helpful told me it was my brother. I'd gathered that and also by the upset that it was serious, but how serious.

"How serious Dad?" I asked quietly.

"He's dead Den," he said with tears streaming down his cheeks and his face haggard and drawn, "he was killed last night in a motorbike accident."

He still couldn't look up.

"We heard that a couple of boys were in an accident on Farningham's Death Hill and that one of them had died. We weren't worried as Derek's bike wasn't working and was outside. Then the police came and we still weren't convinced until they told us that he was the pillion rider on a friend's bike."

"Why did it have to be him?" my Mum wailed in really great pain, "why couldn't he have stayed at home?"

I was stunned, shocked and didn't know what to do or say. My wife held me kindly and compassionately but I still couldn't come to terms with it and never did.

I had never seen my parents so extremely upset and for the first time in my life I realised how much they had loved and cared for us. They didn't allow emotion to show normally. Why him? He was the home boy, bless him. I was the always on the move rebel. They would have got so much more family closeness out of him.

Of course life went on and I was supportive physically but as I had never seen my parents so devastated I always felt awkward and never worked out how to talk to them about it.

So regretfully I never did.

When they had grandchildren, and there were more than a few then they really loved them so that in my own way I felt that I had made a bit up to them.

But they never got over the loss and I never expected them too. A child's life is so precious and he was just nineteen.

Many years and two wives later I was knocking back a bottle of French Burgundy with my partner in a wine bar in Crouch End, North

London. These were the days before the Australian wine invasion and before the setting free of Nelson Mandela in South Africa. That meant I knew nothing of the first and wouldn't touch anything made in the second even though South Africa made a very fine Pinotage. Apartheid was a disgusting Nazi regime to me even though Maggie Thatcher sucked up to it. Not surprising really!

We were in conversation with a group who were celebrating a colleague's birthday, very loudly as it happened.

They were local council social workers.

After a while we teased them on their job as social workers had had a bad press due to an over zealous doctor in the North East putting dozens of innocent families in jeopardy and lots of kids in care. Lack of common sense on the part of the authorities had allowed this nutter of a doctor to carry on far too long with her obsession that most parents in the UK abused their children.

There was a joke doing the rounds, "save a London child, jail a social worker."

Inevitably with the wine flowing tongues loosened and I told the story of my brother.

Oh my goodness I was suddenly transformed into a victim who had suffered in silent torment for years. How sorry they were that I found out that my brother was missed and loved more than me in such a traumatic manner.

Traumatic is such a treasured social worker's word.

I tried to explain that I felt no resentment at all and valued my parents even more because I had found out just how much they loved us both. Of course the focus was on my brother—he had just been killed for goodness sake.

It was no use.

Then they told us of their woes. Not one of them was in a loving successful relationship and some of the stories they told were pathetic.

"I know my husband is being unfaithful," one earnest looking woman burst out, "and it's all my fault. Sex hurts because I stay dry. It's painful for both of us. I can understand him going somewhere else."

All of us drunks nodded wisely and sympathetically.

A doleful voice said quietly, "you can lubricate you know."

"What do you think she is? Only an old boiler needs oiling?" I chuckled but no one else laughed.

"My wife goes away with her company a lot, too much I reckon. Comes back with fancy underwear. Says she can't buy stuff like that in Marks and Spencer. Only wears it when she goes away," said one hippie styled guy.

"Wow!" I exclaimed, "who's the lucky boy then? Fantasy holidays galore."

He gave me a filthy look, "it's not for me is it? I never see them on her, do I?"

"My wife likes to see her undies on me," said an older looking distinguished gent, says it turns her on." We all nodded forlornly in unison looking into our glasses hoping to see an answer in the wine.

My wife and I were left feeling that these were not the people who should be making important decisions about other people's lives and children.

They made us feel normal.

Talk about physician heal thyself.

Out of respect for my parent's feelings I never again bought or owned a motorbike although I was tempted a few times. I had owned bikes before but could never bring myself to worry my parents by behaving so selfishly after my brother died.

Playing Away

O nce again I was witness for the Crown. In this case it was the court at Southwark in South-East London close to Charlie Chaplin's birthplace at the Elephant and Castle.

We had a department store in nearby Walworth Road which was a favourite target for the local lads needing a bit of pocket money.

In this particular case they had stolen a heavy tow truck, backed it up flat out at our metal gates, hooked them up and ripped them out into the street, then roared back again straight through the re-inforced glass doors at the front of the store.

They tore back across the street, trailing wreckage, holding up the traffic, making way for others to drive two Land Rovers through the mess and into the shop. There were seven or eight of them throwing everything of value in sight into the vehicles while one was holding a stop watch timing the whole event.

He called time and they flew away in the Land Rovers minutes before the police arrived, leaving the tow truck blocking the road in the opposite direction.

Brilliant, but they had made a big mistake.

They had left one guy behind in the store. The one with the stop watch.

He was well known to the police so they knew who his mates were and raided their homes almost at the same time as the villains got there.

The police uncovered a treasure trove of stolen property and I was there to identify stolen articles and confirm where they were found.

Our case was a fair way down the list and the police were sure it would be referred up to the criminal court, the Old Bailey, where sentences could be far harsher. They wanted these guys put away.

I sat with a detective sergeant at the back of the court. We could stay there until our case was called.

The magistrate had to get rid of the usual riff raff first.

Number one was an habitual Irish drunk. A regular customer apparently as he greeted the magistrate very cordially. His "honour" was not amused or impressed as the charges were read out along with police evidence.

"Mr. Flynn, you again," he said.

"Yessuh," beamed Mr. Flynn, "'tis me agin suh. How is it you're a feeling today suh?"

"Have no worries on my behalf, thank you. You should be worrying about yourself. Tell me Mr Flynn how are you pleading this time?" asked the magistrate in a deliberate neutral tone.

"Not guilty suh, not at all, at all." stated Flynn.

"Not guilty? Would you like to reconsider because the penalties are high for wasting the court's time you know?"

"Oi knows, oi knows, that's why I'm not guilty so you can let me go roight away." explained Flynn with an expansive gesture of his hands.

"Behave yourself Mr. Flynn, don't try to mock me or this court. I wish to ask you some questions."

"Roight suh, fire away," Flynn said very agreeably.

"The constable says in his written evidence that he found you rolling in the gutter, singing, 'it's the wrong way to fuck a fairy,' at the top of your voice and that you couldn't stand up on your own. Are you disputing that evidence."

"Well yes and no your honour," said Flynn.

"Make up your mind and I'm not your honour."

"I have a bad back suh, an old war wound, and it stabs me sudden like, so I sink to my knees and then roll in agony. Seeing as I'm an old soldier in the service of the King I was, God bless 'im, I was singing, 'it's a long way to Tipperary' but the constable probably heard it wrong due to my groans of agony."

While saying this Flynn was twisting and turning, bending in supposed pain with horrible expressions flooding across his face.

"Mr. Flynn please don't try my patience. We have established before that you served only five weeks in the Pioneer Corps before being dishonourably discharged. You never fought anyone except your ex wife and you were never wounded. The old King would probably turn in his grave at the thought of you having ever served him. You were obviously drunk."

"No suh, I swear sir, ask the desk sergeant, he saw that Oi was foine. Ask him to check his night charge book?"

"The desk sergeant cannot read his night charge book. He said you came in having to be supported by two constables who you were insulting the whole time. Let me see, yes, the abusive language included such graphic descriptions as 'Fucking Flatfoots' and 'Mr. Plod's Pisspots'. As the charges were being read out you apparently spewed up about three gallons of Guinness and two pork pies all over him, his desk and his charge book, which was thereby rendered unusable."

"Suh, I have never used those disgraceful words, I get a bit artistic when in pain is all. The constables were probably tired after a hard day. They are foine fellas indeed."

"They are indeed fine fellows and not surprisingly they are probably tired of you. I find this case proved. You are sentenced to a twenty pounds fine or three months imprisonment. The clerk of the court will work out time to pay or any other details you may need."

"Good day Mr. Flynn, I would be happy to see the last of you but I just know we will be meeting again."

There were a few more similar cases.

One was an old tramp called 'Smokey Joe' who had been on the scene for years pushing his wrecked old bike around on it's rims making a hell of a racket.

He was pulled in every so often on any real or imagined pretense so that he could be given daily baths, deloused, cleaned up, reclothed and fed properly.

The police frequently pulled him in over the festive seasons so as to give him some warmth, comfort and cheer for a few weeks.

He roamed for miles in all sorts of weather and bothered no one until the smell of him caused a lot of discomfort to others but not to him.

When he tried to engage people at bus stops in conversation and they turned away that was when the police decided it was 'Smokey Joe's' bath time.

He hated it.

This particular morning he appeared scrubbed a shiny pink in a second hand shirt, suit and shoes. He refused socks. His wispy hair never laid down, his wrinkled face expressed disdain and his second hand false teeth rattled a lot.

The magistrate welcomed him, admiring his clean new look.

"I preferred my old one," he said in a gruff but cultured voice.

"Now be grateful to the many people who look out for you Mr. Ames, they mean you no harm and wish you well. But you know that, we've been through it many times. I take it you've been treated properly. I have the medical report from the examining doctor. You are well underweight and suffering from lack of proper hygiene."

"I didn't do anything wrong you know, I was just asking the way to Peckham when a young copper came up and run me in. Not right that. Young coppers shouldn't be allowed out alone. They get carried away. Give me an old'un anytime."

"Your behaviour wasn't offensive but your smell was and we all know that you can find your way to Peckham blindfolded. You appeared to be begging. I am proposing a detention of four weeks to make you fit for the road again. Social Services have been notified and are in attendance here to see if they can make another try at settling you down and I think you should accept what they offer. I don't have much hope that you will."

"Don't want it sir. I want the open road and the blue skies overhead."

"Very noble and poetic I'm sure but you should try to learn a lesson from nature regarding fresh air, sparkling clear water and fragrant smells. Leave the insects to feed off the land and not you."

"Where are we now, let's see, August Bank Holiday coming up. I expect to see you again around Christmas time. Look after yourself and behave."

Smokey was led away still complaining about young coppers.

A smartly dressed man in a suit and tie was on next.

The Magistrate looked up and seemed surprised. He conferred with the clerk of the court.

The evidence was read out. Basically the charge was drunk and disorderly and causing damage to property.

"Mr. Barnes, I am extremely unhappy to see you yet again. You have a good education, a good job and are a thoroughly decent young man until you drink.

Until you drink to excess actually. How do you plead?"

"Guilty, I'm afraid sir," said Barnes dolefully.

"Look Mr. Barnes it is about time this was well and truly stopped. On at least two previous occasions you promised this court that it would, yet here you are again. Your behaviour is totally adolescent and unacceptable. How old are you now?"

"Thirty one sir."

"You are a thirty one year old who far too often gets very drunk, roams the streets in an unruly and threatening manner and throws stones and rubbish at anyone who complains. You break windows in buildings and insult the police when they attempt to curb your excesses leaving them no option but to arrest you. If you carry on in this manner you will eventually end up in custody and you will possibly lose your job. I do not wish to do that but if you appear before this court again then you will leave me with no option. I intend to impose a fine and probation so that you may receive some help and guidance. You have got a little too old for this sort of behaviour. Do not let me see you again."

The next up was a clean cut, good looking young bloke, smart and well turned out.

At the same time the court was disturbed for a few minutes as two nice looking girls came in through separate doors both of them with a couple of young children in tow. All were quiet and respectful. I didn't make any connection at the time.

"Watch and listen to this piece of flyboy," said the 'tec next to me, "this is rich."

I looked at the young man as he was put into the dock. He looked around the court, completely unconcerned, saw each of the women, smiled and waved to them but received no acknowledgement.

"See the girls there? One's his wife and the other's his girlfriend, all the kids are his as far as we know. His Mum is the one down the front in the green hat and coat waving to him," another CID guy said.

"What's up then?" I asked.

"Look, listen and learn," said the 'tec.

The charges were nine counts of breaking and entering, several charges of receiving and handling stolen goods and one of threatening behaviour. The evidence presented was pretty conclusive.

He pleaded not guilty!

I chuckled at that.

"Don't worry, every criminal I've ever nicked swore he was innocent and set up," said the 'tec, "well everyone's innocent until proven guilty aren't they? That's why we have a trial. Sometimes the slippery bastards escape but they all go too far and get caught in the end. Time is on our side and when it isn't we just help it along."

"This lad has only been charged with a tenth of what he's done but we stuck to the conclusive one's. If we can get him put away we'll have stopped a fair bit of crime around here. He's a busy boy this one is," said the other cop.

The Magistrate conferred quietly with the clerk of the court, several probation and local council officers and nodded his head.

The Magistrate looked at the guy patiently and calmly, "Mr. Johnson, you have heard the evidence against you but I understand that you have no one to represent you. I am also lead to believe that you intend to present no evidence on your behalf and have no wish to question the evidence as presented. Does that mean that you wish your case to be heard by a jury or want to refer it to a higher court?"

"No sir."

"In that case I have no alternative to find you guilty as charged and I will have to consult as to sentence. Do you have anything to say or anyone to speak on your behalf before I do so?"

"Here it comes," said the 'tec.

"Yessir. This is a mistake sir. I shouldn't be here."

"I don't understand Mr. Johnson. Where should you be?"

"No, I don't mean that, I mean, look I was up before you before sir, wasn't I?

"Yes indeed," said the Magistrate, "and not so long ago as I recall."

"Well sir you gave me a suspended sentence because my wife spoke up for me, showed that she and our children would experience hardship from me being put in the nick. I promised that I wouldn't take any more trouble home to my wife and kids. Me Mum guaranteed that as well. Well I haven't have I?"

"Haven't what?"

"I haven't taken any more trouble home to them?" explained Johnson spreading his hands self evidently in front of him, "I dumped the stuff at me girlfriends and I'm sure you don't want to cause her and our kids anymore hardship than my wife. So you see, I shouldn't be here."

"Mr. Johnson, this case is not about where you live or what your marital arrangements are. I find the Prosecution's case conclusive as to theft and receiving. I will discuss the details of this case and consult as to what custodial sentences are open to me. You will be held in custody until then and brought before me again for sentencing. You will accompany the police officer who will take you down."

"Did you see the look on the faces of his two tarts? If I was him I'd ask for a long sentence. They'll bloody well kill him when he gets out," said the 'tec.

"That's if they don't kill each other first," laughed the CID guy, "anyway we haven't got to worry about what he's up to for a while. We'll have a few beers on that one tonight."

Eventually our case was heard.

Only lawyers appeared, no defendants. The accused required a jury to hear the case at the Central Criminal Court.

No problem. It was referred there.

The police were relieved, just another day at the office. We went to sink a few beers.

Over drinks they asked me about my decision to sack a girl from the Walworth Store Jewellery shop who actually hadn't committed any crime.

I told them that I hadn't fired her. I offered her a transfer, with the agreement of the Store Manager, to the women's fashion department but she had taken offence and resigned.

To the cops there seemed to be no difference.

"OK," I said, "look her boyfriend, as you well know, is a big time hoodlum. You've had him away a few times, so I removed temptation. Crime prevention in action mate."

"Denis, good sir, we are drinking in Walworth right?"

"Yep!"

"Well most days when we sup a bit we'll be standing next to a known villain. We even talk to a few sometimes."

"OK," I interrupted, "so?"

"So we don't expect to be fired because of it," said the 'tec.

"All right, but for crissakes guys, she isn't just standing next to him, she's having his baby!" I cried, "it doesn't take Sherlock Holmes to work it out, does it? Even 'My Dear Watson' would score that in one!"

We all laughed and got another beer in.

Origins

According to tradition a true London Cockney is born within the sound of Bow Bells. I was born about a mile too far away down river but still claimed the honour as the bells could be heard if the wind was in the right direction. Now the title is misapplied to anyone who speaks badly, destroys vowel sounds, misses off aitches and lives anywhere within a thirty mile radius of London.

We were connected to royalty as my Uncle Arthur and Aunt Emily were the Pearly King and Queen of Greenwich. The Pearly Kings and Queens of Cockney London were and still are true royalty as they dedicate so much of their time and effort to helping the under privileged and raising thousands of pounds for charity without pay or security.

I still have a wonderful memory of an aged diminutive Uncle Arthur teaching giant Japanese Sumo wrestlers to do the Lambeth Walk and Aunt Emily achieving media fame by beating up two robbers who were trying to raid a post office when she was drawing her pension.

Don't mess with the Pearlies—they are genuine people!!

We survived the Great Depression and the Second World War but like everyone else we suffered our losses.

Among many memories, two in particular stand out. First I asked my Dad what the newspapers were going to report when the war was over and he said that he expected they would find something. Second my Mum swore she would never worry about anything ever again and she worried about everything until the day she died at ninety one years of age.

There you go—the secret of long life—worry about every day and there will always be another one.

The trouble with that theory is my Dad lived to ninety one also and took every day in his stride come what may.

They were great parents.

We lived in the poor back streets of Southeast London close to the docks, Woolwich Arsenal, Woolwich Dockyard, army barracks and factories.

You can imagine what a fun place it was to grow up in through the war being a daily prime target of German bombers. Six years of air raid warnings, hours of hell, and all clears.

Throughout it all we still attended school when we could.

The pupils of Bloomfield Road School who had survived were some of the first beneficiaries of the Labour Party post war social revolution.

Some of us sat the Scholarship. Neither us nor our parents fully understood what that meant.

The school got a great result—six of us passed. Well done Mrs. Auty, our primary school teacher.

Two of us went to Haberdasher's Aske's School for Boys, one to St Olave's and the other to Alleyns. Two girls went to the Roan.

These were top notch schools who had taken paying pupils and now had to make increasing room for scholarship boys. We were a scruffy lot mixing with the hoi poloi.

The schools later became Grammar Schools and then lumped together into Comprehensive Schools depending on the latest fad of the education authorities until most degrees of excellence had been lost. Statistics say otherwise but when have statistics ever reflected reality?

My parents were so proud and we trotted off to the school tailors, Josiah Messent in Peckham. The tailors for young gentlemen! This was long before the days of Dell Boy and Rodney.

I was measured and the expert fitters piled up the rugby togs, cricket clothes, running, rowing and gym wear and then got around to the uniforms. One for winter and one for summer. Winter entailed school cap, pin stripe trousers, waistcoat and tails while summer had grey flannel slacks, blue blazer and a straw boater. There was a school tie and of course house buttons and badges. A very impressive pile indeed.

The manager added it all up and presented the total. It was the equivalent of more than one year of my Dad's salary before tax and social security deductions.

Silence, then Mum came to the rescue. "We weren't planning on buying today, just seeing what was needed," she said calmly as Dad had gone pale and speechless, "we'll think about it and come back, thank you very much." and we beat a retreat.

"What we going to do, give up the school?" asked Dad.

"Nope," said Mum, "we go down the Co-Op. See what they can do."

We went and they sorted us out with a somewhat watered down two sizes too big version and Mum paid on the weekly.

Some years later Dad passed his Fire Brigade exams for Sub-Officer and turned down promotion as it meant moving seventy miles away. He didn't want me losing my Askean education.

Aske's groomed students for Oxford and the arts, other Universities were not considered good enough for Askeans. I left at sixteen and a half when I realised I was surely destined for Oxford and there was no chance of my family being able to afford it. I left school on the pretext of preferring to earn my own living before coming up to my compulsory military service at eighteen.

It paid off when after five years of serving the Queen and country in full and part time military service I packed away equipment, medals and memories and went to University at night—after a full day's work.

Mum and Dad were at last proud when after seventeen years I ended up with great jobs, two Fellowships and two standard degrees plus a whole lot more.

Unfortunately also with two divorces on the way.

During those years the UK was changing. The beginning of the Sixties was much the same as before. No working class men doffed their caps any more, in fact caps were disappearing, but class barriers had not yet tumbled down.

I went for a job at Harrods. I had applied for the position of buyer.

I was granted an interview.

I was faced with two senior personnel of the company—two right old Hooray Henry's. Now I know that thousands like them were very brave and died like flies in two world wars but the fact is that they made way for those who could really do the job.

This had obviously not worked its way through to Harrods.

After half an hour of questions and interrogations the two of them conferred.

They came back to me.

"Well Mr. Hayes, old chap, I mean well, well, well, what can we say?"

I thought, "why not just say it?"

"Well dash it all old man, I mean, really, you should be interviewing us, what do you say Charles?"

Charles went nasal, "neyeh, neyeh, neyeh," and nodded his head.

"I mean, you are so well qualified, we feel humble, don't we Charles?"

Charles went, "neyeh, neyeh, neyeh," and nodded his head again.

"However, we just have one little reservation dear fellow. What say you Charles," he said.

Charles went, "neyeh, neyeh, neyeh," and nodded his head yet again.

I thought, "bloody hell if that donkey nods his head much more with any luck he'll nod off," but said instead, "Well one small reservation's not bad, sounds good, so let's hear it? What's it all about?"

"Well dear chap, how to say it? I mean what can I say? I mean it's rather difficult isn't it Charles? What do you say?"

And of course Charles goes, "neyeh, neyeh, neyeh, difficult," and nods his head.

"I thought, blimey, this could go on forever," so I said, "look just say it for goodness sake, spit it out, get it over, let's have it, don't hang about. What is it?"

"There you go dear boy, you're doing it, that's exactly it, isn't it Charles?" he exclaimed triumphantly.

I interrupted before Charles' head fell off and said, "What exactly are you talking about, come on at least give me a clue. Very interesting but I'm giving up on the guessing game."

"You see, my man, you just can't help it can you?"

"What?" I almost screamed but managed to hold back. However it still came out somewhat aggressively.

"Well your manner of expression, so direct. I mean have you ever contemplated elocution classes and speech therapy," he said, trying to put a sympathetic and helpful tone in his voice.

What the hell, such a patronising twat!

I said, "look mate, dear fellow, I have studied for years to do a good job. I went to Aske's School and they sent me to elocution classes for two years. This is the best you are going to get it."

I didn't get the job—I was a Harrods reject!!

By the end of the Sixties my accent and others were all the rage, being 'Common' was in.

I remember meeting the Gillette sisters, two of the family heiresses who complained to me that it was so difficult to get help and servants as no one wanted to work anymore. We were near to the Savoy so I took the two bemused ladies outside to the Strand and said, "look can you see that bus there?"

"Yes," was the polite reply.

"Well years ago when you were young that bus was only two thirds the size it is now and there was less than half the traffic on the roads. Then the driver only had to drive because a conductor attended to the passengers, collected the fares and organised upstairs and downstairs. Today the driver has a much bigger bus, much heavier traffic, has to organise the passengers and collect the fares. He also needs another job to make ends meet and you have the cheek to say that no one wants to work anymore. Get real, ladies, get real," I said laughing, to soften the tone a little.

The two charming old girls seemed stunned and I thought, "now you've done it, you've gone and blown them away."

We did separate in a subdued atmosphere.

However they hunted me down a few days later accompanied by a number of friends. They introduced me amid great excitement. "Yes, this is him, so delightful. Do go on, please. Say something, anything, we don't mind."

They then turned to their friends and said, "you won't be shocked will you, he's so dangerous!"

'Common' was definitely in.

I also missed a golden chance to make some big money. I knew Vicky Hutchinson, daughter of the owner of Hutchinson's Press. She owned a racehorse called Flower of Fancy. It had raced a few times with mixed results.

One day she called me up. "Darling put everything you have on my horse," she said, "my trainer says it's time to let her loose, training and initiation are over, we're letting her go this weekend. The odds are 14-1. You'll never get them again so put a packet on her."

I checked with one of our pundits, a security guard, who said, "nah, don't touch it Mister 'Ayes, it's dun nuffin', no previous."

So I didn't. It came home five lengths clear of the field.

I've never taken much notice of pundits since and regard experts with great suspicion.

Our business clients included such a variety, Lady Churchill, Benny Hill, Lord and Lady McLeod, some of the Crazy Gang, a couple of mid European Princes and Princesses, John Lill the concert pianist, a very sinister extreme right wing family and a great young guy who turned out to be Count Tolstoy. He introduced us to his bride to be and we made the Russian Trinity Triple three colour Wedding Ring for them.

He was hesitating over using the title due to modern day criticisms of his grandfather's books. The literary Count Tolstoy was considered a reactionary.

I told him that to me it didn't matter. The Count wasn't living in today's world he was living and writing in a very different era. Great literature was and always would be great literature. He should be proud of his heritage and his grandfather. I hope he still is.

The Eastern Block!

The Cold War certainly wasn't over but it was decidedly less chilly. Some attempts were being made for bilateral trade and some restrictions had been lifted.

Various delegations were paying visits to Eastern bloc countries for a variety of reasons, some actually legitimate and useful.

We were on the way.

We had arrived in Hungary by way of Poland and East Germany. Czechoslovakia was next, followed by Yugoslavia.

We were subdued by the atmosphere and attitude in Poland although there were signs of awakening but it seemed that the Russians were determined to carry on punishing the Germans in their East German sector for as long as possible. Uniformed police, road blocks and sinister looking civilians everywhere.

Hungary was like a breathe of fresh air.

We were met at Budapest airport by a small smiling delegation led by the lady who was to be our interpreter, Ilona.

We were relieved that she had a British accent rather than an American one. It seemed that every Eastern bloc country studied the English language through Hollywood films and even aped some of the gestures.

She introduced us to three minor ministry officials who assured us that over the next few days we would be meeting their bosses in official surroundings.

We were ushered into three Volvo saloons flying Hungarian and Party flags and driven by huge huggy bears of drivers who blocked out the sunlight.

We were to have the same cars and the same drivers every day throughout the visit yet never once did the bears smile or acknowledge our presence.

We checked into the Budapest Hilton and for the first time we experienced proper hospitality as opposed to grudging service.

We had a quick dinner in the coffee bar and joined Ilona in the lobby. She briefed us on the next days meetings.

8 o'clock factory, 10 o'clock factory, 12 o'clock factory. 1 o'clock lunch.

Then the same from 2pm until 6.

We weren't concerned with the intensity, we welcomed it but we weren't counting on Mid-European hospitality.

We were on the move early next morning to visit an Electric Light Bulb and Accessory factory. We were shown into a large assembly hall. We sat down on plush seats set before a long low table. Opposite us across a narrow aisle were more of the same occupied by an Hungarian delegation.

We all exchanged smiles and greetings.

Ilona sat immediately behind us with her counterpart sitting immediately behind the Hungarians.

Almost as soon as we settled a woman came in and took the Chair for the meeting.

She greeted everyone in English and Hungarian.

In front of each person were several glasses, a large number of bottles and some petit fours. Only one of the bottles contained water. Each table was decked out with the Hungarian flag and the Union Jack.

Straight away the leader of the Hungarian delegation, bent down, opened a bottle, poured it all into a glass, stood up, thundered out "Egeshegere" in a loud voice and knocked back the glass in one go. As soon as he sat down the rest of the delegation stood up and did the same thing.

We were stunned. Ilona gave us a few sharp shoves in the back. We were expected to reciprocate.

We did, stood up, shouted "Cheers" in unison and knocked back the drink.

We nearly exploded. We had not looked closely at the labels on the bottles.

Well it was only 8.15am.

With eyes watering and nearly popping out we tried to read the labels. The only bit we could understand was 35% alcohol.

After every greeting, question and answer the result was toasted by knocking back one of the bottles. We tried to survive by seeing which of the drinks carried lower amounts of alcohol but failed to find any. We even grew suspicious of the water!

Much relieved when the session finished we went on to find that every meeting was the same in every factory.

How we managed the last factory tour of that morning without getting killed by the heavy machinery was a miracle. By lunch time we were totally pissed.

When we were offered white wine with our food we all went for it with the traditional die hard English spirit of "well what the hell."

The afternoon was the same.

We finally collapsed at the hotel in the evening with no one capable of going to dinner.

We asked Ilona how she thought the day had gone.

She said that we had made a tremendous impression.

We preened ourselves until she said that they hadn't known the English could drink so much. They wanted to know if we were typical football supporters. We were even worse than the Russians.

We were in no condition to sensibly sort it out that night but did resolve to reform the next day.

No chance.

To refuse the hospitality was to insult the factories which had won merit medals for quality production levels. In vain we argued that we had other factories to visit. We were accused of favouritism by apparently selecting one and refusing another.

We decided to go for it and put ourselves on the list for an NHS liver transplant when we got home.

There was an added problem. The high level of alcohol in the bloodstream was making one or two of us reckless. We were egging on the drivers to show their prowess. We knew they spoke English because of the attention they paid to our conversation and on a couple of occasions Ilona had responded to some complaints before we had even told her.

When we were in the third car we told the driver we wanted to be first. He didn't respond until we asked him why he was so content to be so low in the pecking order. That did it. His ego couldn't take that.

His foot went hard down, our heads shot straight back and the car screamed around the other two and more traffic besides. The driver grunted but said nothing. Neither did we. We were speechless. We had just missed two trucks, a bus, a tram and two cars. We now knew what the official cars and their drivers were capable of. Enough of that we thought.

No way.

Our driver was actually chuckling. We soon saw why.

The other two cars were tearing up to get alongside and ahead of us. Our driver speeded up just enough to keep them level on the other side of the road. If they hit the throttle so did he. If they hit the brakes to slip in behind us so did he.

We had caught a lucky break in the traffic coming the other way due to red lights but the break was over. Tons of stuff was coming the other way.

Our drivers were trained hardcore specialists. None were going to give way.

At the very last minute they all switched on their official flashing red and blue lights and the rest of the traffic swept aside into whatever spaces they could find. Our driver stayed ahead.

When we arrived at our destination we couldn't stop breathlessly and excitedly talking about it all but our drivers said and did nothing. Just another day at the office.

We didn't try to repeat the experience. We didn't have to. The drivers thought us to be good sports and would repeat the spectacle on a daily basis.

One morning Ilona told us we were going to a typical supermarket. We could shop there if we liked. We grinned, yeah sure. A Communist country with supermarkets. We had all read the Western newspapers showing pictures and telling stories of shortages, empty shelves and long queues for even the most basic items. Bring it on Ilona.

She did.

This was one of a chain of co-operatives owned by the members. Anyone could shop there and anyone could be a member and share in the profits by means of a dividend paid out at the end of the year. The more you shopped and put in the more you got out.

There was an ample car park, yep, there were plenty of cars, none were official except ours. Nobody seemed at all worried by our presence nor by the fact that we were so obviously accompanied by party officials and secret police. This was definitely not Poland or East Germany. We would later find Czechoslovakia to be similar to Hungary.

Tito's Yugoslavia however would be something else. Everybody there seemed to be in somebody's secret police!

Ilona was looking around expectantly. Then she laughed and said, "here she comes," and pointed towards the main road.

A gorgeous young girl with blonde hair flying out behind her, wearing a t-shirt and blue jeans came hurtling into the car park on a scooter. She skidded to a halt, kicked down the stand and ran over to Ilona. They hugged and cheek kissed three times then stood apart.

"My eldest daughter," said Ilona proudly, "she's on holiday from college."

"Well done," said Charlie, one of our party, "here or in Russia?"

Ilona smiled, a little puzzled it seemed, "no, of course not, she's studying in America."

The girl lifted up her arms showing the front of her t-shirt which showed the Statue of Liberty and 'I love NY' then she spun round exposing the back which had a map of the USA over written with the words, 'The centre of the free world.'

Everyone laughed including the police and party members.

Most definitely not Poland or East Germany.

We were puzzled. We all knew the paranoia that gripped good ole Uncle Sam. The only good communist was a dead communist. So how come she was allowed to study in the US of A.

"Easy," said Ilona, "contrary to your propaganda we do not restrict travel overseas, you do. We can get out of here but you won't let us in. So we mainly travel round the Eastern Bloc because they do let us in. You are trapped by your own propaganda."

"We are only allowed into religious colleges in America as they chose to believe that if we are christian then we should be untainted by the communist devils. We have to declare our religion."

"And what religion are you?" we asked.

"We haven't actually got one," she said, "we have always been educated but never really religious so we had to invent one."

"This should be good, how did you do that?"

"Well the average American is not very bright so we told them we were Magyar. We are actually but as you know it's not a religion. So they looked it up and found that the Magyars beat off the Muslim Turks in Europe years ago and hey presto we were in. We got others enrolled in the same way. One day the Americans may wake up but we hope it won't be too soon."

The supermarket was fully stocked and doing great business.

We were due in the parliament building in the afternoon to meet two or three ministers of state.

With little ceremony we were ushered into a conference chamber where we were introduced to the Minister of Finance, the Minister of Trade and Commerce and the Minister for Home Affairs. There were a few chuckles over the last introduction, with us wondering how many affairs he had experienced, until we realised that among his departments were the secret police. Not so funny.

We were in Hungary 18 years after the 1956 uprising, in Czechoslovakia 8 years after theirs and 10 years before Solidarity in Poland. It was sensed that some of the ice was thawing but it was not apparent that before 20 years were up Russian Communism would have collapsed and the mid European countries would take an entirely different direction.

We were to get an early insight.

We were subject to the usual bundle of documents and information showing how well the country was performing and how happy everyone was with Communism.

Then it was question time and we could see that they braced themselves for the usual barrage of regime questions that mainly came from a hostile Western press.

We took a different route.

We were a trade delegation looking for business ties and opportunities and also to investigate the allegations of dumping. Import, export regulations were easing between Western Europe and the Eastern Bloc. However businesses were complaining that in order to gain large amounts of foreign currency Eastern Europeans were subsidising their industrial exports in order to gain a price advantage.

The answer was, "no we're not, at least not directly. You impose taxes, tariffs and duties directly as we do, but you offer refund and subsidy deals for exporters to encourage them to increase their overseas trade. You offer direct savings to overseas investors."

"We do not. We offer industry cheaper electricity, less expensive fuel, cheaper rates and rentals, lower interest rates and lower taxation directly. This reduces their costs and consequently their prices. But we offer it across the board not just to exporters otherwise this would lead to unfair imbalances on the domestic market. Next question."

"We have seen supermarkets, restaurants, second hand car lots and markets yet this is a communist country. Do you have a free market sector and if so how does it operate?"

"We are moving towards a more mixed economy in which government and private companies work side by side. We admire the free market and capital but not Capitalism. Capitalism is an ideology not an economic system. It allows and encourages too much wealth into too few hands."

"How do you control it then?"

"Easy," the Minister smiled, "If they get too big and too wealthy we tax them a lot more to dampen down their enthusiasm a little, just like you do. However we don't let them transfer their wealth like you do. They can go but their money stays in the country that helped them produce it."

"Okay," I said, "I don't like ideologies either, they all seem to end in 'ism. Fascism, Nazism, Capitalism and Communism, nasty sounds to me. So can I just use economic terms such as the free market and the command economy? In a truly free market economy any company that doesn't efficiently and effectively produce what the public wants to buy at a price they want to pay fails. Of course there is the problem of vastly unequal incomes, advertising, PR and incentives which distort things but with adjustments and regulations it mainly makes out. The factories by and large produce not only what is needed but what is wanted."

"Yes," said the Minister, "so?"

"Well in a command economy it is decided from the top not led by the bottom. An Official decides what is needed but not necessarily what is also wanted. I have seen in the East German Democratic Republic that all the people have overcoats but little or no choice. They have a coat all right but not necessarily one of the quality and style they would have preferred. How do you know when to start with a product and more importantly when to stop? What about sizes because people will just take a coat to get one. They're not too bothered if it fits. Do you just go on making it forever? Also," I grinned mischievously, "Why do the least democratic countries always use the word democratic in their names?"

Fortunately everyone laughed but our leader looked a bit worried.

"Look," said the Minister, "we want to thank you for the type of questions you are asking. We usually get very loaded prejudicial cross examinations by foreign visitors. They seem to think that we have sold our soul to Russia and Communism so let me tell you that because so many markets are closed to us we sell everything we can to the biggest neighbour which is Russia. We can't say it is our friendly neighbour but it is our biggest. However we sell everything but our souls. I can tell you our souls are still our own."

"As for a comparison with types of market then we believe that the ultimate control should be with an elected government allowing a free market to operate within certain rules and regulations. Not to control the market necessarily but to control human weaknesses and excesses. A command economy works fine with heavy equipment such as tractors, locomotives and military stores and equipment but not so well with food and personal items. We do our best to adjust under difficult circumstances."

This ended the session.

We left with mixed feelings.

We were very impressed with the Ministers and their attitudes but we didn't realise that we were actually being given a look into the future. The Iron Curtain was starting to rust but in the mid 1970's it did not look that way to an outsider. It should have been seen by the outsiders who were inside but it wasn't. As always they were too full of ideologies and propaganda to be able to see the reality. Even to this day American Republicans are too paranoid and selfish to see further than the end of their Pinocchio long noses.

We were taken to an ante room for a debrief. Half of the room was screened off.

We sat down with Ilona and company and discussed what we had heard. It was obvious that the Eastern Bloc satellites realised that Russia was now either unwilling or unable to control them by military might. The countries didn't want to take a chance on outright confrontation having been let down by America's bag of wind before so they had started on a slow process of reforms taking them nearer to a free market and further from Communist control.

I said, "what impressed me most was the freedom in the way they spoke. No fear of the secret police there was there?" and I looked around at the goons who were delegated to us. They grinned and one replied, "nope, we've all been neutralised by James Bond."

Everyone rolled up with laughter.

"Anyway on that subject where's our Russian spy today?" I said encouraged by the atmosphere, "he's so obvious isn't he? He walks around dead suspicious like Peter Lorre, even talks like him. I swear he was trying to recruit me for the KGB the other day."

An embarrassed silence followed.

My face went red and Ilona looked fit to explode.

She was pointing to the screens.

A few seconds later a well dressed woman came in, went behind the screens and led out the subdued Peter Lorre style Russian spy.

After they had gone the Hungarians exploded. He was in fact a Russian delegated to report on all that we said and did. He thought he was in the background, hardly noticed, and I had just blown his cover straight out the window. My joke had been spot on and they loved it.

We were heroes.

That afternoon we were introduced to a middle aged man who spoke English with a very slight Australian tang. He was British with a wonderful survival story to tell. I didn't know it then but we were to become occasional friends over a period of more than twenty five years.

He was born a Jew in pre-war Hungary. His family did not think that Hungary would give up her Jews to the Nazis and even after the start of World War Two and the collapse of France and the Low Countries they were wary but not afraid. When they woke up to the fact that they were on a list for deportment it was too late to safely go West. In fact it was probably too late to safely go anywhere but East seemed a better bet. The family were separated and exploited but a few made it to Australia where they settled and made a new life. They studied and did well conscious of the fact that so many of their friends and relatives had died or were dying. He married and had a family.

After the war he decided to return to Hungary. A free Hungary or so he thought.

Then the Russians and Communism came. No longer a free country and the Jews were persecuted again. Not as bad as the Nazis but he had had enough. Australia had given him a dose of freedom and he was exercising it in Hungary. Wrong place and wrong time. Once more he was on the hit list.

He just escaped and came to Britain. He settled, took British nationality and eventually moved his family to the UK. He was accepted, worked hard, built up several businesses and contacts and was in the process of opening up opportunities in Hungary.

He believed it was a little early but the right time. Communism was on the way out. Because of human greed 'laissez faire' and 'democracy' may not have been ideal but it offered a whole lot more than Communism.

He was back in Hungary. Over a few years he opened up a taxi service, car hire, new car distribution, video rental, jewellery shops and manufacture and was president of the first post war private bank which he opened with the co-operation of the government. I liked Michael and respected him very much and stayed in touch with him and his sons as much as very busy travelling people could. He was never cruel by nature, and was always that European gentleman of past times.

Entering his showroom in London was like entering an Alladin's cave.

A Hungarian Jew who outlasted and outwitted the Nazis, Fascists and Communists. Yeah, great!

When he died it was a loss of an incredible character who refused to be beaten.

As a reward for our diligence we were told we had a free evening.

We wandered aimlessly out of the hotel, strolled around trying to look intelligent but failed. We found a small bistro on the corner. We went in, looked at the menu and nearly fainted.

The prices were not just rockbottom, they fell through the basement. We had game soup, venison steaks in wine sauce and ice cream and fruit for desert.

We queried the bill and asked if this was for government officials only.

The staff gathered round us, asking us about England and the world, and told us that the food was subsidised so that most Hungarian families could eat out at least once or twice a month. Some companies gave their employees vouchers for free meals at certain establishments. We had a whip round and bought another three bottles of red wine. Bulls blood of course.

As we crawled back to the hotel we passed a few ornamental trees and bushes stuck in pots in the middle of the wide pavement.

Suddenly we heard, "psst, psst."

We were actually well pissed and we looked around to see where the comment came from.

No one. No where!

Again, louder, "psssssst, psssst."

We looked closer and saw a woman's facing peering at us through a gap in the bushes. We went over and saw that she was dressed in a red plastic mack and white thigh length plastic boots. She smiled, opened her coat and displayed what was on offer. It was a lot and it wasn't all covered up. She asked, "English?"

"Yes," a couple of us gasped.

"I love English, had some before," and smiled, "do you have bed? You want sleep with me, come to my place?"

Only a couple of us could see what was happening but everyone could hear.

"Wow!" exclaimed George, "they're so friendly, these communists, they're even concerned that we may not have a place to stay?"

"Down George, that's not what is going on," we laughed, "the accommodation on offer may be more than you can afford and the activity at bit too strenuous. Don't lose your pills. Come and take a close look."

George and a few others did and their jaws dropped. "Oh good lord," exclaimed George, and backed away.

"Go for it George, give yourself a treat," we shouted.

"No," said George, "I like where we're staying better, thank you," and walked smartly away followed by the others.

I looked at the girl, smiled and said, "Sorry lady, the English decline." I joined my colleagues. We told Ilona the next day that we were accosted by a prostitute and she looked surprised.

"Sorry," she said, "there are no prostitutes and crime in communist countries, you made a mistake."

Right, okay, so sometimes even Ilona had to follow the party line.

Our job was done in Hungary and it was time to see a bit of the city and countryside.

Budapest was in fact two cities on opposite sides of the river Danube, Buda and Pest. Both were full of historical buildings a number of them still pockmarked by shell and bullet holes not from the Second World War but from the Russian Army putting down the 1956 uprising. There were wide boulevards along the centre of which ran public tramcars.

Pest was the flatter part of the city while Buda occupied the heights. They were connected by a number of ornamented bridges. The grand style of the buildings and apartments, inherited from the Austro-Hungarian

Empire, were similar to those in Vienna in Austria and Prague in Czechoslovakia.

Buda was dominated by the castle and palace on the hill adjoining the Danube.

We would be headed there the next day but today would be a morning of wine tasting and an evening of Ancient Roman Villa hospitality.

First we went to Lake Balaton.

This was a huge inland stretch of water used as a resort and watersports area. There were water skiers, jet skis and power boats but we went more sedately in a little paddle cruiser which we were told had been used for nearly a hundred years. Some of us felt a bit whimpish but most felt safe.

It was actually a welcome calm relief after the hectic days and weeks of travel.

That was it. We were soon bundled into our cars and we were off again. We were on our way to a low mountain area which contained a lot of caves—some natural and some man made.

The hill slopes were ideal for growing grapes and most of the Hungarian wine was produced in the region and stored in the cool all year round even temperatures of the caves.

On arrival we were at first sat down on benches outside a Winery waiting for our guide. It was explained to us that this particular place specialised in producing the famous Bulls Blood. This potent red wine was supposed to have been the brand that had fired up the Magyar Warriors before they went out at first to hold back the Mongols and in a later century to defeat the Turks. We did the usual tour which included a little tasting.

Then we moved on to the serious stuff.

We were taken deep into one of the caves and got a great surprise.

There waiting for us were the all Ministers and staff we had met on our trip along with a Gypsy Orchestra and Dancers.

We sat down at long trestle tables literally covered by glasses, bottles and plates of food.

At first everyone kept note of the wines that we were tasting but as we could ask for a bottle of our favourite along with numerous top ups the whole place soon became a free for all of toasting, nibbling and drinking.

We were shortly singing Gypsy songs in languages we had no idea of and were doing the twist to the tango.

The Minister of Industry, Trade and Commerce swept grandly over to the substantial and statuesque lady leader of our delegation, a well known British Cabinet Minister and took her by the arm. He led her onto the floor, caught a rose thrown to him by a colleague, put it into his mouth and swept her into a sensual tango.

We were all on our feet roaring them on.

Before she could catch her breath she was delivered onto the lap of another Minister who serenaded her with a Gypsy love song in a wonderful tenor voice.

She was entranced and we had bets on whether she had an orgasm. The general opinion was that she wouldn't know even if she had so all bets were off.

We were there four hours and by the end all the capitalists were sworn blood brothers of the communists and all the communists had pledged to become capitalists at the first opportunity.

Everyone was a happy but a complete and utter mess.

My business colleague and I were in a car with a young MP who was being given a chance to be blooded. We were asked to take him under our wing and see him safely back to the hotel. We had managed to get him into the car after a struggle but frankly he was so far gone he didn't know what planet he was on let alone which car he should be in.

Luckily for us he had brought up most of what he had in him in the toilet before leaving. We had been encouraging him by showing him how to heave and also by sticking our fingers down our throats. At one time it had been a close run thing as to whether we would be sick before him but he obliged us at just about the last minute.

We were upset that he didn't seem to appreciate it.

In the car he came round a little and wanted to snooze. We were relieved until he woke up just before the hotel. He wanted to get out of the car and wanted to go to bed. He didn't want to wait for us to arrive. We sat on him until he told us he was bursting for a piss.

The driver was actually chuckling, the first since we had the race through the streets. "He wouldn't be the first," he said over his shoulder, "we had a group of Germans from East Berlin once who nearly flooded the car."

"Not this car though eh?" I said hesitantly.

"Yes of course, it was out of service for a few weeks after."

We looked at each other and our MP decided to hang onto it but we all lifted ourselves up off the seats a little.

As we scooped ourselves onto the pavement our young man told us with great relief in his voice that he was glad that it was the end of the day as he was going to bed to sleep the whole night through.

We eventually managed to get him to focus on us so that we could tell him that this was only four o'clock in the afternoon and that we had an evenings entertainment starting at eight.

His face went even paler and his legs gave way.

He made us promise to see him through. We agreed, knowing that we would have enough trouble looking out for ourselves but what the hell?!

We prepared for the Roman Villa.

The government had restored a small Roman community, including a villa and posthouse. They had rebuilt on the ancient ruins in accordance with paintings and plans of the area at the time. A letter posted there in the morning would be in Rome the next day. Roman and Greek civilisation and influence had spread over an incredible area until swamped by horde after horde of destructive barbarians from the east. What the East called Civilisation the West called the Dark Ages!!??

All just a matter of perception.

The Post House was complete with Inn, rooms and stables.

We occupied a large room on the first floor. All the usual suspects were there.

Our Hungarian hosts seemed fresh and ready to go. We seemed done in and already gone.

Although we had another full day before leaving this was by way of being our official farewell party.

We kept tight hold of our young MP protégée who was in danger of sliding under the table as soon as he sat down.

As soon as the food was served the toasts started. We first of all saluted each other's country, each other's future, each other's systems and leaders and then we started to toast each other individually.

At first everything and everyone was perfectly synchronised. Standing up together to toast and sitting down at the same time to recharge our glasses.

Then our protégée started to slow down. He was just getting up when everyone else was starting to sit. When he finally found his feet he triumphantly thundered out a blurred version of cheers or egeshegere and then went into a backwards freefall. We managed to catch him and keep him on his seat but in the meantime the crowd had thought that this was a new toast and were on their feet celebrating once more. Our fine fellow decided to join in, staggered to his feet with a benign grin on his face and toasted one and all. Unfortunately the toast had finished and they were all sitting back down but not to be impolite and outdone they all stood up as our guy was sitting down.

This may have gone on for ever but my friend and I decided to sit on him. Even then he still struggled to get up and join in the toasts. For a while everyone was looking to see where a sort of strangled voice came from but gave up when a body did not appear behind the strange sounds.

By popular request the Gypsy Orchestra appeared with one of our wags saying, "so the Nazis didn't gas all of them then."

Luckily one of the Ministers was singing loudly again, by popular request, so that only a few of us heard her.

We swiftly got her to join in singing along with us to a song none of us had ever heard before.

At the end of the evening we were literally shovelled into our waiting cars.

We sped back to our hotel where the staff had been alerted to be on hand.

They ushered us into the lobby and lifts making sure none of us escaped to cause mayhem in the streets.

Within minutes everyone of us was either sound asleep or unconscious.

For those of us who made breakfast it was a lonely, silent, melancholy affair.

The staff took great delight in being loud, over co-operative and noisy. Even in servitude there were opportunities for revenge.

Most of the members of our party staggered into the lobby more or less on time, a few never made it much to our hypocritical disgust.

None of us matched our guides enthusiasm for our coming tour of Buda.

We saw the mediaeval and old towns and finally arrived at the Palace.

This group of magnificent buildings had survived a number of vicious totalitarian wars due to the magnanimity of the opposing sides. Agreements had been made that if the buildings were evacuated by the defenders then the attackers would cause no damage. Some damage had occurred needing renovation and during one such set of repairs the builders had discovered the old Roman remains deep down.

Just such an agreement had been made against Hitler's wishes over the fall of Paris as Germany steadily lost the Second World War.

We toured and toured, steadily going down until we had passed the mediaeval remains and were joining the ancient Roman city at a very low level.

It was at this point that two or three of our party sat down on some marble blocks and asked the guide if she came back the same way later. She did. Our reluctant tourists said that was great and requested that they be woken up and picked up on her return. They could go no further.

We accused them of being wimps which had no effect whatsoever as they agreed totally.

That afternoon we all rested but it was more like a collapse.

The next morning we were ready bright and early for our journey to the airport. In the lounge we saw Oliver Reid, Racquel Welch and others who were leaving after filming in the country. I have never been one to disturb or harass celebrities, only rarely being tempted.

I figure they should be entitled to their own private lives and not invaded by a load of goggle eyed idiots every time they went out. I have always wanted to lead my own life not live it through others. Each to his own I suppose.

When our tour was completed we made our report and as far as we know it was never acted upon. Basically all countries practice protection of their own industries in one way or another. All protect their own currencies to a certain degree and try to equate them to the US Dollar. What is acceptable is purely one of definition.

Events were to accelerate anyway into the eighties and beyond where old rules, conventions and attitudes had to change. Communism hadn't worked. It hadn't represented the free will of the country and almost from the start had become another form of repressive, vengeful dictatorship. The original theory had in fact removed thousands from poverty but eventually found itself in a blind alley going nowhere.

Capitalism does the same. Although usually operating in a democracy it is conveniently and wrongly confused by some with the free market and sensible acquisition of capital. A free market cannot operate efficiently or effectively when around 90% of the wealth is possessed by 10% of the population. That resembles more of a closed market, not a free one.

Something will have to give.

I returned to Hungary several times in later years. This was to a free Hungary but I was never sure that the country and it's people were ever enslaved and defeated.

It seems that you can herd them, harass them and make them fear you for a time but can never defeat the spirit.

Life for me also was changing.

It was nearly time to say bye, bye to those Big boy, Baby boy Blues and say hello to those Hard Travellin' Man Blues.

THE END
Or the end of the beginning!

The Hayes Family wish you all a beautiful life.